A GRASP FOR LIFE

A GRASP FOR LIFE

The continuing story of Howard Walker

D.H.Clark/I.B.Long

iUniverse, Inc.
Bloomington

A Grasp for Life
The continuing story of Howard Walker

iUniverse books may be ordered through booksellers or by contacting:

iUniverse
1663 Liberty Drive
Bloomington, IN 47403
www.iuniverse.com
1-800-Authors (1-800-288-4677)

ISBN: 978-1-4759-5491-3 (sc)
ISBN: 978-1-4759-5492-0 (ebk)

Library of Congress Control Number: 2012918642

Printed in the United States of America

iUniverse rev. date: 10/04/2012

Howard D. walker has grown into a handsome young man who has been drafted in the U.S. Army and he finds love and romance. It is during their marriage that they find there are many bumps in the road. Howard finds himself reflecting back on his childhood life while his wife Sueanne takes her loneliness into the arms of a friend. Howard is tossed back and forth from army to navy to army again as he searches for a grasp of life.

Cast of Characters

Fort Holliman: Baltimore, Md.

Howard D. Walker
Jim Thompson
Peter Cavanaugh
Carl Upton
Lester Johnson
Sueanne Walker: (Howard's wife)
Korina Walker: (Sueanne's elder sister)
Marilyn Walker: (Sueanne's Mother)
Allen Walker: (Sueanne's Brother)
mother Sanbornton Bridge, N.H.)
Linda Noyes: (Howard's young girlfriend in N.H.)
Jerry Darnell: (Linda's Uncle)
Brian Moulton: (stole Joanne Walker: (Sueanne's younger sister)
Justina Rose Walker: Sueanne's Gramm)
Ted & Nancy Sanderson: (Howard's friends from N.H.)
Brian Westford: (Korina's boy friend/husband)
John Andrew Westford
Samantha Noyes: (Linda's Howard's girlfriend, Linda Noyes)
Robert Evans: (Howard and Sueanne's best man)
Anna Patiello: (Maid of Honor)

Supporting Cast

Gunners Mate second class: Norman Gleason
Regina and Alexandros Stephanotis: (Sueanne's friends)
Marina and son Apolodoris Kotsiopoulos:
(owners of Grecian Travels, Baltimore, Md.)
Miriam and Jeffrey Collingswood: (Howard's mother and
step-dad, Gossville, N.H.)
Thomas and Charlene Walker: (Howard's elder brother in
the Army)
Tom Jr. and Dennis
Seth and Yvonne Walker: (Howard's younger brother
in the Marines)
Lorelei and Sabrina
Edward Jr. and Brenda Walker: Third youngest of the boys
in the Army)
Edward the 3rd and Sheila
Aunt Mary & Fred Bakersfield: (Rumford, N.H.)
Andrew (In the Navy
Aunt Sarah & Lloyd Carpenter: (Capital City, N.H.)
Lloyd Jr. Steve and Katrina
Aunt Alice & Brian Brown: (Penville, N.H.)
Joanne and Philip
Aunt Gloria & Arnold Bakersfield: (Rumford, N.H.)
John and Karen
Aunt Eunice & Fred Robinson: (Rumford, N.H.)
Tamara and Danielle
Sol and Anita Caruso: (Howard's first foster home
Waterford, N.H.)
Alberto and Regina

Machinist Mate 2nd class: John Morrison: (Baltimore, Md.)
Captain Skinner: Howard's Group Leader (Vietnam)
Lt. Colonel John Johnson: Commanding Officer of city (Vietnam)
SSgt. Andrew Pineo: Chickasaw Indian, Howard's Squad Leader (Vietnam)
Mrs. Cummings: (Capital City, N.H.)
Roger Beamer: Sueanne's biker Friend turned lover, (Baltimore, Md.)

Chapter 1

The year is 1966, March 18th to be exact. Howard Walker is now a young lad of 20. He has matured to a height of 5 feet 10 and one-half inches, thin at only 130 pounds. His once blonde hair has turned brown, and it seemed to flop over his brow that almost hides his dark blue eyes.

He truly has emerged into a very handsome young man, who is now a Private First Class (PFC) in the U.S. Army.

Howard had been drafted just this past September, just four short days of his twentieth birthday. Howard's heart sank into his chest just knowing he was going in the service and leave his girl friend and a family he has gotten to know well. Besides, he was working at a hard but enjoyable job in Laconia, New Hampshire making molds for Laconia Malleable Iron. The job is hot and the weights used to lift and shift from one mold to another was back breaking. Howard loved this job for he was out on his own and making money in order to pay the Darnell's for living there. He and his foster brother with Linda and her mother would head out by car to Boscawen where they would catch a drive-In Movie. Linda Noyes is the seventeen year old daughter of Mary Noyes and the granddaughter of Mrs. Ruth Darnell who Howard calls Grammy. Howard would sneak in as much cuddling and kissing as they felt they could get away with. Times were fun and now it is going to end due to having to report to duty at Fort Dix, New Jersey.

He had completed his Basic Training at Fort Dix, New Jersey and then Transportation School where he learned everything from driving the Deuce and One-Half, Stake and Platform trucks to the M151A1 Jeep to the M38A1 Jeep. After graduation, he was given orders to report to Fort Holliman which was located in Baltimore, Maryland. Ft. Holliman was founded in 1918 as a Camp for the US Army's first motor transport training center and depot in southeastern Baltimore City. During World War 1, Holliman supplied the American Expeditionary Force in France with Detroit-made vehicles. Thousands of military personnel were trained here to drive and service the automobiles and trucks. It is said that on 2 July 1919: a U.S. Navy blimp the C-8 exploded while landing here injuring about 80 adults and children who had gathered to watch. Windows in homes a mile away were broken by the blast. It is here, that the now famous Jeep was tested and refined. In 1942, it was renamed Holliman Ordnance Depot by 1947 it is renamed to Camp Holliman. Later: renamed as a fort. The U.S. Army Intelligence School and Counter Intelligence Records Facility.

Before he settles into Ft. Holliman, Howard is given a ten day leave in which to report to his new duty station. During his leave, he takes a bus and returns to his last home in Sanbornton Bridge, New Hampshire where he had lived before he was drafted. There, he spends time with his foster family; the Darnell' family.

The Darnell's is the last home he lived in after he left the Martin's in which the state had placed Howard and Tom his eldest brother whom Howard depended on so much in protecting him from the bullies back at the Orphans Home as well as the Martin boys who were always picking on him due to his Enuresis (blatter problems in which one is unable to hold the urine). But tom left and joined the army, this left Howard to take on the abuse from the four brothers. Howard had made a promise that this was the last home he will live in if he ever found a chance to get away. When time came that he felt staying with Mrs. Darnell and his son Jerry who he got to befriend, he asked the family if he could stay and get a job to pay his way because he could not get along with the Martin family. While at the Darnell' home, he got to date Mrs. Darnell's granddaughter: Linda Noyes. She had been on his mind the whole time he was away in Basic Training and in Transportation School. Howard loved Linda (or Lin the name she preferred). Howard and Lin would go with her mother Samantha and Grandmother to the drive-in movies where they would hold each other and do a little kissing. The two would get into his 1954 Chevrolet Station Wagon and drive around Sanbornton Bridge and to West Southbridge where her mother lived. Occasionally the two would drive up to the White Mountains and ride the Kancamaugus trail. It was shortly after Samantha divorced her husband, when Lin moved out of the house and in with her Grandmother and Uncle jerry. At this time, Howard and Lin were able to see much more of one another until the two had fallen in love. Howard had begun to feel as though he had been accepted as another member of the family by the way he was treated and the love that Lin as well as her mother and Grammy Darnell have taken him in to become one of theirs, as Walker and Jerry would get along as if they were brothers, until the day had arrived when Uncle Sam sends a draft notice to report for a physical for the army in Derryfield.

Howard could not wait for the bus to arrive at the Sanbornton Bridge bus station just outside the inn at Sanbornton Bridge. Running down the sidewalk and south toward the apartment, Howard runs up the steps skipping every other one. Taking a deep breath, he knocks on the door Jerry opens it and surprised to see Howard states out loud "Look everyone its Howard and he's in uniform." Exiting from the Living room are Samantha, Lin's Mother and Lin whose golden blonde hair shined from the sun streaming through the window, she is dressed in a brown skirt and a white blouse. Her hair swayed from side to side as she runs to see Howard who reaches out to give her hug only to be just short of receiving one in return. Howard then notices an old schoolmate Brian Moulton.

"Hi" states Howard reaching to shake his hand

"How are you doing?" asks Brian walking back into the living room where he sits next to Linda.

Looking around the apartment as everyone was welcoming him home, all he sees are Linda and Brian on the sofa.

"What is this Lin, you and Brian? How could you do this to me?" yells Howard approaching the two sitting on the sofa. We were going steady, I missed you every day."

"You never wrote, and when you did all you wrote about was what you were doing in basic training, Not once did you say you loved me or that I was on your mind and that you missed me"

"B-but you knew I loved you. I still do. Please, don't do this to me?"

"I'm really sorry, but we are planning our engagement"

"Engagement!" screams Howard, This is quick, are you pregnant?"

At this time Linda slaps his face, "How dare you say that to me, you know damn well I would never act that way before I got married."

Rubbing his face as it reddens, Howard asks "Then why the sudden engagement? Why can't we go on as we did before I got drafted?"

"Things have changed. I don't love you anymore, I'm sorry but that's the way it is."

Turning to Linda's mother, Howard states, "Please tell her that she is making a mistake. She has been the only girl I've loved."

"I cannot tell her who to fall in love with and run her life for her. I'm also sorry Howard, We love you like one of our own."

"Oh sure you do but not enough to be a Son-In-Law. I'll always love you Linda (Lin).

Howard continued to beg to Linda as she and Brian got up and kissed her mother and Grandmother in order to excuse them as they would have to be going.

Linda and Brian brushes passed Howard as Brian remarks "Sorry Howard just let it go."

Linda turns to Howard who was showing tears in his eyes and says, "Sorry, Bye Howard."

Howard joins Jerry in his bedroom where the two closes the door and talk of what was the relationship of Lin and Brian.

Howard remained the ten days with Mrs. Darnell and her Brother Jerry Davis although there was a lot of resentment between him and Linda. Howard would listen to Lin and her date leave and then later Lin would reenter the apartment to prepare for bed. She slept in the living room on the couch while her grandmother slept in a bed in the living room. Howard bedded with Jerry in his room. Much like his years past, only this time Howard would bury his head into his pillow and sob until he fell asleep just one room away from the girl he loves and had come back home to see.

The ten days go by quickly as Howard and Jerry would find different things to do. Jerry worked at the town dump where Howard would join him in collecting rags, iron, and aluminum as well as tonic bottles to be sold to the junk dealer that arrives and pays Jerry for the items. He gives Howard some money as well as the bottles where he turns them in the store for cash.

Howard would feel uncomfortable as Lin and Brian would gather together in the apartment and enjoy each other's company, but not show too much affection whenever Howard was around.

Howard was invited down to Samantha's trailer for dinner along with Brian, Lin' Jerry and his Grandmother Mrs. Darnell. The dinner went very well as the conversation was set on his time in Basic Training. Howard tells of the harsh times he had to go through as well as rifle firing, bayonet practice, gas attack and hand to hand combat. The exercising and long march before the sun was up.

Soon it was time to return back to his duty station. Lin and Brian had left earlier that morning in order that they would not see Howard leave in a sad way. Hugging Mrs. Darnell and shaking Jerry's hand, he then hugs Samantha saying, "Tell Lin I still love her and I hope for the best. I'm going to miss her."

"I'll tell her. But whatever she chooses it's up to her. I'm not interfering with her life. She's a big girl now."

'Ok, I won't interfere with her either, it just hurts."

"You have a good trip back. And don't forget to write."

"I will. Love you. Bye" at that Howard accompanied by Jerry leave the apartment, go down the stairs and head up the bus station where Howard boards, waving bye to Jerry. The bus then heads out of town.

On this night, he had arrived at his new duty station at Fort Holliman and is assigned to the U.S. Army Intelligence

Command (USAINTSC) his billets is up on the second floor, there he unpacks his duffel bag into his assigned wall locker and foot locker according to the picture that is posted on the inside of the wall locker door and foot locker top. As he goes about unpacking, he pulls a notebook where he opens it up to show that he has begun writing a book of his childhood days and life in an orphan's home. The book consists of a lot of scribbling and editing. Why he chose to write this story, is unclear to him. He believes in writing this down would help him unload a heavy weight that he has been holding for the past thirteen years. The story is for just his eyes only and not to be seen by anyone else. Especially the way his one-half cousins: Tamara and Danielle Robinson treated him growing up.

Upon finishing unpacking and placing his items away as they should be, he goes downstairs to meet the Command Sergeant Major. There he is given his new assignment of projectionist for the School. His job will consist of showing films and slides to the individual classes in both Samuel and Hubbard Hall, As well as going over to the Command Headquarters Building and setting up for any ceremonies that may occur. He is as well responsible in the maintenance and repair of the projectors: ANPFP-1 and the AS-2, and the Kodak carousel slide projectors. Each day he would read a board that contained a projector to be placed in an assigned room for the day, he would then proceed to place the proper equipment in the room and stand by in case he was to run and show the designated film to the class.

Howard enjoys his work, for each day he is able to get out of doing police calls, which is looking for cigarette butts and candy wrappers strewed along the lawn and walkways of the parade grounds. He would arrive at the projectionists' office wearing his greens which really makes him stand out.

Here, He would get his plans for the day and write them down in his little book before heading out to the different buildings where the different classes were held and he would go to a specified office that held his projectors, carousels, and view graphs as well as the speakers for the projectors. Here he would clean the selected item and take it and the film or slides to the room where he would set it up in the back of the room and wait for the class to enter and be prepared to start the projector.

Howard was learning a lot from the films and the slides he was showing to the different classes. Most of the films were on safety tips on those going to Vietnam or others Southeast countries. Just seeing what the films were showing on how the Vietcong and the Vietnamese Army were setting traps that the American patrols were easy to fall into made your stomach very queasy.

Howard felt very lucky to be on the side showing the films and slides to the outgoing classes than being one of the class members who would be soon heading overseas to any one duty station.

The difference between the big city of Baltimore, Maryland and that of his hometown of Penville, New Hampshire causes Howard to remain close to the Fort. The largest city he could recall roaming freely about in was when he lived at an Orphans Home in Derryfield, New Hampshire. But compared to this larger than life city of Baltimore, Derryfield was very small, though at the time when he was but nine-years old he felt very small amongst the high buildings and crowded streets and sidewalks as he made his way from Derryfield Home for Orphans in search to find his parents who he believed still lived in Penville: some thirty miles to the north.

When Howard did finally reach Penville almost a week later, and climbed those stairs to knock on the door to what was once called home, it was Mrs. Anita Caruso who had opened the door to the wet, hungry dirty nine year old who collapsed into her arms. The Caruso's had taken Howard and his three brothers home to Waterford where they lived as a family for almost three years before Mrs. Caruso suffered a nervous breakdown and was hospitalized. From that first Foster Home, the four boys were separated from one another once again as they were placed in different homes. This separation continued right into Howard's adult life.

Howard and his brothers never did have a normal home life. The five children: Howard, Thomas, Edward (JR), Seth and Anna Marie, were born in Penville, N.H. Howard being born the second child, on September 28th, 1945. Although loved by their father very much, he found more interest in the bottle while their mother loving all the males of this small community. This caused a lot of friction and fights between their parents, and when the state of N.H. stepped in the children were taken away and placed into an orphan's home while their twelve-week old sister was placed into a foster home's care. This constant shifting from one foster home to another instilled in him an unwanted feeling that his own parents didn't want him so he became a loner, Howard would continue wetting his pants and his bed getting punished for it instead of help. Even in school his work suffered due to fact that he figured that he wouldn't be there the following school day.

When Howard Finished Eleventh grade, He got a job at a Rexall Drug store on main street as a fast food cook "Have you the experience?" asked the man behind the grill.

"Oh yes" replies Howard faintly.

"Okay then I'll give you a try. Put on this apron and just put on the grill what customers ask for."

"Yes sir" replies Howard tying the apron around his waist.

Soon customers started swarming in asking for hamburgers, cheese burgers, and toasted cheese sandwiches. Howard throws the burgers onto the grill, places a piece of cheese on several burgers before flipping them over to grill. The smoke from the melting cheese begins to fill the room as the customers begin to laugh and poke fun at him. "I thought you told me you could cook?"

"I just wanted a job. I wanted to make my own money. I'm sorry." states Howard ripping the apron and throwing it on the floor.

Just when it looked as though he was to reach the door and run out, he hears, "Wait a minute, can you handle a broom? If so you can sweep up the store and place items on the shelves." calls out the owner to Howard as he scrapes off the grill to begin the orders all over again.

"Yes sir, I can handle a broom." states Howard sheepishly as all eyes are on him as he accepts a broom from a gentleman behind the medicine counter.

"You can sweep the store down than go down stairs and bring up the items that are on the sheet tacked to the door and place them on the shelves where they belong."

Just when it looked as though he was to reach the age to get out from under the custody of the State of NH which had held a tight control on his life for so long, he now finds himself drafted into the U.S. Army and under an even tighter control of the Federal Government. Here once again he is placed with more strangers and not only is he taken from the quiet rural countryside that New Hampshire offered, he now is thrown into a hustling, bustling Life of a large megalopolis of which he never knew existed except in school books.

So it is here at Fort Holliman, Baltimore, Maryland, that Howard more or less stays to himself in the fear that making friends would only lead to the loss of them just as quickly with the next set of orders.

But as fate should have it, one evening as Howard sits in the day room in his billets watching television and downing a Dr. Pepper, he is approached by a fairly medium-built young nineteen year old who Howard had talked with many nights as they both either watched television or played a game of foosball with this young man, by the name of Jim Thompson, seemed somewhat restless as he constantly rises from his chair and makes his way over to the window at the far end of the room where he peers out the window that overlooked the rear of the billets and up the road toward the main gate where the Service Club was. It was there that each Friday evening a dance is put on that draws the regional bands that draw the public in to give entertainment to the troops.

After several minutes looking out the window and up towards the Service Club, Jim would return back to his chair. This went on for some time, but this last time, Jim takes a chair next to Howard. Leaning in towards him, Jim asks in a low voice "Care to go over to the service club?"

Without taking his eyes off the television, Howard answers back shaking his head negatively, "Not really."

"Oh come on, let's go, it'll do you some good" pleads Jim as his voice rises along with his body when he once again heads over towards the window.

"No thanks Jim." replies Howard turning to pose a stare at Jim who was now leaning into the window, "I'm watching the Wild, Wild West show."

Turning his back to the window, sporting a sheepish grin that reached from ear to ear, Jim states, "We could go over just to see what's going on and check out the chicks."

By now, Howard was becoming somewhat annoyed by Jim persistence due to the fact he was as well missing his show that he blurts out, “Okay! We’ll go, but if it’s too crowded, I’m coming back with or without you. Now shut up and let me finish watching the rest of the show. There’s only fifteen minutes left, please.”

“Sure!” replies Jim turning to take one last look out the window before taking a seat and slinking back in the chair where he remains silent for the next fifteen minutes.

When the show had ended, the duo rise and head toward their respective wards where they retrieve their coats and head downstairs and out of the building. The service club is but about a hundred yards up the road. During this walk, all Jim could talk about was getting to meet some girls, maybe even to go home with. Howard listened to Jim rave on about his episodes with picking up single girls and going with them to their apartment for the week-end or to a bar. Howard wasn’t into drinking, and he really had no intentions on meeting any girl. He just went to shut his friends’ mouth.

As the duo approach the service club, Howard could almost visualize the entire building sway to the un-Godliest, hard rock music that has ever befits ears.

Upon entering the building, Howard cuffs his ears to prevent them from rupturing from the loud music and deafening noise. Howard becomes very uneasy and uncomfortable with going into the mass of bodies that lay before him.

He wishes to himself that he hadn’t accepted Jim’s invitation and should have stuck to his guns. “Brother!” exclaims Howard nervously looking all about him,

“This place is really packed.”

“Yak!” agreed Jim with a large grin spreading from ear-to-ear, “I’ll bet there are a lot of single girls here tonight, just waiting to be picked up.”

"I'm not here to pick up any single girls." growled Howard, giving Jim a look of disapproval.

The foul smell of tobacco, perfume and the assorted mixture of shaving lotion, along with the odor of coffee, popcorn and potato chips all seem to linger in the room, thus causing Howard to become somewhat nauseated. His eyes begin to burn from the cigarette smoke that hung in the air like a heavy fog. This as well results in his vision to become watery and blurred. To add to his blurring, is the fact the only lights inside the building comes from a string of multi-colored lights that projected it's dimly luminosity that was strung above and around the bottom of the band's staging. As his eyes become more accustomed to the darkened building, Howard begins to notice the colored streamers of blue, red and white stretching above him from one corner of the building to the other.

Between the band's singing and its instruments, along with the chatter and laughter coming from the crowd within, Howard was unable to make out one word that was being spoken by Jim, who was trying to help him manage his way through the crowd.

As he tries to continue his way through the sea of human bodies that were dancing, Laughing or just milling around talking and yelling, he finds himself having to side-step his way through, stopping just long enough to find an area for him to continue his journey and to keep Jim in his line of vision.

It had come to a point, that he had thought about giving up this idea in trying to stay with the fleet-footed Jim, who at this time was well ahead of him and probably already at the far end of the building.

Frantically he looks about him in the hopes that he would catch a glimpse of Jim so that he would have some indication in which direction he would travel, only to see the mass of bodies all about him. This caused him to begin to sweat and his heart rate begins to increase. "Damn!"He mutters under his breath, "Why did I ever let him talk me into coming here."

At this time, he felt himself step on what seemed to be someone's foot. So to be safe, in case this person would start trouble in a way of pushing or hitting him, he remarks just loud enough for that one person near him could hear him, "Excuse me!" then under his breath, he states his true feelings, "Damn!"

Oh how he wished he could end this torture and look for the nearest door to remove him from this frustrating endeavor. As he searches for an escape route, he suddenly hears his name being called out from his left. Looking towards the voice, he spots an outstretched arm which belonged to Jim. Jim was leaning over a table waving his arm calling out, "Howard! Howard. Over here."

Disappointed that Jim had spotted him before he could find his escape route in order to get out of the building; Howard turns around and heads toward the outstretched arm muttering to him,

With a deep sigh, he continues towards the raised arm of Jim's, passing tables covered with assorted sandwiches and cans of tonic. He pauses just long enough to pick out his choice of sandwich and drink before continuing on his way through the crowd until he arrives at the table where Jim is seated with three other people.

As Howard finally arrives and approaches the table, one of the three rises up and pulls a chair from behind him and places it at the table next to Jim, motioning to Howard to take a seat and join them, which he does.

At this time, Jim introduces his three friends as: Peter Cavanaugh, Carl Upton and Lester Johnson. He goes on to tell his three friends that "This is Howard Walker from New Hampshire. I'm trying to get him set up with a chick."

Howard sits in awe with what he has just heard, but before he is able to comment on the subject, the band, which is off to their left, some twenty-feet away begin to pick up their tempo as a sea of mass bodies make a beeline to the dance floor. Howard could only cover up his ears.

Looking in the direction of the music, all he could make out are the silhouettes of the band members which were highlighted from the flashing of multi-colored lights that enveloped the stage from above as well as below.

"How the heck can anyone keep from going nuts from all those flashing lights and loud music?" asks Howard, to anyone that may have heard him.

"You'll get use to it after awhile." come a voice from the other end of the table, it was Lester. And he was really grooving to the beat, as he drummed his hands on the table, "Every Friday night it is like this, only the bands change, not the crowds or the girls. Don't you just dig on this music?"

Looking at Lester banging away on the top of the table, trying to keep with the drumming of the band, Howard suddenly begins to feel as if he may have gotten mixed up with such kind of people that he has often heard about, but had never really met before. H now feels if he says the wrong thing, then he could become an outcast from people he just has gotten to know.

Swallowing hard, Howard right then and there was not going to allow these new found friends, if indeed they really are friends, to have him lie about his true feelings. He had learned from an early age that being you is always the best way to get through life's barriers.

"Not really! I'm a Country and Western fan myself." He remarks as he looks around the table expecting them to start laughing and begin ridiculing him in his taste in music.

Howard is somewhat taken aback when he was surprised by Lester's remark. "That's cool. We have that type of music sometimes as well."

About this time, Howard's eyes are getting accustomed to the ill-lit dance hall, as he begins scanning the dancers who had jammed-packed the floor. In doing so, he takes notice of two girls leaning against the center of three posts that sectioned off the stage and the dance area. The two girls were talking and laughing with one another. One of those girls had caught his eye as she flung her long hair back to keep it from out of her eyes."Mmmm!" thought Howard to himself as he sized up the two. One girl was taller than the other for her forehead stuck above the one with the long hair. Plus she was a lot thinner than the one that had caught his eyes. The thinner of the two wore a light blue pant suit as compared to the shorter one wearing a blue navy skirt with a matching blouse. But, Howard knew that it was the long wavy hair that was his weakness. He just loved running his digits through that long hair. "What beautiful hair and such a pretty face." thought Howard, unable to take his eyes off her.

It was at this point, that he realized he was allowing his mind to get away from him. So he quickly breaks his contact with the two girls and sweeps across the dance floor. His focus comes to set on a couple enveloped in one another's arms as they danced in what could be called, a world of their own.

Although he desperately tried to avoid the two girls, his eyes would not allow him, it was as though they were controlling him as they would dart back to lock on the two girls still leaning on the center post. As he watched the two girls, he notices that whether it is due to their own wish or to the fact that the dance floor was very crowded and that they were unable to leave their spot, they were not dancing, just standing around talking and laughing.

The sudden eerie silence about him, snaps him from his focus on the two girls. Looking about the room he discovers that the band has ended their song and was leaving for a break.

"How long have you been in?" It was Peter Cavanaugh. Focusing his eyes towards Peter who was looking at him as he chews on a sandwich and then washing it down with his tonic, Howard asks, "Excuse me. What was that you just asked?"

"I asked, how long have you been in?"

"About six months."

"Are you in the school or the command?"

"The command, I'm a Projectionist for the school's classes."

"You're a Projectionist? What do you do? Show movies?"

"Uh uh, I show different training films to different classes."

"Do you show films up at building 320 as well?"

"If I'm assigned there, I will. I generally show them at Samuel and Hunter Hall."

"Sounds like good duty." smiles Pete, looking around at the others.

"Wish I could get that type of duty, rather than getting ready to go to Vietnam." Remarks Lester Johnson "I'll be going over next month. I'll be taking a thirty day leave starting next week and then, it's off to kill some gooks."

"I have my orders also," informs Carl Upton.

As the three begin talking about their orders and when they would be reporting there, Howard steals a glance on the dance floor where he spots the two girls talking to a third one.

"Are any of the films about Vietnam?"

Again Howard looks to the others and quietly answers," Yes."

"We are scheduled for a film Monday." states Carl, "Will you be showing it. Samuel room 110."

"It all depends on the schedule. I'm not the only projectionist. There are five others that show films in other classes at the same time. I won't know what film or what class I have until I go in Monday morning."

The band had gathered back on stage and was beginning another number. Howard, getting tired of answering all those questions, turns to glance at Jim in hopes that he would get his message. But he was deeply involved with talking with the others that he never looked Howard's way.

The music begins with a slow waltz. This gives him an opportunity to get away from all those questions. Excusing himself, he rises from his seat and heads over to the spot where the two girls were. As he sets out towards his rendezvous, he finds himself in a mass crowd of dancers. He excuses himself as he bumps into couples also making their way onto the dance floor. Nearing the girls, he feels a large lump in his throat. To himself, he fights with the thought of loosing himself in the crowd and head to the nearest exit or ask one of the girls to dance. Looking behind him, he notices that he was being watched by his friends at the table. He knew now that his only choice was to keep walking towards the girls and hope that one of them would dance with him, or he would never be able to show face with the boys back at the table.

The nearer he closed in on the girls, the more his heart quickened, to a point that it actually begins to hurt. Perspiration begins to form on his forehead that trickled down his cheeks. Before he knows it, he was standing in front of them. The two stop talking, turn and face him. The shorter of the two girls and Howard's eye meet. "Would you like to dance, Maam?" He asks struggling to find the words, and hoping she would refuse him so that he could get back to the table and just tell the guys that she was waiting for someone.

The girl looks at him and then to her friend. Handing her the drink in her hand, the girl tells him, "Sure! I'd love to have this dance."

Howard receives her hand into his and as they start out to the dance floor, the girl turns back to her friend and says, "I'll see you later, Korina."

Once they find an open spot on the floor, he takes her into his arms and they both proceed to waltz. "Oh!" remarks the girl looking up at him, "You are sweating, hot isn't it?"

"Sure is.", all the time hoping, that she is not too aware that it is his nerves and not the actual heat that is causing him to perspire so.

As the two danced, his free hand begins stroking her long, silky auburn hair while trying to keep tempo to the music.

This task was somewhat hard for him, seeing that he was tone deaf, and this only added to his nervousness. He trips and stumbles over her feet, having him constantly apologizing. As she laid her head on his chest, beads of perspiration would flow from his cheeks, landing on top of her head.

Just the thought that she may hear his heart pounding out its own rhythm became another worry to him, but he continued to dance as the perspiration flowed freely, molding the two into one.

"Oops! Sorry." states Howard, stepping on her feet.

When the girl doesn't respond, he begins to think to himself that this young girl, whose head is buried into his chest, is thinking how thin he was and that she would go back and tell her friend that maybe he was some sort of drunk in need of a drink.

While deep in his thoughts, an eerie silence had fallen about him. He suddenly notices that the music had ended and Sueanne has raised her head and was looking up at him." Thank you!" she remarks breaking the embrace between the two. "You're welcome!" he replies.

As the two retreats from the dance floor, he notices that her hair and her blouse were soaked with his perspiration. Arriving back to where he had picked her up, he stutters, "Thank you again." The girl answers back, "You're welcome... again." The response from her catches him off guard; for he was almost certain that she would laugh or say something about how foolish he had acted.

Leaving the two girls, he heads back to the table where his friends are still seated and chatting. Upon his arrival and taking his seat, Lester, leans across the table and asks, "Who was she? Did you get her name? How was she?"

"Not bad! Not bad at all" smiles Howard relaxed in the knowledge that they had not seen how nervous he really was. No sweat" he adds, "As for her name, I'll tell you after I find out."

"You didn't get her name or her phone number?" barks Jim.

"Oh I will "murmur Howard gazing over towards the two girls. "Wait until the next dance."

As time goes on, and the music continues, Howard sits with his new friends talking about their past lives before the service. Somehow he felt that their lives were full of adventure and fun compared to his. He was hoping that they would not ask him what type of life he had, he really did not like talking to total strangers about his life in an orphans home and his constant moving around to different towns and schools.

Although he did pretend to listen to the conversation that was going on, by agreeing with them when they looked at him and laughing when something funny was said, but his real attention was on those two girls that were laughing and chatting up a storm. As he notices the girls looking his way, he would look away. Then return to watch them laughing and giggling between one another. His mind begins once again to wonder if they were talking and giggling about him. Could she have told her friend how nervous he was, about how he had gotten her soaked with his perspiration? How he had made a total fool out of himself by pretending to be able to dance when he knew nothing about dancing. His mind going a hundred miles an hour causes his throat to become dry, his face flushed. "You feel okay Howard? You're face is really red." asks Peter.

Snapping out of his vivid thoughts, Howard responds, "I'm okay. It's just a little warm in here."

"Here, take a few swigs of my soda." states Peter handing him his can.

"Thank you!" reaching across the table and taking the soda, he then takes a long gulp before wiping his mouth with his sleeve.

"Boy! You were thirsty weren't you?" states Carl as he watches Howard gulps down the soda.

Handing Peter the can of soda, Peter notes to him to keep for he was going up and get some more. "Anybody want one?" Those that did shelled out the money to Peter before he got up and left.

In his head, Howard had worked out a plan to see if the girls were talking and giggling about him. H peers over towards them and waited until they looked back at him. When the shorter of the two looked his way, their eyes locked onto one another. It was then, he slowly spreads a grin, and he waits for her return grin, and he waits, and waits as her eyes stay transfixed on his. Just as he was about to believe that they were talking about him and how foolish he had acted, she grins back. Thus assuring him that all was well between them and just maybe a second dance could make up for the first.

Howard allows several songs to go by before he allows himself to believe that she would dance with him again. Rising from his seat just as another waltz was starting, "Oh! Excuse me." He states, "I almost forgot. I promised this chick a second dance."

"Get her name and phone number this time." responds Jim.

"Yuk!" added Carl, "Find out if she has a sister?"

"If I don't come back, don't look for me." Smiles Howard, for he knew if he was rejected, that he would exit the nearest door rather than showing himself a fool that he presently thought he was.

Proceeding onto the dance floor, he could feel his legs weaken. His thoughts were speeding through his head so fast he had no time to think things out. Before he could unscramble his thoughts, he was there, looking into her hazel eyes. "Would you care to dance again?"

"Sure! I'd love to." reaching out her hand as she had before.

Howard encircles his hand around hers and leads her into the crowd where he finds a spot and without letting go of her hand, he takes his other arm and brings it around her waist thus bringing her body into his. As they dance, he releases her hand and begins to run it through her hair. "You have something about long hair?" she asks looking into his eyes.

"I'm sorry if I bothered you. But yes, I love long hair and I love running my digits through it."

"It's alright if you run your digits through my hair if you want, I kind of like the feeling."

At that she rests her head into his chest and as they dance, his digits walk through her long strands.

As they danced, Howard notices as he looks down upon her head, he watches the multi-colored lights casting its mirror images as if playing silly games of darting between strands of hair that reflects back into his dark blue eyes. The two danced as if they were in a world of their own. Howard felt at ease and couldn't remember when he felt so comfortable dancing with anyone before.

His thoughts were interrupted by his very own nervous, barely audible voice asking her, "Do you live here in Baltimore."

To answer his question, the girl raises her head up from his chest, looks him in the eyes and replies in a voice that sounded just as nervous as his, "Yes I do. I've lived here all my life, which so far has been seventeen years? Where are you from?"

"I'm from New Hampshire." He replies with more of a steadier voice.

"What's your name?"

"Howard, Howard Walker."

Her eyes seemed to sparkle, as she asks him to spell his last name.

"W-a-l-k-e-r"

"W-a-l-k-e-r." she repeats. "That's my last name."

"Really, Well I'll be."

"My name is Sueanne Walker."

"Well, hello Sueanne walker. Sure am glad to know you."

"Are you really?" she asks as she tightens her hold on him and lays her head back on his chest, as they continue to dance.

"I really am Sueanne; you don't have any idea how glad I am to know you."

Without taking her head from his chest, she asks, "Do you have a girl friend at home?"

"I did once, but she is getting married to my best friend."

"Do you miss her?"

"I did for awhile. We knew each other for a couple of years. She was the niece of a friend where I use to go to get away from one of my foster homes. It was more like a home, and the family accepted me."

"You were in a foster home?" she asked raising her head up.

"Yea, several foster homes."

"Did your parents die or something?"

"No. The state came in and took me, my three brothers and twelve-week old sister away and placed us boys in an orphan's home and my sister into a foster home."

"I'm sorry! It must hurt to talk about it?"

"A little, but maybe someday I'll tell you all about it."

The two stay out on the dance floor and danced to the waltzes, or just stood talking to one another when the fast ones came up. But, when they did dance, there wasn't as much perspiration, and his dancing, although not much improved, becomes that much easier for Sueanne to take. While dancing, He bends down, in her ear he whispers, "Sueanne that is a pretty name."

"Thank you!" she responds burying her head deeper into his chest. "Mmmm!" he remarks, "What is that perfume you're wearing?"

"Why! Do you like it/"

"Sure do, it smells really good."

"Good because I like it too. It's called Chanteuse."

"Do you have a favorite perfume?" looking up into his eyes.

"There is one I like. It's called Intimate." Replies Howard, hoping the answer doesn't hurt her feelings.

"Did your last girl wear it?"

"Yes she did. But that's not the reason why I like it."

"Intimate, huh, do you know who makes it?"

"Revlon makes it"

"Intimate, by Revlon, I'll have to check it out."

The music ends, and before Howard could say another thing, Sueanne grabs his hand and heads him off the dance floor and toward her friend who was still waiting, but was met with another girl that she was talking with. "She'll never believe this in a million years when I tell her this." States Sueanne hurrying the two off the floor. The closer they got, the quicker her legs moved. She moved pretty fast for her weight. In Howard's mind she must outweigh him by some thirty pounds if not more.

"Korina, Korina!" shouts the gleeful voice of Sueanne. "Take a guess what his last name is."

Turning to the now out of breath Sueanne and the trailing Howard at the end of her hand, the girl looks quizzically at them, and states "Don't be silly Sueanne. There must be a million names and it's impossible to come up with the right one in such a short time we have left."

"Come on Korina." Who now holds his one hand in both of hers? "Just take a wild guess, please. "She begs.

"Oh alright." states Korina Glancing over Howard, taking a quick look up and down. "Let's see could it be Presley? Newton? Humperdinck?"

"No! No! No!" cries Sueanne jumping up and down. "It's Walker, just like our last name. Meet Howard Walker, from New Hampshire. Howard, meet my older sister: Korina."

"Glad to know you Howard Walker, from New Hampshire." holding out her hand to be accepted by Howard. "This is our cousin Wanda."

"Glad to know you Wanda." replies Howard offering his hand to shake.

The four stand together and talk for awhile, before Wanda asks to be excused to go off and find her boyfriend.

An announcement is made that the last dance will be a waltz. Howard and Sueanne excuse themselves from Korina and tell her that they will meet her at the car when the dance is over.

Leaving Korina to fend for herself Sueanne and Howard dance the last dance embraced in one another's arms, with little or no conversation. As the last dance ends, Howard gives Sueanne a big hug before pulling apart. Looking up at him, she states, "I've really had a good time tonight. Thank you."

"Me too!" replies Howard, "and to think I wasn't really into coming here. But, I'm sure glad that Jim: my buddy talked me into it."

"I'll have to thank Jim, when I see him."

"Before you go, can I have your address and telephone number?" Howard asks hurriedly as the two begin the slow process of finding the exit door out of the building.

"Sure, if you promise to call me."

When the two return to where Korina was, Sueanne rummages through her purse where she finds a piece of paper and writes down the address and telephone number. Handing it to Howard, she remarks, "The address and number is our Grand mom's. Don't let it be seen by anyone."

Howard escorts both girls out of the building to an awaiting 1957 red Chevrolet impala where on the hood of the car were Wanda and her date.

Korina, alone with no date, slides into the back seat while Howard and Sueanne gets into the front seat to await Wanda to finish saying good night to her friend.

"What are you going to be doing tomorrow?" asks Howard placing his arm around the back of the car seat and onto her neck. "I have a pass for this week end, and no place to go."

Thinking fast, Sueanne states gleefully, "I know what. I'll walk down here to the front gate around ten o'clock. And if you're here, we can walk up to my Grand mom's apartment where we generally stay on weekends. Okay?"

"It sounds good to me." replies Howard allowing his arm to close over her shoulders. "I'll be waiting right here at the main gate. Ten o'clock sharp." Before he knew what he was saying, he asks, "Anyone hungry? There's a pizza place across the street." At first he looks at Sueanne Before looking around in the back seat, where Korina has spread herself across the whole seat.

"I'm not really hungry. Are you Korina?"

"No thank you. I'll get something when we get to Grand moms."

Howard was somewhat relieved, for having asked the question, he realized that he was broke, for he had left all his money in his wall locker.

"You sure you're going to be there at the main gate tomorrow? I don't want to walk down here for nothing." remarks Sueanne, stroking his digits that lay on her shoulder.

"I'll be here. I Promise." replies Howard as he takes his free hand and brushes back her hair from her eyes. "Tonight, I think I've found something that I was never looking for and I don't want to part with it. Not this time, not ever, I want this night to go on forever."

"Maybe it can." She replies as she increases her stroking of his digits as she gazes into his deep blue eyes. "I know that I'll always treasure this night, no matter what happens tomorrow."

Pulling her body closer to his, he repeats," You needn't fear about tomorrow, I'll be there at the main gate waiting for you. I promise."

Laying her head on his shoulder, Sueanne releases a deep sigh as she states, "I hope so, Howard, I really hope so."

From the back seat, Korina adds, "Let's not get too mushy up front. I'm here in the back seat alone."

Howard and Sueanne snuggle even closer and give each other a kiss just as the front door of the car opens. Wanda gives her friend a kiss and gets behind the wheel. Looking around the inside, she states, "Everyone ready? We really must be getting back before Grand mom begins to worry."

Howard removes his arm from around Sueanne's neck and reaches to open the door so he could slide himself out. As he was doing this, Wanda turns to look in the back seat at the sprawled out Korina, and remarks, "No hidden men anywhere in here."

Closing the door, Howard leans into the window and plants a kiss on Sueanne's lips. "See you tomorrow. Ten o'clock." assures Sueanne reaching her arm out to touch him. "I'll be here. See you then, good night and thanks again." Shouts Howard as the car begins to roll away, leaving him standing there alone in the parking lot.

For some time he stands in the darkened lot waving as the car exits the main gate and takes a left hand turn up Holliman Avenue. Standing there, looking out the chain-linked fence as the car drives out of sight brought back vivid memories of yet another chain-linked fence that he as he could, but, this time he wasn't running scared. Would watch cars go by and wished that one of them would be for him.

Turning towards the billets, he allows his mind to wander with the thoughts of all that had happened this night. Flashing a big smile, he jumps and lets out a loud yell as he ran as fast as he can.

Chapter 2

THE FOLLOWING MORNING, HOWARD AWAKENS at seven o'clock. Before dressing, he makes his bunk and picks up his area. From his wall locker he takes out his shower kit, proceeds down the hall where he showers and shaves. Returning to his locker, he pulls out some clothes that he will wear for breakfast. He plans on returning later in the day to put on some more appropriate attire for when he goes to meet Sueanne.

Once dressed, he heads back into the shower room to comb his hair, before hurrying down the stairs and out of the building. The mess hall was about a five minute walk from his building. Entering the mess hall, he shows his identification badge and is checked off from a list that the duty watch has before him. He picks up a tray, cup and silverware and heads down to join a line of others gathered to wait their turn in receiving their food.

When it came his turn, he asked for two scrambled eggs, sausage, and bacon. Going further down the line he gets some SOS and a cup of coffee. After getting what he wants, he heads over to an empty table. There, he places his tray down, pulls up a seat and sits to eat his breakfast. As he eats, his mind flashes back to the night before and every now and again, a grin would cross his face.

After he had finished all he could, he picks up his tray, drops the paper waste into a trash container, scraps his food scraps into a garbage container and places the tray with the dishes onto a conveyer belt that looped into the wash room.

Exiting the mess hall, he heads down the road towards his billets, but then turns left, on his way to the School's mess hall where he hopes to run into his friend Jim.

The school's mess hall was about a fifteen minute walk from where he turned. Although he would need a school identification badge to get in, the command personnel are permitted to enter as long as they give a reason why they are there and show their badges.

Arriving at the mess hall, he is stopped by the duty personnel and is asked his reason for entering. Howard informs them that he is here to visit with Jim Thompson, a buddy, if he is here. One of the duty personnel look about the room, finding him, he goes over and talks to him. Howard notices Jim look his way shaking his head up and down. The guy returns and states that Jim knows him and that it was okay for Howard to enter.

Approaching Jim, Howard sits down at the table and explains, "Jim, about last night. I'm sorry I left without seeing you, but, after meeting this girl, I just couldn't get away."

Before he could explain anymore, Jim cuts him off by saying, "That's alright. I saw you and her together. She's real cute, but a little plump. I hope you got her name and phone number?"

Taken back by his remarks, Howard replies, "Her name is Sueanne Walker, and the friend with her was her sister: Korina and their cousin Wanda. I'll be seeing her in a couple of hours. She's going to meet me outside the main gate. Boy! She is some girl."

"Didn't I tell you that you'd find a chick?" snubs Jim in-between biting off a piece of his toast.

"Yes you did. But, I had no intentions of looking for anyone at the time."

"Maybe not" replies Jim shrugging his shoulders, "But that is the main reason those types of girls show up to the dances. They are looking for someone in uniform that will spend their money and insurance on."

"I don't think Suanne is one of those girls."

"They are all the same. They are you're girl friend until you receive your orders to ship out. Then they go looking for another easy picking. Believe me, they are all alike. Just don't get too hooked up on her. She will break your heart later."

Howard was a little uneasy, listening to him saying these things. He wanted to argue with him, but, he knew he wouldn't be able to change his mind.

"Look Jim, I've got to get back to the billets and change these clothes. I'll see you when I get back. That is, If I don't get back too late."

Rising from his seat, he thanks Jim again for taking him over to the service club the night before.

Turning to leave, Jim gulps his coffee and reminds him, "Remember what I said, I don't want to see you get hurt." He then raises his arm, wave's bye to him as he continues eating his breakfast.

Looking back, Howard waves and replies, "I'll be okay. See you later."

Leaving the school's mess hall, Howard heads back toward his billets thinking about what Jim, who is supposed to be his friend, had told him about girls such as Sueanne. In his heart he felt that the meeting between him and Sueanne was genuine, but could it be that just possibly, they do this on a weekly basis? The very thought of it weighs heavy on him as he enters his billets to freshen up. Climbing the stairs, he feels that it is a job in itself. How could he allow his friend, if he really was his friend, to make him feel so uncomfortable? Should he ask Sueanne what her intentions were? Should he just ignore what Jim had said?

Troubled with his thoughts, Howard opens his wall locker and takes down a long-sleeved black turtle-neck shirt, a long-sleeved red button down shirt, black trousers and a yellow long-sleeved wind breaker. Shedding his shirt and t-shirt, he once again grabs his shower kit where he heads down to the shower room to once again, washes up, brushes his teeth and combs his hair, leaving a slight curl that falls slightly from his forehead. Once satisfied, he splashes on some Pub after shave lotion. He then exits the wash room and returns to place his shower kit back into his locker.

Still troubled with Jim's remarks, and mumbling to himself, he proceeds to pull on his turtle-neck shirt, red button down shirt and pulls on his black trousers, tucking his shirt tail into them. He finishes dressing by pulling on his yellow wind breaker. He shuts the locker door and places his combination lock in place, spinning the combination numbers. Looking around his cubicle, he makes sure everything was in order. Running his digits along the sides of his hair, he exits the ward. Passing the clock hanging on the hall wall he notes that it was nine forty-five. If he walks slowly, he would still be early. But it would not be him, instead he increases his stride and as he quickly descends the steps, he jumps the last two and quickly is out the door.

Walking briskly, he wonders to himself if maybe Sueanne had already been there waiting for him. If that was so, he would have to apologize to her for having her wait on him. Then, again, he rethinks that thought, what if she had no intentions of coming down. If she wasn't there, how long should he wait for her? What if Jim was right, when he told him that these girls sometimes play the guy as a fool, just to see what they would do?

Passing the Service Club, his heart rate shoots up a beat or two, as he quickly recalls the dance from the night before. Smiling, he tells himself, not Sueanne, she would not do that to him. She would be here just as she said she would. Stopped at the guard house, he shows the Military police (MP's) his identification card and his pass. He is waved through the gate. Looking both ways along the chain-linked fence, he doesn't see anyone there. S he takes a few steps away from the main entrance and he waits for her. And he waits, and he waits. Looking at his watch, he now notes that it was ten-fifteen. Becoming nervous, he ponders that dreadful thought once more, that just maybe Sueanne had been jesting him about coming down to meet him. He wonders maybe he should go back to the building and call her. Deciding against this idea, for maybe this is what she had intended in the first place, for him to call her so she could only laugh at him and tell him she had never said such a thing.

Again, this thought is short lived, he would allow her more time, in case she had gotten tied up on something, or perhaps she had forgotten how late it was getting. Whatever the circumstances are, he had decided to wait her out as he peers both up to the left of the avenue and to the right, in hopes to catch a glimpse of her coming his way.

Still leaning on the chain-linked fence, he notes that another fifteen-minute has gone by. Then a figure of a female is seen turning a corner on the other side of the avenue, to his left. Squinting in order to make out the on-coming figure, he wonders if this could be her. Drawing closer so that he could make out the figure, he mumbles, short, heavy set, long hair, yes! It is her. She did show up.

Howard crosses Holliman Avenue almost at a run, slows down to a quick step and reaches up and brushes his sides of his hair once again, closing the gap between the two.

The figure approaching, is wearing a white blouse with a dungaree knee-length skirt. As she comes within arm's reach, she is wearing a large smile and holds her arms out for Howard to run into.

They give one another a large hug, and when they pull apart, it was Sueanne who states, "I really didn't think that you would be waiting for me."

"I told you I would wait for you right here at the main gate. "

"I'm sorry I'm late. I had some work to do for Grand mom."

"Think nothing of it. I just got here myself and thought that maybe I had been late and probably had missed you. I see I didn't have to keep you waiting though" assures Howard as tries not letting her know how foolish he had been thinking as he waited for her. This would be one secret that he would keep from her.

The two place their hands into one another's, turn and proceed up Holliman Avenue, happy and spirited as if they were two young teen-agers on their first date.

"We turn right here." states Sueanne swinging their clenched hands to the right. "It's only about a half-mile up this hill."

As the two walk, they exchange stories and their feelings of the night before. When the two top the hill, they turn left onto Groveton Way; this led them into a housing development known as Sheraton Heights. Continuing their way down the narrow way, they arrive at apartment one-o-five.

There behind another chain-linked fence surrounding the back yard of the apartment, was Korina; she was in a pair of dungaree shorts and a light blue shirt sleeve blouse, on her hands and knees trimming the tall grass along the fence. "Looking up when she saw the two, she states, "I see, he was there waiting for you." She then goes back to her clipping the grass.

"Hi Korina." waves Howard with his free hand.

"Hi!" responds Korina without looking up.

When the two had passed Korina and they had entered the walk way to the porch, Sueanne informs him, "Pay no attention to Korina. She's a little upset with me. I was to help her with the grass clipping for Grammy, but I wanted to come down to see if you would really be there waiting for me." She then reaches up and kisses him. She then turns and knocks on the door.

Sueanne notes the bewilderment in his eyes, and she explains, "Our Grandmother always leaves the door locked whether or not someone is home or not. She's 70, and spends all her time in her bedroom watching television and she cannot hear when someone comes into her apartment."

"Makes sense to me." replies Howard, "If I lived in this big city I'd keep my door locked too."

Grinning, Sueanne remarks, "You really must be from a small town." Just then an elderly, short, white-haired lady in a blue with white flowers appears at the door. "Oh! It's you dear." She backs up to allow the two to enter the doorway.

"Grand mom this is Howard Walker. The boy I was telling you about last night at the dance." This is our Grandmother. Justine Rose.

"Hello!" replied the elderly lady as she heads down the hall to her room where there is heard a television. When she arrives there, she closes the door.

"Sit down, motioning him towards the multi-colored sofa, while I go and make us some drinks. Would you like ice tea with or without lemon?"

"Neither." Replies Howard, taking a seat on an old, worn out brown sofa. "But if you have hot tea, I'd like some."

"Hot tea I think I can do that."

As soon as Sueanne disappears into the kitchen, Howard scans the room from his position on the sofa. It is small but very quaint. Its walls are covered in ripped or missing brown and white wallpaper. In one of the corners there is a small round bellied stove. Above and right next to the stove is a knick knack shelf that holds dozens of different sizes and shaped salt and pepper shakers. Next to the front door and against the wall, sitting on a chipped brown and gold—trimmed table is a gray and white record player, on which Sueanne had placed several 45 records just before heading into the kitchen. On the floor, were scattered several multi-colored oval and rectangular carpets.

While taking in the room, he is startled by Sueanne's voice, as she had returned from the kitchen and was placing a cup of hot steamy tea before him on the coffee table.

"Here you go." She states placing down the cup and a bowl with sugar. "You can put your own sugar in. Do you take milk?"

"Thank you. Yes I do. Do you and your sister stay here with your grandmother?"

Shaking her head, as she places her ice tea on a coater that was on the table, she replies, "No! Not really, only when we go to the dances or when we are going to be out late. Sometimes we will just come up here and spend the weekend with gram."

Sueanne goes on without giving too much detail about their family problems that exists between their father and mother and how she and her sister were kicked out of the house at different times by their father. This act, forced the girls to move in with their grandmother until they are able to get their own apartment.

The conversation continues as Sueanne talks about how they have a younger brother and sister still living at home. She speaks of how their mother is really living a life in hell by constantly being brutalized and degraded by their father in front of the younger children. That she is denied having any life of her own and when she is able to do anything at all, it is for the sake of the children. Their mother becomes a sounding board taking responsibilities for all the pressure, heartaches and pain, bearing them all and yet still finding love and forgiveness within her which is shared by all.

She goes on to tell him that they have a younger brother: Allen, and a younger sister: Joanne still at home. She informs him of how their mother is really living a life in hell by her constantly being brutalized and degraded by her husband in front of the children. Their mother is denied having any life of her own, and when she does do anything at all, it is for the sake of the children. Sueanne tells Howard that their mother becomes a sounding board, taking responsibilities for all the pressure, heartaches and pain, bearing them all and yet still finding love and forgiveness within her which she shares with all.

"Do tell me about your life. You have a family don't you?"

"I had a family, but we children, four boys and a girl were taken from our home and parents and placed under wards of the state."

"Didn't your parents fight for you?"

"My dad was an alcoholic and my mom wanted men around all the time.

"Did you brothers live together in a home?"

"We were in an orphans home for three years. My two younger brothers on the baby boy's side of a chain linked fence and my older brother and I on the other.

"What about your sister?"

"My sister Anna Marie was twelve weeks old when the state took us from our home. She was eventually placed into a home that took good care of her.

"My dad couldn't care for us after they separated due to alcoholism and my mother loved just too many men. My dad had a wonderful aunt and Uncle who cared for my dad when he was growing up. The state thought we would be better off in an orphan's home with the hope a good family would take us in."

While the two talked, Korina knocks to be let in. entering, she snarls at Sueanne, "Thanks for your help in cutting the grass."

"I'm sorry." Apologizes Sueanne, "Time, just got away."

Saying hi to Howard, Korina shuffles past them on her way down the hallway where she enters her Grandmother's room.

Looking at Howard, Sueanne remarks, "She'll be okay in a little while. I was supposed to help her cut the grass along the fence line. Grand mom wanted it done this weekend."

"I hope I didn't cause any problem between you three?" questions Howard uncomfortably.

"No! Not at all, everything will be alright." States Sueanne, motioning him up from the couch. "Be right back." She then leaves him standing in the middle of the floor as she heads down towards her grandmother's bedroom, where she enters.

Howard could barely hear what was being said over the noise of the television.

Sueanne returns and passes him on her way to the door. "I told them that we were going for a walk around the block."

As the two head out of the apartment, Sueanne snaps the lock and closes the door. She turns the knob and pushes the door making sure that it was closed tight and locked.

Walking down an alley that stretched the length of the many apartment buildings that lined both sides, the two continue with one another's life story.

"Please continue with the story of your family." asks Sueanne holding onto his arm as though he was going to run away.

My childhood, why would you want to hear any more about that? If you really insist in hearing it, I promise you this, it will make you cry."

"Because I picture you as a sad little boy, looking to grasp life before it got away from you." replies Sueanne he arm tighter around his, "Come on tell me about your boyhood".

"Well! I have three brothers and a younger sister, my father loved his drinking and my mother . . . well, and she loved her men.

"You already told me that part. I want to know about what you were like as a little boy." "After placing us into an orphans home when I was six, I never again saw my mother until I got drafted. When I was nine, I ran away from the Orphans home in search of my parents.

I had mingled with the visitors and was able to sneak away, and guided by areas that my father had pointed out to us during bus rides into town, I looked for them and finally found my home. But neither my mother nor my father was there. It was my 'Lady of Charity' Anne Caruso that had met me at the door. "

"What about before you and your brothers were taken to an orphan's home?"

"When I was born in Capital City, we lived with my Aunt and uncle in Penville until I was three then my Mother and father moved into their own apartment building in the center square. I recall my Grandfather, my dad's father living with us until he was placed in the Merrimack County Home, because they couldn't care for him either."

The two had walked the end of the alley and were entering a playground. There, the two find a spot that is free of people, the two sit down upon a grassy area, where she asks, and "Were the caregivers at the Orphans home mad when the Caruso's returned you?"

"Somewhat, but what could they do. The Caruso's had already petitioned that we boys go and live with them."

"Was there any happiness in your young life?"

"I had some good times especially when Anna Marie was born, I was able to look after her almost every day. I watched when my mother fed or dressed her and how she would warm her milk bottle under hot water. When she stuck it into my sisters' mouth, and propped it up with blankets, I would make sure it didn't fall out."

"What did you boys do for fun?"

"We had this garage in the back of our house that the town of Penville would keep their tar and salt as well as other stuff in there for when needed. One day my neighbors: the Clark's and my brothers were playing in the shed when Randy Clark dared me to dump the bucket of tar over my head. Well guess what?

"You didn't tell me you didn't.?"

"I'm afraid I did. Yup right over my head. After that I was known as the Tar baby of Penville."

Laughing hysterically Sueanne tried covering her mouth, but she couldn't stop the laughter as she stated."Tar Baby just like the one in the movie: *Briar Rabbi*t."

"I guess you could say that, although I didn't think it so funny walking through the square on my way to the doctor's and everyone laughing like you are right now."

"I'm sorry it just sounded and probably looked funny at that time."

"Did you and your brother's ever feel you were loved or felt as though you had a family?"

"Not until I was able to leave the orphans home and go and live with the Caruso's. That was one family I had wished I could have lived with forever."

"So what happened to the first foster family? Are they still around?"

"Sure! They live in Waterford, New Hampshire. After a couple of years there, Mom Caruso had a nervous breakdown. But we didn't know that at the time. We thought that maybe when she returned from the hospital we would return to them. As it turned out, we were separated, my brothers and I, and placed into different foster homes."

Sueanne shakes her head back and forth causing her long hair to swing from shoulder blade to shoulder blade. "They really have left a mark on your heart, for it shows in your blue eyes and in your voice." implies Sueanne clasping his hand tightly. "It's okay to feel that way when you are taken from someone who loves you that strongly."

"You love your sister dearly. Don't you?"

Howard brings her hand up to his lips, kisses it and places it on his heart. "Other than my brothers and the Caruso family, she is the only person I had in my life to love."

Dropping his head as she removes her hand, she begins stroking both sides of his face, lifting it; she gazes into his deep blue eyes. "Thank you for telling me this." She then leans into him and pulls his head where she plants a kiss upon his mouth. Dropping their hands, they both become locked into a long hug and deep passionate kiss. Sueanne can now sense the need in him as she has tapped into his hidden emotions.

Breaking their hold on one another, both Sueanne and Howard have tears gathered in their eyes. Biting his lower lip, Howard responds, "I love them all so very much. I just wish we could have grown up together, under one roof."

Kissing both sides of his face, Sueanne responds, "They are very fortunate to have you."

The two have been away from the apartment long enough to get Korina and her grandmother worried. "We'd best get back before grand mom becomes sick with worry."

Howard rises from the grassy spot and begins to brush his seat of any grass residue that may have collected on his pants. Sueanne holds her arms up to him. He lifts her gently to her feet. Together, with arms wrapped around one another, they give each other one last long kiss. Then with their arms around each other's waist, they begin their walk back to the apartment. The bonding of the two was just beginning.

Once back at the apartment, the remainder of the day is spent listening to records, dancing, and playing card games and talking, having a good time. Soon it was over before they had realized it. The time was eleven-thirty p.m. "It's time I get going."

"Dang!" replies Sueanne looking down the hallway towards her grandmother's bedroom, "Grand mom's light is still on, and she's probably ready to go to bed."

"Will I be seeing you tomorrow?" he asks holding her around the waist as they head toward the door. "How about ten o'clock?"

With a big smile and nodding his head up and down in agreement, the two stands transfix onto one another as they stare deep into one another's eyes.

Making their way out onto the porch, the two feel one another's emotions begin to stir deep within. The new moon glimmered in the blackened sky, almost translucent in its pale beauty. The scattered distant stars winked down upon them as they hold tightly onto one another.

Howard kisses the top of her forehead, then her lips and when he raised his head and kisses each eye, Sueanne was taken aback, until, he states, "God bless you."

It was then, a tentative smile spreads across her face as she replies, "And you too."

Lowering his head, his breath mingles with hers, he lightly brushes a kiss over her lips then states," I really had a good day today."

Sueanne draws in a quick breath and releases it as a deep sigh, "I enjoyed it very much." She then pulls Howard closer to her, kisses him with a strength and passion that catches him off guard. He then regains control and it was his time to return the power kiss back to her. The power that is given off between the two ripples through the two bodies as if it was about to rip one another apart.

Howard had never felt so strong a desire as he was getting this night. This passion so all-consuming, a need so powerful, and he felt somehow that she has that same feeling. Both feel that this was only a moment of what could be a long life ahead for both.

Relaxing their hold, he whispers good night in her ear, as she continues her hold on him, trying to squeeze a few more precious moments.

When she does relinquish her hold, he steps out of her arms, turns and begins to walk away, while Sueanne remains standing by the door waving until he is out of sight. She then enters the apartment, shuts the door, locks it and turns off the porch light.

Chapter 3

THE WEEKS SEEM TO PAST fast, and every night after duty, Howard would head up to visit Sueanne and together, they would spend many happy hours either going bowling at Kingstown Bowling Lanes, going to see a movie, dancing down at the Service Club or just sitting around the apartment talking about anything that they find interested in talking about.

On one such occasion, the two decide to take in a movie in Dunwalk. Playing was Bonnie and Clyde. The two walk down to catch a bus for the fifteen minute ride to get there. The movie really brought out the emotions in both of them. They had become mesmerized with the action, and when it was finally over, they and the other viewers exited the theatre with tears rolling down their cheeks.

Crossing the street, the two enter a small park in the middle of the town. Here, the two sit on one of the benches to await the bus that would take them back home. While waiting, the two talked of one another's past, and hopes for the future.

Glancing over his shoulder, she notes a pale form of moon, the twilight sky and the first glimpse of a twinkling star. She then places her head on his shoulder.

Looking down upon her, he smiles, lowers his head and gently reaches up to run his digits through her long auburn hair.

“That feels so good. Thank you.” whispers Sueanne, giving a large deep sigh.

Laying there with her head on his shoulder, she could not imagine any woman not wanting to be in her place at this moment in time. He was quite handsome, tall, thin, and so debonair in his black pants, blue and white-striped shirt and navy-blue wind breaker. In the pale moonlight, his brown hair is blown lightly from the cool night breeze that sort of felt good upon her exposed skin.

Howard had noticed as he was looking around him, that up in the center of one of the many trees in the park, there hung a large flood light. Its beam of light cascaded throughout the trees branches. This light encircled the tree in the misty, blackness of the night.

Looking up into the tree, Howard has Sueanne look to where he was pointing as he states, “That tree sure looks spooky! Doesn’t it?”

Sueanne raises her head and looks in the direction that he is pointing. Seeing what he was seeing, she replies, “It sure does. Funny I’ve never noticed it before, and I’ve been coming here all my life.”

“I wonder if that light was hung up there just for that purpose?” asks Howard unable to take his eyes off the tree.

“I don’t know, but I do know one thing, it sure is creepy. And right now I’ve got this eerie feeling.” stammers Sueanne, edging closer to Howard.

Nudging him to his attention, for he is still grossly involved in dissecting the tree, Howard looks at her and notices what she was trying to do. Reaching his arm around her shoulders, he informs her soothingly, “Spooky or not, I’ll keep you safe.”

After hearing what she wanted to hear, she snuggles deeper into his arms. Looking up into his bright blue eyes, she states, "I trust you, Howard, I really do."

It was here in the park, under the watchful light of the spook tree that the two come to realize that they had something going and did not want to lose it. The two have discovered one another. They knew that each other was theirs if only they could hold onto it. Could this be real love? Or was this feeling just temporary? Only time would tell. But for now, time was on their side.

Every night after duty hours, Howard heads up to visit Sueanne at her grandmother's. The two would play records and dance in the living room, go for walks, head out to see a movie, or just hang around the apartment sitting and getting to know one another . . . The nights were never long enough for them. But not long enough for Howard, who finds that he was always rushing off and running down the hill in order to get into his billets before midnight.

One Friday night, the two had arranged to take Korina to a dance at the service club. The purpose is to introduce Korina to one of Howard's projectionist friends.

The three arrive at the club early in order to obtain a good table. Upon entering the building, they scan around until they find a good spot. Approaching their table, Howard notices his friend that he wishes to introduce to Korina. His friend is seated in the rear of the building talking to two others that weren't seated, but leaned over him as he listened to them shaking his head. His friend, is a rather good looking young man, with a very short hair cut, he is dressed in a black shirt with a red trim around the collar.

"There he is!" remarks Howard, "Care to go over and meet him?"

"Do we have to?" replies Korina, looking back to the table in the corner.

Without answering, Howard takes Sueanne's hand and calls on Korina to follow them. Arriving at the table, the trio notices that the two guys that were talking to him had departed. He was seated alone.

"Hi Brian!" smiles Howard approaching the table, "Mind if we join you?"

"No! Have a seat. The guys wanted me to go down to the `Keg of Ale` with them, but I'm not in the mood for drinking out when I can quench my thirst right here."

"I have someone here I want you to meet. This is Korina, Sueanne's sister. Korina, this is Brian Westford. He works in the projection room at building 320."

"Hello!" remarks Korina rather softly.

"Hello! replies Brian, with a big grin on his face, "Heard a lot about you from Howard and Sueanne. I see they tell no lies."

Korina's face begins to turn blush-red as she looks over toward Howard, "I hope it wasn't all bad."

"I can assure you, Korina, that what they had to say was all good."

Howard rises to his feet bringing Sueanne up with him, saying, "You two will have to excuse us, we would like to get this first dance in. Wouldn't we dear?"

Sueanne at first gives him a surprise glance, and then quickly picks up just what Howard was up to. Shaking her head in a positive way, she replies, "Oh! Oh yeah! This is one of my favorite songs." leaving an astonishing look on Korina's face.

Waving, the two disappear into the already gathering crowd, thus leaving Korina and Brian the chance to become acquainted with one another.

While Howard and Sueanne danced to the song, `In a World of Our Own`, sung by the Seekers, his mind goes back to when he was eighteen-years old, living in Sanbornton Bridge, N.H. While visiting a friend, he had met Linda Noyes; she was two years younger than he was. She was 5'1" weighing 98 pounds, long blond hair and eyes of green. She had walked into the room as he was listening to a stack of 45 records that he had placed on spindle of a record player. Howard was seated on the sofa listening to the songs as he waited for his friend Jerry Darnell to return from the store with his ailing mother.

Howard had known Linda for several years as he befriended Jerry. He would visit the family every chance he could just to get away from his foster home.

Entering the living room, she notes that Howard was seated alone on the sofa. Looking around, she asks, "Where's Grand mom and Uncle Jerry?"

"They went over to the A&P, Jerry went to help her."

Linda sits down next to Howard; soon she had taken his hand and was talking about nothing. "Want to dance?" she asks, rising up to her feet and pulling him up with her.

Slowly the two approaches circle their arms around one another and begin to waltz.

Howard liked Linda very much but while he came to visit, he really never thought of her as his girlfriend. It was when he and Jerry had come home from working at Laconia Malleable Iron that Linda wanted to show Howard a hole in the wall that has shown through to the other apartment which happened to be her uncle's. Once the two were lying across the bed to peer through the hole, Linda gives Howard a big kiss and tells him how she feels about him. This is a beginning of a two-year relationship that was beginning to blossom until things had fallen apart upon his return home from Basic training.

Now it is Howard and Sueanne that encircle one another as the song continues. The two hold one another close as they shut out the rest of the world. The two were literally in a world of their own.

By the end of the evening, Howard and Sueanne find Korina and Brian waiting for them by the exit door. "Mind if I walk with you to the house?" asks Brian.

"I would think it would be up to Korina, not Me." replies Howard giving a quick glance to Korina.

Turning to look at Korina, and before he could open his mouth, she responds with a quick acceptance.

The four exits the building, make their way out the main gate and head up Holliman Avenue. Making their way up the avenue and the hill, they discuss their evening.

Upon arriving at the apartment the girls unlock the door and yell out to their grandmother that they had arrived home. The four talk for awhile and say their goodnights before the two boys begin heading back down the hill towards the billets.

"What do you think of Korina?" Howard asks curiously.

"She's a really nice girl, and we'll be seeing more of each other as the time goes by."

"She talks much about her home life?"

"She did say some things, but didn't go into too great a detail. She did say that their father kicked them out of the house and that was the reason they were staying with their grandmother."

"They are staying there until they are able to get an apartment of their own. Their father is a real B—, always beating on their mother and little sister and brother." As the two reach the end of the hill and turn up the avenue towards the post.

After showing their id card, the two enter the main gate and head toward their billets in silence.

Sueanne was able to get a job working at a nearby sub shop where she filled in as cook, submarine maker, taking orders and served as a waitress.

During Howard's off duty hours, he would walk up to the shop and there, he would sit and drink tonic while he waited for her to finish work. Every night and on the weekends he was there making like a customer, waiting for her to finish her scheduled time at work, and he would walk her home.

Both Sueanne and Korina worked hard until they were able to afford their own apartment at 1144 Steelton Avenue, just a short distance away from the post. The four of them now had their privacy, as they went about entertaining one another as well as having their friends over to visit.

On some occasions the girls still would spend time over their grandmother's just to let her know that they had not forgotten her when they needed a place to stay.

Both couples had become almost inseparable. They would go places together, to all night drive-in, or over to visit with friends. They would ride around Baltimore and Washington, D.C. Then there were the times that they remained home to play records, or cards and board games.

Howard is invited by a friend and another Projectionist, by the name of Ted Sanderson to his apartment for supper and to meet his wife Nancy. Ted and Nancy Sanderson had moved off post and into an apartment in Essex, just a short six miles from Fort Holliman. Ted, a tall, thin, sandy-haired man, and his wife, Nancy, a vibrant bubbly, tall, short-haired witty girl, had reported to Fort Holliman and USAINTSC a year earlier than Howard had. Nancy arrived just six months later after Ted had searched for an apartment in order to bring her out from Seton Falls, New Hampshire, some three miles north of the Massachusetts border.

As the threesome sit around the dining room table eating chicken, mashed potatoes, cream corn, coffee, chocolate fudge cake, Ted mentions to Howard,

"Nancy and I are thinking about going to Sherwood Gardens and Liberty Dam on a picnic this coming weekend, seeing its Memorial Day, and we don't have to show any films, we thought you would like to join us?"

"Sounds great!" replies Howard, filling his mouth with chicken. "Would you have room if I asked my girlfriend along? That is if she is able to go."

"You got a girlfriend?" states Ted almost choking on his food. "Who is she?"

"Her name is Sueanne Walker. I met her at the Service Club dance."

"If I had known that you have a girlfriend, we would have asked her to come by for dinner."

"I think we could find room for one more." states Nancy. "If you have her number, you can call her from here if you'd like" she said wiping her hands with a napkin that she retrieves from her lap.

Ted points to where the wall phone is, as Howard rises up from his seat, wiping his mouth with a napkin, and strides over to the phone. As he begins to dial the number, he turns towards the two who watched him as he dials, and gives them the thumbs-up. The two return the jester. He returns to finish the dialing.

When the voice comes back online, Howard, with a gleeful "You can? Great." He then turns once again to face the two for a third time, grinning, with his free hand he holds up the a-okay sign.

Into the receiver, he informs her, "We'll pick you up Saturday around . . . ." turning to Ted, he awaits for a time as Ted and Nancy decide on the best time. Ted then replies, "Eight-thirty?"

Howard repeats the time into the receiver. "You will? Great Oh! So how was your day? That busy huh? I had a great day. You'll just love the both of them. Okay, Say hello to Korina and your grandmother for me. I'll see you Saturday. Love you. Good night."

Arriving back at the table, Nancy asks pointing to the large dark brown chocolate cake sitting in front of them, "Want a piece of my homemade chocolate cake?"

"I'll save a piece for later. I can't eat another bite."

"I think someone is in love." Smiles Ted, winking at Nancy, getting up to clear the table.

The trio breaks out in laughter.

Sueanne is waiting for them outside on the porch when the car arrives. Howard opens the rear passenger door to allow her to enter. Before she is fully seated, she waves back to her sister and grandmother who had arrived at the doorway.

"Bye Korina, Bye Grand mom."

"Have fun." Yells Korina just as Sueanne enters the car and shuts the door. Rolling down the door window to extend her arm out in order to wave as the car drives away. After rolling up the window, she slides over toward Howard and the two kiss.

Howard introduces Sueanne to Ted and Nancy. "Ted is also a Projectionist with me at the Command Headquarters. He's been here about a year and they are from New Hampshire."

Sueanne settles herself into her seat as Howard brings his arm up around her neck.

"Pleased to meet you." states Sueanne to Ted and Nancy.

"Nice to have met you." replied Nancy. "It seemed as though he couldn't stop talking about you after he talked to you on the phone."

"Hope it was all good." Jokes Sueanne, as she smiles up at Howard.

"I assure you, it all was." Answers Nancy.

As they drove toward their destination, the two couples talk and get to know one another. As the vehicle crosses the Chesapeake Bay Bridge, which has a length of 7.7 miles and two lanes having a twenty-eight-foot wide surface. It has two towers that reach three hundred forty-eight-feet high, Sueanne slides even closer toward Howard, causing more space between her and the vehicle's door. "This bridge always scares me."

"There's nothing to fear." replies Howard hiding his own feelings for he was just as nervous as she was as the vehicle crossed the bridge.

Howard retrieves his camera and begins taking pictures of the bridge, Ted and Nancy and of Sueanne. Howard is hoping that this picture-taking would help take her mind off of being on the bridge, and she would become more at ease.

Upon arriving at Liberty Dam, the two women head for the rest room while the guys search out a grassy area that would be a good spot to spread the blanket. With the basket of food sitting on the blanket to await the women, Howard grabs his camera and heads over toward the restroom to wait for the two women to emerge. When they do exit the building, he snaps several pictures and runs back to the grassy knoll with both women on his heels. Once back at the area, both couples begin chasing one another around, rolling in the grass and acting more like children.

Soon, they settle down. While the two women unpack the food basket, the two guys sit and talk as they take in the size of the dam.

What they learn from reading displayed signs, that the dam was completed in 1954, its waters from Liberty Reservoir flows by gravity through its 12.7-mile long 10-foot diameter tunnel to the Ashburton Water Filtration Plant for treatment in Baltimore City. The Dam's crest elevation is 126-feet above sea level. Water overflowed the crest for the first time on February 6, 1956.

When the girls had the picnic ready, they call the guys to the blanket. The foursomes enjoy their meal and time together. After they had eaten their fill, and picking up the area, they stroll along the trail that leads them alongside the Dam, while Howard snaps more pictures of the Dam and of them.

The two couples lie down in the grass and take in the beauty that lies before them.

Turning to the others, Howard notes, "This place sure is beautiful. I'd love to come back here again."

"I'm sure we will. We have a long life ahead of us." Answers Sueanne as she encircles her arms around him and bringing him down to the ground with her. There, they hug one another and kiss. Seeing this, Ted and Nancy follow suit.

The four sit and talk and enjoy one another's company until Ted informs them, "If we plan to visit the Sherwood Gardens this day, then we had best get started."

"Oohhh!" remarks Sueanne lifting her head up from Howard's lap, "I really hate to leave here. It is just so beautiful."

Reluctantly, they get to their feet, pick up the basket, fold up the blanket and head back to the car.

It was forty-minutes later, just after two o'clock pm when they arrive at Sherwood Gardens, this place is nestled in the Northeast part of Baltimore, in Guilford County. It comprises of seven acres of planted one hundred thousand tulips and other bulbs. The three walk through some of five thousand Azaleas, English boxwoods, Flowering Cherry and Crab-apple, Dogwoods and other Flowering plants. All along the pathways which led to different types of plants. Ted and Nancy walk past the pansies and stop where the Chrysanthemums or Mums are. They purchase a couple of the Mums to take back home.

The trip to the Gardens brought back the memories Howard had of when he and his brothers visited his Great uncle's mansion when he was living at the Derryfield Orphans Home. At that time, it was the most beautiful flower garden he had ever seen.

He had been very proud to be a relative of someone as famous as his great uncle Edward McLaughlin who had made the New Hampshire magazine back in the 50's for his beautiful gardens of flora and fauna. He was one of the richest men in Derryfield. He had a mansion, chauffer, maid, butler and a Gardner that took good care of his home and garden. Howard remembers seeing this when his uncle would bring him to his place on several weekends while he was at the Orphans Home.

Chapter 4

HOWARD HAD ARRIVED AT THE girl's apartment one Saturday where he was to join them over to their mother's house to celebrate her birthday. The old man had gone to West Virginia, which he does every time there is a family event.

After knocking, he lets himself in, "Sueanne! Are you here?"

'I'm in the living room. I could use your help." Entering, he sees her bent over a cluttered oak bench struggling to keep its many fragile items from falling to the floor and breaking. Her skimpy blue dress rides high on her thighs, revealing short, shapely legs the color of tea laced with cream. As she stretched further forward to catch a falling glass unicorn, her hemline inched even higher. All Howard could do was to freeze in his tracks and stare.

"Excuse me; I really could use your help here." Without turning around to see what he was doing?

"Oh yeah." remarks Howard after being alerted to Sueanne's dilemma, "Here, let me help you, lurching forward and catching an item that was about to go crashing to the floor.

Upon straightening up, she faces him, he stands in amazement, and she is just as attractive to look at as she was from the rear. Howard has always been more attracted to slender women, but at this time in his life he felt that there was something to be said for this particular female who was generously round in all the right places, especially this day when all her roundness is displayed in a clingy blue dress that reveals her every dip and swell.

Tugging her dress down, she replies "Thank you. You got here at the right moment." Fluttering her hand at the collection on the bench, she states, "I was just trying to get Heidi: my dog outside to go do her thing before leaving to go to mom's, but the leash got tangled around the leg of the bench, and as you can see what happened."

Glaring, Howard wasn't listening to one word she was saying. His being was finding it hard to find the words to describe he beauty. Her curly long brown hair cascaded over her shoulders and wrapped around one side of her face. Her shoulders were bare except for her black spaghetti wide dress straps. Her mouth was lush, soft and defined with deep burgundy gloss. Above the bodice of her dress, frill, creamy breast bulged upward, thus displaying a cleavage that had captured his stare. From that point, his eyes dropped to her legs. Her smell of Chanteuse perfume rattled his senses even more.

Smoothing down her dress once more, she gives him a look, her eyes lock onto his and he notices where he is looking. Smiling, the two come together in an embrace that ends in a hard kiss.

For a moment there, Howard couldn't recall why he was there. Breaking their hold from one another and with a deep sigh, she regains her composure and with her infectious smile states, "Korina and Brian went to the store to pick up a birthday card for mommy from all of us."

"Guess I arrived in the nick of time"

"Want to come along, while Heidi does her duty?"

"Lead on, I'll follow. By the way, you really look beautiful in that dress."

"Why, thank you."

In taking her hand into his, he notices that her digits were much plumper than his, as he slips his long slender ones in-between hers. "Come on Heidi, let's go out."

Once outside, Heidi runs out on the lawn looking for a spot to do her duty, while she was busy sniffing the ground, Howard and Sueanne stand locked arm-in-arm as they keep a watch on Heidi.

Sueanne realizes that she was squeezing him as if he was going to get away from her. But when she tries to loosen her grip, he squeezes her stating, "Don't let go." Then as he looks down the road, he utters to her, "here comes Korina and Brian."

"Hello Howard" states the duo as they come upon the two who had been reaching down for the dog."Hello" replies Howard, "really is a nice day isn't it." The two shake their heads in approval.

"Sueanne, you are going down to mom's, aren't you?"

"Sure I'm going down. Howard's going down with us."

The foursome gets into Korina's car and head down to Marilyn Walker's house. There, Howard gets to meet the rest of the family. There were Allen and their younger sister Joanne. The party lasts all day, as they sat around the back yard talking and getting to know one another. Later in the day, the family gathered together for a game of volleyball before heading over to Francis Scott Key Junior High School to watch the fireworks. Though it is only July 3rd, 1966, it is much more than celebrating Independence Day, it is family day, a day that has brought Howard into what he has wanted since he was a young lad with the Caruso family in Waterford, N.H.

As the fireworks burst over his head, and Sueanne hugged his arm, his mind goes back to when he had run away from the Derryfield Home for Orphans, and had made it back to his hometown of Penville in hopes to reach his mom and dad. As he climbed the steps up to the porch of his apartment, he notices the Maynard's, waving him on. Below him, the town's people had shown up through word passed down, to watch this young lad make the climb that would finally end his journey in the search of his parents.

Approaching the door to his apartment, he knocks calling out to his mother and father to open the door. When the door finally opens, Howard follows the sight of remembered soft blue shoes up the yellow print dress which he had sat upon so many times, then his scan continues upward and as he looks upon the smiling face that was looking down on him, and just before collapsing into her lap, he cries out, "Mommy!". The smiling face that had met him at the door was none other than that of Anita Caruso, she and her family had known where he was heading and they had arrived earlier that day to await his arrival.

The Caruso family had taken all four Walker boys to live with them. They stayed with them for three years before Mrs. Caruso had become hospitalized with a nervous breakdown. The family that had been his for awhile was now in his past. The state moved in and moved the boys to different foster homes, never to be living with one another again.

The memories that had flashed back in his mind, as well of the love that he continues to have for them causes a tear to slide down from his eye and dribble down his cheek. Looking about him, he sees Joanne and Allen running around while the fireworks burst brightly in the air.

After the fireworks, the family went back home where Marilyn and the girls sit in lawn chairs talking female talk, Brian, Allen and Howard are bent over an old Buick that Allen and his father are restoring when they have the time. Everything is great; Howard hopes that nothing could break up this new found family.

All that week and into the weekend, Howard had come to feel welcomed into his new family as Brian and Korina take them on long drives to see everything they could see in the area, are the rivers, forests, beaches, lakes where they could spread a blanket and enjoy a picnic. They found good spots in grassy meadows full of flowers or covered areas with clover. Some of the areas, they stayed long enough to actually lie back and converse before taking a nap. Then they would arise and go on short strolls through the trails.

Howard had found himself in an incredible relationship with this very pretty woman who never once pressed one another for anything more than holding hands, wrestling or playing tag, walking through the forests when the earth is soaked in sunlight. They danced in the open air with the wind providing them with music. Other times, they would just sit together drinking in the panoramic views of the region. Then there were those summer days they would drive somewhere, anywhere just to hold One another and scanned the beauty before them occasionally spotting a squirrel or deer bounce as they tenderly caressed each other's skin through their clothes.

As the summer continues, they would leave the Baltimore area and drive into Washington, DC, or head into Pennsylvania where they would spend the day hiking the trails that climaxed into incredible views below them.

On August 25th, 1966, Howard is in the dayroom watching television, it is just before 2pm, (1400 hours) and the final launch of AS-202, which is the Apollo-Saturn/AS, 2=Saturn 1B launcher and the 02, a particular launch. This is to be the second launch in the test of the unmanned launches of the Saturn 1B. It is the test of the S-4B upper stage. It is also hoped that a successful mission will relieve worries about spacecraft/launcher compatibilities in hopes to give a final man-rating to the command module reentry vehicle.

If all goes according to plan, it will open the way for AS-204, the first manned mission of the Apollo program. Virgil I "Gus" Grissom, Edward H. White and Roger B. Chaffee will be the first to fly a fourteen day mission designed to test all CSM systems; (Command and Service Module).

Howard's mind goes back to his early childhood when the thought of spaceflight would bring him exciting adventures into outer space. Just the thought of jumping around in a gravity-free world, knowing when you fall from a tree or atop a building that you will only bounce back up even higher than where you had fallen from. As an astronaut, he would get to look outside the spacecraft's window to witness the whole world below him.

To become an astronaut was Howards' dream ever since he witnessed the launch of Freedom 7 as Astronaut Alan Shepard takes America into manned space for the first time,

The Soviet Union had not only placed a man in space, but as well placed several spacecrafts into orbit of the Earth. But he knew that he would have to buckle down in school and study a lot harder. But it was the constant interruptions that he would face from going from one school and one town to another. This put his studies even deeper in the hole. So by the time he had finished his junior year, he was going to have to repeat it the following year, and he could not show up for another junior year as he prepared for his twentieth year. No way, not even.

Howard knew that his dream to become an Astronaut would never amount to be reality. So it had come down to reading and rewriting on each space mission as he goes about collecting space patches, pins, models and all sorts of artifacts for his collection as well as his personal knowledge on space and the life of an Astronaut grew.

Space is new to man and the thought of going into space becomes a world conversation when on that fateful day of October 4th, 1957, the Soviet Union successfully launches into space a 180-pound artificial satellite known as Sputnik. The whole world is able to listen in to its BEEP—BEEP as it circled the earth. It was only a matter of a couple of weeks later, when a second satellite is launched known as Sputnik-2, but this time there was something added to the satellite, aboard was a dog named Laika and it was also orbiting the earth.

Howard, twelve years old is shown by Alberto and Regina Caruso as the two points out to him a twinkling orb as it passes overhead on its ninety-minute journey around the earth.

The United States never got a chance to counter this new communist threat until it successfully launches its own artificial satellite: Explorer-1 atop a Jupiter-C rocket on January 31st, 1958. So it was. Howard has become smitten at the rough young age of twelve, knowing that an Astronaut was what he wanted to be.

By July 29th, 1958, President Dwight David Eisenhower officially creates the National Aeronautics and Space Administration (NASA). This agency is to develop a program that would clearly define the United States as a top leader in the space race.

When Howard is in his sophomore year of high school, he writes a class paper on his knowledge of just what the future of NASA was going to be for not only the United States, but for the entire world. He as well envisions himself graduating from high school, going to Massachusetts Institute of Technology (MIT) and into the Aeronautical Engineering, and imagining that he would be playing a vital role in man's conquest into space.

Howard watches the mission perform flawlessly; it has been a repeat of its predecessor AS-203 which had flown first. The AS-203 first flew due to a minor hardware problem. As he follows the mission on the television, he hears a voice outside the dayroom informing him that he had a telephone call. Leaving his chair and exiting the dayroom, he pulls up the phone that has been hanging by its wire. "Hello!" he states into the receiver. It was Korina, she was calling for Sueanne. "Howard, could you come by tomorrow? We are having a Birthday party for Brian."

"Sure! I can make it. I'll be there after I clean up from work. Does Brian know anything about the party?"

"I don't think so, although he's been dropping hints that his birthday was coming up. Mommy, Allen, Joanne will be early in the afternoon to help decorate before Brian arrives."

"My last film is at 4:30. I should be there around six o'clock. Is Sueanne off for the weekend?"

"I was told to tell you that she's off all weekend and will see you when you get here tomorrow."

"Okay. See you tomorrow. Thank you."

Excited by the news, Howard hangs up the phone and returns back to the dayroom where he sits down to finish watching the rest of the space mission.

Thanksgiving, 1966, sees Howard joining Brian gathered at the girl's house, helping to pitch in the preparation of the turkey dinner. Each had a chore to do. They looked liked a mass of ants gathered to get their jobs accomplished.

During the meal, they had to separate due to the kitchen being small, Howard, Sueanne and Joanne eats in the living room that had been set up with TV trays. They would be seated on the sofa.

Though they may have been separated, they could still talk to one another. It was a very homey dinner and very family oriented.

After the meal had been eaten and the dishes picked up, the rest of the family joined the three in the living room.

Dismissing herself to go to the ladies room, Korina had sneaked into the kitchen retrieved the hidden cake and lighted the candles. As she enters the living room everyone broke out singing;"Happy Birthday."

"Wow!" Exclaimed Brian with a big smile on his face "What a beautiful cake. "

"I can't take all the credit" replies Korina placing the cake with lighted candles on the table, "Mom made the cake, and we just frosted it."

"Any way, thank you."

"Okay Hon' states Korina," just cut the cake 'handing him the cake knife they used during their wedding.

"Hurry I want a piece." States Joanne jumping up and down with her plate.

"Me too I want a piece." seconds Allen holding his plate as well.

Once the cake and ice cream was eaten, Korina and Sueanne bring out the presents and Brian has a field day unwrapping and thanking everyone. It truly was a wonderful day, very family oriented. Just what Howard dreamed of as he watched everyone and felt attached to the family.

In December, Howard was going home on a ten-day leave. While there, he visited with his half-brother Jerry Davis in Sanbornton Bridge where he tells the family he was to spend the day than head to Gossville to visit with his real mother. He informs them that he has a girlfriend and her family has been treating him like one of their own, "But you are my family and I love and miss you all."

"What about Linda?" asks Jerry?

"We had a good time and I'll always have feelings for her, but she made her decision."

While Howard visited, he found out that Linda and Brian Moulton had married and had built a house, Brian was a musician and was playing in a band.

Howard stays the day before heading to Gossville to visit with his real mother and step-dad Jeffrey Collingswood who were living in a trailer park just outside the town of Gossville. He was surprised to find his brother Edward Jr, who also was in the army, was visiting as well. His younger brother Seth was thinking of joining the Marines.

Their step-father worked across the divided road at *the Circle Nine Ranch* where they held country dances on the weekends. Jeffrey had used a tractor and tore up the entire field and cut down trees in order to build an area where they had Indian powwows. Both the country dances and the powwows brought in a lot of guests and Howard and his brothers had enjoyed the family of Sid and Barbara Anne who previously played at the Sanbornton Bridge Town Hall and on television channel nine as the *"Sid and Barbara Anne Show."*

The boys loved going over and dancing and mingling with the crowd, looking at the girls and just having a good time.

One Saturday evening the boys decided to go over in their uniforms in which they looked very smart and proud. They mingled and got wolf calls from some while others shook their hands and stated how they looked up to them. There were those that brushed up against them and showed disgust in their uniforms. There were these tough looking guys who were from Pinebrook. The next town over approached them and one said. "You look like sissies in those rags. Why don't you just go back home and take them off or we will."

"You're not going to do anything of the sort and we are not going back." remarked Edward Jr.

As the crowd begins to stop what they were doing, some of the Gossville guys began to surround the Pineville guys both town disliked the other and before anyone knew it, a punch was thrown and the five Pinebrook citizens were thrown out by Sid and Jeffrey who had heard the commotion. The rest shook hands and helped Howard and Jr. to the bar. Jr. took the free drink but Howard refused, saying, "Sorry fellas, I don't drink, but thanks for the help, we were about to be Pell melled by those guys."

"Let's forget them and get back to having fun, By the way, the name is Artie Murphy."

"Artie Murphy? Any relation to . . . ." asked Howard before he was cut off in mid sentence.

"Somewhere down the line, At least that was what I was told. "

As the dancing and fun continues, at the same time carloads of Pinebrook citizens must have been about twenty or so bent on a fight pulls into the parking area and unload and together.

Enter the building where they were first met by Sid who demanded that there be no trouble.

Pushing him aside, saying, "Get out of the way old man." Looking around the room one of the guys points toward Artie and states to the lead guy, "That's him over next to the two soldiers."

The group push their way towards Artie and begins to bad mouth him, Jr. butts in saying, "Your so called moron buddies started that fight and I suggest that you either leave on your own accord or we'll have to send you home in ambulances."

Artie holds his arm out so that Jr. couldn't start anything." I think you boys had best leave now or you won't be going anywhere."

"That soldier boy or should I say killer of innocent children has no right to call us Morons."

"Then I suggest that you hooligans don't act like one and leave while you still can."

Suddenly all hell broke loose the Pinebrook boys began whopping on Artie and Jr. and Howard defended him by jumping on the lead guy and punching him while the girls and the ones not in the fight back themselves up against the walls of the dance hall. Fists are flying everywhere, tables are uprooted, and chairs are thrown while bodies are piled on top of bodies one could not tell a Gossville citizen from a Pinebrook citizen.

Soon the brawling winds up outside the dance hall as the rest of the crowd gather to watch.

Howard finishes off two of his attackers and looks around for his brother. Yelling out his name he hears his voice coming from under a pile of three Pinebrook boys. Rushing over, he belts a guy that tries to stop him. Thinking his brother really needs help; Howard reaches the pile and begins pulling the bodies off Jr. Howard hits one that falls backward down the embankment that leads to the street lucky no cars were coming up the road. By the time the last body is removed from Jr. He gets to his feet; his uniform is ripped and dirty. Brushing himself off, he says to Howard who was straightening out his tie and dusting himself off as well, "Why did you do that? I had the best of them"

Looking around he notices the ground is strewn with badly beaten boys from both towns. Sirens are heard in the background and Jeffrey leads Howard and Jr. away from the Dance Hall and into the area where he was working clearing the land of trees for the Powwow that was to take place next week.

The police helped the injured into the dance hall where they were to wait for medical assistance. One body was found in a gully with a knife wound to the stomach that body was of Artie Murphy. Watching from their safe location the three overhear from the police that there was a body of a young man presumed murdered.

"Dad," Says Jr. We have to go and see who it is."

"If you are even seen by the police you will never get back to your outfits you'll be serving time in prison. And besides you're not out of it yet. Wait until your mother sees you two. God forbid."

Jeffrey was able to keep the two boys from being found out and when everything seemed quiet the three make their way back to the trailer park where some of the residents were still watching and talking about what they thought was happening at the dance hall.

As soon as the three enter the trailer, Seth asks what happened up there.'

"You really want to know? Glad you didn't come with us. It was those darn Pinebrook morons who crashed the barn and started a fight." replies Howard taking of his jacket, loosening up his tie.

"Don't you just look like a pair of washed up kitty cats." Says Miriam as she enters the dining room from her bedroom. "Get out of those clothes quickly and I'll see if I can get them to the cleaners down the rotary. And just where were you when all this was going on? Probably on one of your drinking binges again?"

"Mom" Yells Howard," dad helped us he broke up the first fight with Sid and after the second fight he hid us from the police."

"Well, he can be of some good can't he?" states Miriam taking the boys clothes as they strip them off.

"Both of you get ready to get into the tub and clean yourselves up."

Jr. prepares the tub first while Howard goes through his travel bag to find something to wear. Finding a pair of fresh boxers and t-shirt and he lays them aside. The clothes he does find will be worn tomorrow while his uniform goes to the cleaners where they will be repaired and cleaned. For tonight after his bath, he will go around in his boxers.

After a few days there, he travels to visit the Caruso family in Waterford. While Edward Jr. travels to visit one his foster parents in the other direction it is here that Howard receives the warmest of greetings. He remains for a day and night, before asking them to take him to Rumford so that he could get a car registered which he had previously purchased from one of his friends at Fort Holliman just before he was to end time in service(ETS).

With his license and registration in hand, he says his goodbyes and returns back to Fort Holliman with two days left to put his plates on his 1952 Ford which he calls "Fang" due to the fact that the vehicle has no grill and the bumper looks like two teeth on each side of it.

Now with having his own vehicle, he no longer has to rely on Brian or Korina to take him and Sueanne different places away from Dunwalk. Two now have their privacy, of which Sueanne had before, to go where she wanted. Two would drive outside the Baltimore city limits, without having to catch a bus to get there. Yes, life was beginning to be good to them. There was no one that was going to come into their little world, which the foursome had built for themselves.

But, there was an outside force just waiting for the right moment, and that moment comes on March 25th, 1967 when Korina Lynn Walker becomes Mrs. Brian Howard Westford. The two become husband and wife in a ceremony at the Eastern Assembly of God Church, located on Wise Avenue. The best man was one of Brian's friends who came down from his hometown in Ohio.

Sueanne was the Maid of Honor; Allen and Howard were the ushers. Joanne was the Junior Brides Maid. After the ceremony, the wedding party was whisked away to a reception held at the Non-Commissioned Officers (NCO) Club on Ft. Holliman.

The Bride and Groom leave the reception around seven—thirty pm to begin their journey to Ohio for their Honeymoon. The remainder of the party breaks up around midnight.

Sitting in the car as they await to take her mother, brother and sister home, Howard and Sueanne talk about how beautiful the wedding and the reception went. "Sure it was beautiful." Recalls Sueanne looking up into his eyes, "and awfully sudden."

"Come to think of it, it is quite sudden, isn't it?"

With her eyes fixed onto his, she remarks, "I suppose, that when they come back from their honeymoon they will want the apartment to themselves."

Trying to search for an answer that would help console her, he replies, "We'll find you another apartment. At least you can stay here until they come back, and that won't be for another thirty days. By then, we should be able to find something. I'll be around to keep you company."

The two look at each other as if they could read each other's mind. The two hug and kiss as her hand slides down and settles into his midsection area. Just then her hand is brought back up as her mother; brother and sister arrive, tugging behind them their cousin. Entering the vehicle, the mother asks Howard if he could drop her off in Dunwalk. Howard Okays the wish and they depart the area. As they proceeded on their way, the mother informs her, "Don't worry about being alone, Joanne, Allen and I will be staying with you until Korina and Brian returns."

Before Sueanne could get a word out edgewise, her mother stops her short and states, "You are not staying in that apartment alone, and if you fight me about this, than you will have to move back in with grand mom."

Looking at each other, Sueanne places her hand on his knee and rubs it as close to his midsection without giving away what she was wishing for. They knew it was a losing battle to argue with their mother. Once her mother has made up her mind, there was no changing it? She has fought with the devil and that was her husband.

During the time that Korina and Brian were away on their honeymoon, Howard finds it very difficult to spend time alone with Sueanne. Soon he begins to feel intruded upon as does Sueanne. Wherever they wanted to go somewhere, the rest of the family wanted to go as well, and Sueanne just couldn't say no to her family.

When the two could get sometime alone, they would question the family's actions. "Do you think they know something about Korina that we don't know?" asks Howard with his arm around her neck as they sat upon the couch.

"I don't know." states Sueanne, snuggling tighter into his arm. "But I think she just might be pregnant."

"You really think so?"

"Well think about it. They spent more time together than we could, they got married with a burning fever, and they've only known each other less than a year. Yes I think she's pregnant."

Laying her head on his shoulder, she places her hand between his legs and murmurs, "I would like to see what you have there." rubbing her hand on his now swelled lump, she looks up into his eyes, and says, "I've never had a man before. I've never seen one except my little brother's. Can I see yours?"

Uneasy, because the family was still in the kitchen, he allows her to slowly unzip his fly and place her digits into his pants and under his shorts. Carefully she wraps her tiny plump digits around his enlargement and brings it out into the opening where she gets a birds' eye view of it. "Wow! It is big. I think I could really enjoy this." After stroking it and viewing it for some time, she slowly places it back into his pants and zips up his pants. With a twinkle in her eye, she looks up into Howards' eyes with a look as though she were ready to devour him. After awhile, her mother calls them into the kitchen for something to eat. Howard tries whatever he could to hide the bulge that wanted to be released, as Sueanne puts on a little smirk.

As they sit, Sueanne kept her eyes on him as his face was fully flushed from her activity.

Howard had never met any female in his whole life, other than his cousins were when he was a little boy and not really knowing what they were doing, that was interested in seeing, playing, wanting his body as did Sueanne Walker. And one day when that time comes she will get to know all of him.

When Korina and Brian did return, Howard and Sueanne were able to find an apartment just a couple of blocks up from the Westford's. Howard helps her move into her apartment on the evenings that he has off from his duties. The two have become so involved with one another, that by June, the two have become engaged and down to the jewelry store at Kingstown Shopping Center they go.

"Oh Howard!" exclaims Sueanne trying on several types of rings before deciding on one special set. "It's beautiful, I love this one."

"It is beautiful. You do have good taste." Calling over the saleslady, "We'll take this set. No need to wrap it. She'll wear it out."

Exiting the store, Sueanne marvels her stones as Howard holds the door open for her. They reach their vehicle, and as she adjusts herself into her seat, she ponders, "What do you think mom is going to say about all this?"

"How old are you?"

"Eighteen. Why?"

"She can't say anything. You are old enough to make your own judgments."

"But, I've never had to make them before."

"Life is new to the both of us, but I'm sure with a few mistakes and problems, we will overcome them."

"I am so happy and know everything will be alright. I love you very much."

Howard was a little taken back with those words. He had never been told he was loved by anybody except Mrs. Caruso.

As the vehicle sped back to the apartment, Sueanne whispers in his ear, "Let's pull over somewhere before we get back. I want to do you a favor that is if you want me to."

Once again her hand begins stroking his leg and inside the thigh. As his bulge begins to swell once again, her hand strokes the length of it through his pants. "Do you like me doing this?" she asks looking up at him and then down to his bulge.

"Yes, But it's not easy to concentrate on driving."

"So hurry and find a parking place."

After awhile, Howard spots a dirt road going off to his right, "Do you know this road? Or where it will take us?"

"No, but we don't need to go too far off the road."

The car veers off the main road onto the dirt road, the whole time Sueanne is rubbing and squeezing his bulge.

As soon as the car stops, Sueanne has his zipper undone and asks, "Lift you fanny up off the seat so I can get your pants down."

Doing as he was asked, Sueanne slides his pants down so that she was able to see the whole of him. Taking his bulge into one hand she begins to squeeze and jerk her hand up and down on it. "How does this feel? I've never done this to a boy before. I don't know what to expect."

"You are doing just fine. Do you really want to finish me off?"

"I don't know. I've never done this to a boy before! What do I do?"

"Do you have a Kleenex in your purse?"

"I think so." searching in her purse, she comes across a handkerchief. She then proceeds to stroke his bulge which was ready to explode. Just then Howard lets out a huge grunt and Sueanne quickly covers the top of the bulge to catch his ejaculate.

"Wow," replies Sueanne that was sure some fun. Did you like it? Will it hurt me when we . . . when we do it?"

"Yes, it will hurt the first time, but after it will feel real good just as I was when you finished me off and you will know just what I experienced this day. I want to thank you for caring."

"It was more for my curiosity, but I love doing it for you. I want you even more now that I know what love will be like."

After discarding the evidence, the two straighten out his clothes and proceed to head back to the apartment with a new lease and knowledge of one another. "Have you done it with many girls?" she asked quizzically with her hand still between his legs

"I really haven't had sex, if that's what you mean, but I have been relieved a few times."

Before the two head off back to the apartment, the two decide to head on down to her mother's to show her the diamond ring. Arriving at the house, Marilyn comes out of the house to meet them at the car. This was a warning, that the old man was home and that they were not welcome in the house. As Marilyn approaches, Sueanne holds up her left hand to show her the ring. As though lightening had struck, Marilyn throws an ugly stare towards Howard before turning around and heads back into the house without so much of a how do you do.

Knowing that it would do no good in following her into the house and causing uproar between her father as well as her mother, the two head back to the apartment as tears stream down Sueanne's face, then she says to him, "With or without her blessing, we are going to get married.

After all, I love you too much and I now have a life of my own to live."

Without saying a word, Howard shakes his head in agreement and just knew that she would work things out between herself and her mother.

For the remainder of the ride home, Sueanne kept fingering her ring. "You do love me. Don't you?"

"What a thing to ask. I do love you very much."

"I've never known love until I met you. You make me feel like a woman and I love that feeling.

"You've shown me love that I've never had before as well and I love that feeling."

"We are going to be good for each other, you just wait and see." At that, Howard reaches an arm across her neck and brings her head to rest upon his shoulder.

"If you stay the night, I'll show you a good time." smiles Sueanne,

"Sounds as though I have created a monster"

"Just wait until I get you home, I'll show you what kind of monster I am, and remember it's your entire fault."

"Oohhh, you got me wondering what I'm up against."

"Keep in mind what you just experienced and then think twice that feeling. That's what you are up against."

When the two did get home, Sueanne did not disappoint Howard, nor did Howard disappoint Sueanne as they both got to know one another. Love comes to both of them this night.

Chapter 5

On August 19th, 1967, while Korina was in the hospital giving birth to a boy by the name of John Andrew Westford, Howard and Sueanne were being married at the Lutherans Memorial Church on Wise Avenue. It was a rather small wedding as compared to the exclusive of the Westford's. But it was all they could afford at the time. The entire wedding party consists of a best man: a close friend of Sueanne's, a neighbor of hers, by the name of Robert Evans, a maid-of-honor; another close friend of Sueanne's who they visited quite regularly, by the name of Anna Pitiello. The guests include Marilyn, Allen and Joanne, and because of the birth of Andrew, the Westford's were unable to make the wedding.

There was to be no reception afterwards. Howard and Sueanne dropped the family off at their house, and went on to their apartment. Obvious to the two, that their marriage was not approved by Marilyn. But yet, their association with the Westford's was much more openly and friendly.

Howard moves out of the barracks and moves his belongings in with Sueanne at 1210 Gilmanton Avenue. The apartment consists of one bedroom, good size living room, a moderate size kitchen and a small bathroom. Plus, it was above their Best Man's apartment.

While living there, the two would go downstairs and spend time with Mr. Robert Evans and his wife Janet. When it seemed quiet on the home front, the two would visit the Westford's and get to see the new addition to the family.

Two weeks before Howard was to end his term in service, Brian is preparing to move Korina and John Andrew to live in his hometown of Oneida, Ohio.

When time had arrived for Howard to end his time, he was hoping Sueanne would change her mind and let him stay in. He knew it would be rough out there and getting a job that he was not trained to do would be almost impossible for him to get. Besides, he wanted to return to his hometown in New Hampshire and Sueanne wanted to remain in Baltimore near her family. What with Korina and Brian in Oneida, her mom and siblings were alone and she would have to be around to assist them whenever the old man goes on one of his warpaths.

Disappointedly, Howard is discharged to Baltimore, Maryland and immediately seeks out employment. First, he applies at Signor Steel, the Chevrolet plant, and the Fisher Body plant. After taking the required physicals for each of the jobs, he is turned on each. "I just don't understand it." States a disgruntled Howard, upon returning home one evening throwing his jacket onto the couch.

"What is the reason they give you for not hiring you?" asks Sueanne coming into the living room wiping her hands on an apron.

'The doctors doing the physical claim that the tests all show that I have an enlarged heart."

"An enlarged heart," exclaims Sueanne shockingly," wouldn't the army have told you about this during your physical to get into and out of the service?"

"The army would have never drafted me if they had caught it, unless it could have happened within the past two years, of which I very much doubt that it had."

Sitting down next to him on the couch, Sueanne places one arm around him and asks, "So what can you do about finding out about this, now that you have been discharged from the army, and they are no longer responsible for your health?"

"I can go down to the Veterans Administration and tell them what I was told, and see if they could do something to help me. Don't worry hon. we'll figure something out"

True to his word, Howard arrives at the Veterans Administration where he explains his problem to the proper authorities. They give him a complete physical and inform him to go back home and wait for the results to arrive.

The whole month is spent waiting for the test results from the VA, and each time Howard calls in for verification, he is again constantly being told that he would be notified when the results of the tests become final. The whole time that Howard is waiting for the test results to come in, and still unable to find a job, Sueanne continues searching before they too far behind in their rent and bills.

Being pregnant, Sueanne finds a job in the toy department store on Channel Drive located in the center of Baltimore City.

The thought infuriated Howard just knowing that his wife had to go to work while he feeling healthy was unable to. This caused him to become a major cause of all the heated arguments and frustrations which seemed suddenly begin to befall upon them.

Sueanne being pregnant was having enough problems just carrying the baby. She didn't need these arguments that kept cropping up for no known reason. In each of the arguments that had come between them, Sueanne's family was quick to accuse Howard and rush to her side whenever she needed a shoulder to cry on. But, there was no one there for him to turn to. This loneliness that Howard felt is the same he had when he was at the Orphans Home when he was growing up, and it caused the arguments to boil over more than was necessary. Howard believed that their problems could have been solved between the two if the family had not interfered or if Sueanne hadn't run to mommy every time see shed a tear.

Life was looking a little bleak for Howard and Sueanne as they daily got into an argument for one reason or another.

One evening after work, when Howard picks Sueanne from work, she informs him," I talked to my boss and he said if you didn't mind working in the shoe department, you could come in with me tomorrow morning and he would you a try."

The following morning, Howard goes into work with Sueanne and talked to the boss. By the time he exits the office, Howard has a job.

Though selling shoes was not one of his most likable jobs, he learns the business fast and learned to love his work, only because it was the only type of work he could get.

During his lunch breaks, Howard would go up to the fourth floor and together he and Sueanne would eat their lunch while they talked of what happened to them during their work time.

It was during one of these social conversations, which Howard had mentioned about the hope that he could continue his education, get into MIT in the hopes of getting a degree in Aeronautical Engineering. But in doing so, it would take him away from her and her family, and that he would need another six years to finish schooling before he could ever benefit from his training.

Sueanne was against this idea right from the beginning and gives him a hard time about him even wanting to leave the job she had gotten for him or leaving her as well to go back home.

"No, I don't even want to hear about moving to New Hampshire. I don't know anyone there and if something happens I'll be all alone. Besides it seems as though you have bad remembrances of the people in New Hampshire." This split in decision, would tear their marriage apart, and with her soon to deliver their baby, Howard could not risk the loss, so in Baltimore he stays.

Then, as fate would have it, On December 17th, around one o'clock in the afternoon, as Howard sat upon the couch relaxing and putting together one of his space models, Sueanne notes that she was going down to visit the neighbors. Five-minutes later, she returns, sits down next to him, watching what he was doing. Howard then returns the look and as they face off squarely, he asks putting his model aside," What's wrong? I thought you were going downstairs to visit with the neighbors?"

"I decided not to, besides, I'm not feeling too well."

"You do look a little peaked, you want to lie down?"

"No, but I do have to go to the bathroom. I am feeling a lot of pressure down below."

Rising up from the couch, Howard helps her into the bathroom. Once she is seated securely on the toilet, he returns to the couch to wait for her call for assistance. Suddenly, he hears her shout out to him. Leaping to his feet, he almost stumbles over his own feet, before obtaining balance, in doing so; his model that he was working on flew up in all directions. Heading towards the bathroom, he notes Sueanne sitting there quivering in pain as tears stream down her face "What is it?" asks Howard nervously, "Why did you scream out like that?"

Looking up at him, she points downward stating, "My stomach, it feels like it is falling out of me." She reaches out to him, drawing him closer to her, as she rocks back and forth in pain.

Examining the situation, looking for whatever he thought might be causing her this terrible pain. As he looks closer he states, "There is what seems to be what looks like a bag hanging. It looks as though it has water in it."

"Oh God, no" yells out Sueanne, "It's my water bag, I'm Going to lose the baby." Trembling uncontrollable on the toilet, she tells Howard, "Run downstairs and ask Janet to call mommy up and let her know what is happening."

Running downstairs, Howard misses the last step and lands against the banister before falling onto the floor. Quickly he regains his balance and enters the Evan's apartment to ask for the use of their phone. After informing Janet and Bob of Sueanne's condition, Janet heads upstairs to be with her while Howard gets Marilyn on the phone to inform her of what is happening with her daughter.

Bob has agreed to take Howard down to pick her up. Howard knew that Sueanne was in good hands and that he would not be missed in a situation as this.

When Howard and Bob arrive back at the apartment, Marilyn runs into the bathroom where she consoles Sueanne. It was at this point, that Howard had realized that no one had called a doctor. Heading back down stairs, Howard dials the doctor's office only to get his secretary. After finally getting the doctor on the phone, Howard explains to him detail by detail of what was going on with Sueanne. But before Howard could get everything out, he was cut off short by the doctor when he heartlessly states, "There was no need to get upset, and that neither should worry. Sueanne and the baby would be alright."

"Bull shit" yells Howard slamming the phone back down onto its cradle. He then thumbs through the phone book for another hospital. He comes across Harbor Hospital. He knew that this hospital cared for the unfortunate and those on welfare, but he needed help now.

When he is connected to the doctor on call, Howard informs him of what is taking place with his wife who is only six months pregnant. The doctor informs him that he has never heard of a water bag, if this is the water bag to fall down so low and yet not break

"Well, it may have already broken for as long as I've been down stairs trying to get a doctor to help her."

It was at this moment that he is told to bring Sueanne in as soon as he could. "We'll be right up." States Howard clumsily hanging up the phone and running back upstairs to inform Sueanne that she will be going to Harbor Hospital to be seen there.'

"Harbor Hospital!" remarks Marilyn, "I don't want my daughter going to that hospital."

"Too bad," remarks Howard, "She is my wife, and this hospital agreed to see her, so if you don't mind, get her things together, and Bob . . . ." But before he could finish the sentence, Bob remarks, "You get her things together, and I'll get the car ready. Just take it easy. Everything will be fine."

"Ok, thank you."

Arriving at the hospital, the doctor quickly takes Howard into an office where he was asked all sorts of questions. One was why they hadn't called their own doctor who would know about her case. To which Howard replies, "I did call him. But he told me there was nothing to worry about. And you, yourself told me to bring her right up here because you had never heard anything like this before."

"We can't touch her because she is under another doctor's care, and if we did, it would mean trouble for us."

"You mean that you're not even going to look at her?"

"I'm afraid it's out of our hands."

By now, Howard is getting very angry and soon is beginning to yell at the doctor who was trying desperately to back himself out of the room.

"Well, what kind of doctor are you? Are you just going to let her lie there?"

Knowing that Howard's hollering was being heard by those in the waiting room, the doctor asks, "Who is her doctor?" taking out a pencil to write his name down.

Dr. Waters" replied Howard as his voice rises throughout the emergency room. The loud voice brings a security guard into the emergency room just outside the office.

After giving the doctor the information, he retreats back to the sofa where he sits himself down where he can watch the doctor and the security guard through the glass doors.

"Howard, you've got to get a hold of yourself." Consoles Bob as he sits down by his side,

"You're temper isn't going to help Sueanne. Don't you think she can hear you as well as all of us out here?"

"I know you're right, but these doctors and their so called damn rules. They make me mad."

A few minutes go by, when one of the doctors come out to the waiting room. Confronting Howard, he remarks that he had reached Doctor Waters and that he was going to see Sueanne out at St. Joseph's Hospital.

"St. Joseph's." screams Howard jumping to his feet, "That's thirty miles away.

Bob, who was the only one that seemed to keep his head, asks for directions and informs Howard that he would take them there.

Howard enters the emergency room keeping his eyes on the security guard following closely behind him. Entering Suanne's room, he informs her that she would be going to St. Joseph's Hospital. Helping her up, he retrieves her coat while Marilyn helps Sueanne to get dressed. Howard helps put it on her the whole time complaining about the way they were getting the run around to Marilyn, who, had been very quiet throughout the whole ordeal.

With directions in hand, Bob, holds the door as they begin to exit the hospital, suddenly Howard turns to look back at the doctor and the security guard still standing in the room by the glass doors watching them leave the building. "Thanks for nothing. You'll never see us coming back to this dump again. And if anything happens to my wife and I can prove you could have done something for her . . ." Bob pushes him along cutting off the rest of his sentence, in hopes to prevent him from saying something that may get him arrested. "Don't threaten them Howard." Placing his arm across his shoulder as Marilyn gingerly escorts Sueanne ahead of them to the car.

Howard joins Marilyn and Sueanne already in the rear seat. As the vehicle prepares to exit the hospital in the front, Howard notices the security guard still watching them from inside the building, as they pass in front, Howard gives the hospital and the guard, 'The middle finger'.

"Howard" exclaims Sueanne after witnessing his gesture in giving the security guard the "finger".

"I'm sorry honey, but they made me so damn mad."

"Getting mad didn't any of us anywhere, did it?"

"Maybe not, but I feel as though I got their attention."

Once they got on the Jones Falls Expressway, Bob puts the pedal to the metal, thus arriving at the hospital in just twenty minutes. Upon checking in at the desk, Howard is told that Dr. Waters had not arrived yet, and to take a seat and they would be notified when Dr. Waters arrived.

So they sit, and they sit, as one patient after another come into the waiting room, sit for a short time before they are called to the emergency room.

Pacing back and forth, Howard tries desperately to keep his cool. Four hours has gone by, yet they still are told to wait.

At eight-thirty pm, Dr. Waters arrive and calls Sueanne into the Emergency room.

A short time later, Dr. Waters arrive in the waiting room.

"How is she?" asks Howard as the doctor approaches him.

"She's going to lose the baby and there is nothing I can do to save it."

"With his mouth wide open, and Marilyn dropping her head into her hands, Howard states loudly, "You told me five hours ago that there was nothing to worry about, and now you tell me she's going to lose our baby, and there's nothing you can do about it. Bullshit doc, you are going in there and you are going to save our baby or sooo help me."

I'll need two hundred dollars by morning if I'm going to even touch her."

"What. Now you want two hundred dollars to save the baby."

"That's just for me to begin to care for her."

"I can't come up with two hundred dollars by morning or even by next week." states Howard now leaning up against the doctor.

Bob rushes to Howard's side and pulls him away from the doctor.

"We were going to pay you like we said we would when you first saw her, but we never expected anything like this to happen. Now you tell us to get you the money in a few short hours. That's impossible, and besides, you give us the run around, get us up here thirty miles out of our way, keep us waiting for another five hours and now demand two hundred dollars."

Raising his fist to land a blow at the doctor, he is stopped by Bob, as Sueanne yells out, "Howard, stop it right now, just cool it."

Turning, at hearing her voice, Howard witnesses Sueanne exit the Emergency room to the waiting room, looking very displeased at what just took place'. Howard runs over taking her hand he leads her to a chair, "Don't worry hon. everything is going to be alright." Turning, he points towards Dr. Waters and in a loud stern voice remarks, "You, go to hell with your two hundred dollars. For you are no longer our doctors."

At that moment, the nurse had arrived with three other doctors and a security officer; they stood at the door to see what was going to take place. Again, Howard becomes belligerent as he continues yelling at Dr. Waters. At this point in time, to protect the others in the waiting room from hearing his verbal abuse, the security officer enters through the Emergency room instructing Howard to keep his voice down or go outside the building with it.

I want him taken off my wife's case and placed in the care of the hospital."

The three doctors look at one another and ask Howard to join them in one of the offices for a conference. Entering the room, Sueanne somewhat shaken up cries on her mother's shoulder as Bob rubs her back.

Shortly, Howard emerges from the office, enters the waiting room with one of the doctors and the security guard. Sitting down next to Sueanne, he informs her, "They want you to return to the ER. You are now under the care of the clinic. They will take care of you and the baby." Howard remains in the waiting room with Marilyn and Bob, as Sueanne is escorted back into the ER and into one of the rooms.

Marilyn never looked at Howard or said a word to him. She thought to herself that Howard had made things worse by his vulgarity. Being a Catholic, she never believed in swearing and if things didn't work out the way she wanted them to, then that was the way it should be. She had learned as a young girl then you can't change things by getting upset or mad. Thus the reason she is still married to her husband. It would be sin if she disobeyed him or left him.

Howard, by growing up in the world he had known, believed if something is not going right for you than you should stand up for them and use any source available in order to make it happen, and although his vulgarity was louder than it should be and his jesters were uncalled for, he got what was needed and that was care for his wife and baby.

It was shortly after midnight when the doctor enters the waiting room and informs Howard and Marilyn that Sueanne had delivered a baby boy and that both were resting comfortably. He then states, "Because the baby is three months premature and weighing only two pounds, he couldn't see much of a chance in the baby living through the morning. But would do all he could to save him."

Marilyn had been wringing her hands together as she listens to the doctor's words, placing her hand into Howard's as she thanks the doctor before she too begins to weep.

Placing both arms around the both of them, the doctor instructs them, "I think it would be for the best of you to go home, get a good night sleep. "I'll call you if there is any change in your wife or the baby."

Bob leaves his address and phone number with the nurse at the desk before escorting Howard and Marilyn to the car. It was an eerie feeling that had overcome Howard knowing that he had to leave his wife and new born son in the hospital and travel thirty miles away from her.

Upon arriving back at the apartment, the two thank Bob for all his help and asked if he would care for any money for the gas and time accrued. Bob refused ushering them upstairs so he could inform Janet what had taken place before going to bed.

Marilyn helps Howard prepare for a shower and then into bed before she takes her shower. While Howard lies there in bed, he prays, "Please Lord let everything be alright with both of them for I need them so much in my life." He then falls into a deep sleep. Before Marilyn retires to the couch for the night, she checks in on Howard where she finds him sound asleep.

The alarm startles Howard awake, sitting up in his bed; he stares at the dials on the clock. It reads 7am. Wiping the sleep from his eyes, he stumbles out of bed, goes into the bathroom, washes up, does his teeth. Back in his bedroom he dresses up for work, makes his bed and enters the kitchen to prepare himself breakfast. Shortly, Marilyn joins him at the table. Howard pours her a cup of coffee. Quietly they sit, both thinking the same thing, but neither wanting to talk about it.

Howard was the first to speak up, "Do you want me to take you home before I go to work?"

Without looking up from her coffee cup, Marilyn shakes her head in the affirmative, "If you want to." "It's not that I really want you to go home, but I'm afraid of what the old man is going to do. Plus there is Allen and Joanne who need you there, states Howard taking two pieces of toast out of the toaster and spreading them with Apple Butter.

Holding her coffee cup with both hands, Marilyn answers, "Right now, I really don't care what the old man thinks or does, just as long as he does not take it out on the children."

Just then, there is a knock on the door. Howard rises from the table, enters the living room and opens the door where he meets Janet Evans. "Howard, you have a phone call."

"Thank you." And he rushes past her and down the stairs in a single bound. Picking up the phone he nervously answers, "Hello. Yes, this is Mr. Walker." Listening, his face becomes ashen white as his body falls into the nearest chair. Tears begin to trickle down his face as he says, "Yes doc, I'm still here. How is my wife doing? Did you tell her yet? Good, could you wait until I arrive before you tell her? Thank you, we'll be there just as soon as we can." Howard just sits in the chair taking everything in before hanging up the phone onto its cradle. Turning, he sees Mrs. Evans standing in the doorway holding her hands to her mouth. She had overheard the conversation and had forecasted the worse from the hospital.

Advancing towards Janet, Howard states chokingly, "Our son is dead"

Slowly, Howard climbs back up the stairs, trying to hold back the tears that threatened to burst from his eyes. Approaching Marilyn he informs her of the news as the tears run down his cheeks "The Baby is dead; he died this morning at seven-thirty. The doctor said his lungs had collapsed."

Laying his head on her shoulder, together they both weep, one for his son and the other for her grandson.

"Do you want to ride up with us or do you want to go home?"

"I want to ride up with you. I want to be with my daughter."

"I'll go downstairs and call the pastor and see if he could meet us up at the hospital." states Howard heading off in the direction of the door and down the stairs.

While Howard uses Mrs. Evans's phone to call the pastor, Janet, Bob and Marilyn stand outside the hallway and console one another. "Would you like me to ride up and keep you company?" asks Mrs. Evans.

"No, I'll be alright. But thanks for the offer."

After everyone had finished dressing and Marilyn had packed a bag containing items that Sueanne would need while in the hospital, they met Bob who was ready in the vehicle waiting for the two.

Janet comes out of the building, approaches Bob's side of the vehicle, leans in and kisses him. He then says something to her that was not audible to the two in the rear seat. Bob then looks behind him and asks if they were ready. Seeing all was, he drives out of the drive and heads toward the hospital. The trip was not very conversational due to the feeling of gloom, but they tried to make the best of the trip.

Arriving at the hospital, the trio enters and takes the elevator up to Sueanne's room. As they entered, they see Sueanne in tears. Howard and Marilyn both rush to hug her, but it was Marilyn that Sueanne reached out to as she lets it all out." My baby boy is dead."

"Who told you?" asks Howard standing beside the bed waiting his turn to get to hug her.

"I knew when the nurses brought the babies in for feeding."

Marilyn again bends down and gives her daughter another hug and words of comfort, just as a nurse appears at the doorway of the room and motions Howard over with a wave of her index finger.

"I'm terribly sorry. I didn't know until it was too late." Without saying a word, Howard shakes his head yes, as though to let her know that he understood, and pats her on the shoulder. He then turns to Sueanne, just as the Pastor comes in. Together, they all stand around Sueanne and pray, as tears of sorrow fall upon the bed. The tears falling from Howard's eyes were especially more painful, for as Sueanne's husband and the father of their lost baby boy, he had yet been able to hug her and help her in her consoling. After the prayers were said and the family thanking Pastor Taylor, Howard takes his turn to sit on the bed and holding her hand he hugs her all the while Marilyn was eagle-eying him.

"I'm so sorry about the baby."

"The baby's name is Norman Edward Walker."

"You named him already?" asked Howard holding tightly to her hand.

"Named him right after he was born, named him after mommy's Uncle and your dad."

"Thank you hon. I will write to my dad, he'd be very pleased to know that his grandson carries his name."

The family and friend stay the day taking turns going to the cafeteria and keeping Sueanne occupied. They would arrive in the morning and leave after hours.

Three days later, Sueanne comes home from the hospital and her life begins to change drastically. She becomes unbearable to live with, no matter how Howard tries understanding her moods.

The doctor's orders were that she was not to go out of the house or do any type of strenuous work. In the meantime,

Howard loses his job at the shoe department, for in all his haste he had forgotten to notify the department store as to what was happening.

The frustration of losing the baby and the outbursts from Howard and her family has Sueanne talking about leaving Baltimore for it has nothing to offer her anymore. Howard mentions that "Maybe going to New Hampshire and getting into MIT", which has been his dream since boyhood," and to graduate in Aeronautical Engineering, that the change might do them some good."

Sueanne ends his thoughts of moving to New Hampshire before he could even get the rest of his thought out. "I want to move to Ohio and be with Korina and Brian"

"But we're not sure about Ohio. I am sure about New Hampshire, as you are of Baltimore. I've lived there and know more about living there than I would in a state I or you know nothing about."

"I want to move to Ohio, Korina and Brian will help us, plus I'll be able to babysit my nephew."

"Think about it. Please, before you make up your mind."

"I've thought about it since I lost the baby."

"You thought about it! What about me? You've never said anything about moving." yells Howard getting a little hot over what he is hearing.

"I talked to Korina about it when I was in the hospital; she thought it would be a great idea in moving out there"

"You talked to Korina before you talked to me?"

"Because you always yell and lose it. No one can talk to you when you get upset. Look at what you did to Dr. Waters."

"You are blaming me for yelling at Dr. Waters? It was his negligence that resulted in the loss of our baby."

"It was your fault. Even mommy agrees."

"Sueanne, you don't mean what you are saying."

"Yes I do. Either you move to Ohio with me or you can get out of my life, your choice."

"Sueanne please let's not leave it like this. We can sit down and talk this over."

"My mind is made up Howard, either you drive me out to Ohio, or I'll take a bus. Either way I'm going to Ohio.

"Okay! I'll take you out." remarks Howard, as he decides that what she is going through, maybe Korina will be able to help get through her suffering."Will you be sorry about leaving Baltimore?" asks Howard making sure Sueanne was aware of what she was about to do.

"No, not really, I'll miss mommy, Allen and Joanne, but other than that I'll not miss this place at all."

"What about your mom and grand mom? Will they be alright?"

"When the old man goes on his warpath, they will head down to grand moms as usual."

"Then, why doesn't she just leave him, if he is so abusive to them?"

"Mommy has her beliefs. She believes that her marriage is sacred and when two people marry, they remain married forever and what happens in the marriage is part of it."

"Well! If that's the way it's supposed to be, then there is nothing anyone can do to help them." states Howard.

With that remark, Sueanne glares at him, and then says, "Sometimes, you make me so damn mad that I want to slap you. I'm not my mom so if I find this marriage upsetting, I will walk away from it." She then walks away from Howard.

Standing there, with a puzzled look on his face, he asks himself, 'What did I say'.

Chapter 6

On January 20th, 1968, Howard and Sueanne stop at Marilyn's house to say good-bye to her family. They were packed to head out to Ohio. At around 5:30 am, as snow begins to fall.

Marilyn scurries from the house to see them off.

"The old man is gone to work so it's okay to come out and say goodbye."

"You could have waited until we came into the house to goodbye." replies Sueanne.

"Are you sure you want this?"

"I miss Korina and being around my nephew. Yes, I'll be fine."

Reaching through the door window, Marilyn kisses Sueanne and waves to Howard. She really believes Howard was taken her daughter away from her as much as Brian had taken away Korina. Her family was falling apart and she felt like she was alone without her two oldest daughters who were always a part of her life.

"You take good care of my daughter, you hear?

"Yes Maam I will do that. I love her very much and this is what she wants to do so I will go along with her."

"Get along now the snow is beginning to fall harder, I love you." States Marilyn as Sueanne rolls up her window as tears fall down her checks.

The two set their sights on what is hoped to be a new beginning of life in Ohio.

The drive out is long and treacherous, at times they wondered if old Fang, loaded down the way she was would even make it out of Baltimore leaving them stranded on the side of the highway.

"You think that this old car will make the trip?" asks Sueanne with a puzzled look

"I have faith in her as long as we don't get into traffic jams, then we'll wind up with vapor locks and we'll have to wait it out for awhile."

"Sure hope we don't get half way there and have to call Korina and Brian out to pick us up." stats Sueanne not looking over at Howard.

"Well don't you worry your head off I have no intentions in calling your family for any help. This car will make it."

As Howard drove along, he would reflect on when he was going to take a friend of his, head to Lorain, Ohio where Francis is already employed aboard an ore boat, but Howard had to wait for physical and information on which ore boat he would be employed on. Francis helped Howard with a month's rent at the Lorain Hotel. Just hoping he would be called before the month's end, for he no money and his car had cracked a block so when the wrecker came to tow it away, not having the money to repair the engine, he signed the car over to the tow truck owner and the two had to take a cab to the hotel since they had been only eighteen miles away. The month was just about over when finally a letter arrived telling him to report to the docks where the 580-foot ore ship

Alva C. Dinkey was docked. He was to report to the cook in the galley where his job would be cook's helper and helper in exchange of linen when in port. Howard traveled from Lorain on Lake Erie up Lake Huron through the Sault Ste. Marie locks between Escanaba and Canada into Lake Superior arriving at Duluth, Michigan where their precious cargo is unloaded and a new load of iron ore limestone to be ferried back to either Milwaukee or Lorain, Ohio.

Throughout the night and into the morning hours, the tired old Ford carried them through. It was almost twelve hours later when the couple had finally reached its destination and arrived in Oneida, Ohio, around five pm with the Ford still running.

"Sueanne!" yells Korina running out of the house and into the snow that had accumulated to about eight inches. Korina throws her arms around Sueanne as she gives her a big hug and a kiss. "Are we glad you made it alright? How was the trip?"

"Long and tiring" states Sueanne trudging through the snow, making her way towards the house.

"Leave the stuff in the car. Brian will help you unload when he gets home from work." Inquires Korina to Howard, who was about to begin reaching for stuff to unload. "Just bring in yours and Suanne's suitcases."

Once in the warm house, Korina goes about making something quick for them to eat, for supper would be ready when Brian arrives home.

Howard sits at the table and listens to the girls' talk of Baltimore and their family, as Korina bounces John Andrew on her knees.

By the time Brian arrives home, the snow had really amounted so deep that as Brian had been halted by the deep snow and unable to get up the driveway. Howard joins Brian outside in removing the snow in order for Brian to get his car up the drive. Brian then helps Howard bring in what they could from the car for they had run out of daylight.

Howard and Brian enter the house where they remove their wet clothing and take turns in cleaning up before supper.

The girls prepare the supper while Brian and Howard entertain john Andrew as he goes about crawling on the floor in the living room.

Some reason Howard feels uncomfortable being around Brian. His conversations about hunting, trapping, guns was not the talk that Howard was use to. Ohio seemed like a backward state, there is so much open land that it seems no matter where one hunted, the owner never complained.

This from Brian who was now showing Howard the new Rifle Magazine he received in the mail. Howard just pretends to be interested in his conversation.

When supper was on the table, and all had taken their seats, Brian asks, "How long are you two planning to stay with us?"

Korina quickly gives him a disapproving stare as if to tell him that there was no need for such a remark.

Looking at Sueanne and then at Korina, Howard states, "You people invited us up to live here, I hope you will help find us a job and a place to live if you don't want us living here with you and your family"

The conversation around the table suddenly became very quiet. Then Korina asks "What was it like growing up a foster child?"

Howard, surprised at the sudden question explains to them, "There was a lot of moving around, having many different families whose own children would like to fight you because they didn't want to share you with their parents."

"Was there any particular foster family better than the others?" asks Brian sipping on his coffee

"Sure, there was the Caruso family; they were my first foster family. It was them that rescued me from running away from the orphans home to look for my real parents."

"You ran away? How far was it? Weren't you scared?"

All these questions thrown at him at once began to confuse Howard as he sought out what to say next. "I was around nine years old when I joined a crowd of visitors and got outside the home before making a beeline down the road following landmarks that I had remembered when my "Lady of Charity" who just happened to be the Caruso's would take us home for a weekend and I would remember the bridge down the road from the Home when we crossed it made this whining noise. It was later told to me that I had traveled some Thirty-eight miles from the Orphans home to where I had lived in Penville. I was scared the whole journey, I was afraid the police would pick me up; I hid in bushes along the river, in backs of stores where I could get something to eat and in barns. During the journey I was picked up by a few families that took me to their homes to be cleaned up then upon hearing they were calling the authorities, I took off again."

"What kind of home was the Caruso's home?" asks Brian.

"What was the Lady of Charity?" asks Korina getting up to get more coffee.

"It was a farm, a dairy and chicken farm, I recall one day when it was snowing like mad outside and we were told to move the chickens from the second floor down to the first, my oldest brother Tom tried to get in front of them and wave them to the stairs, but we three waved ferociously at the chickens where they crowded into a corner crushing one another. We were really in trouble now, so my oldest brother thought of throwing the dead chickens out the barns back window into the snow where they would be hidden from view. That was fine until spring came and shortly one after another chicken was spotted when Mr. Caruso started to work the back field. Of course we blamed it all on Tom, and he got punished.

"The Ladies of Charity were normal family members who came to the orphans Home and assigned to certain children who had no one to take them out on weekend jaunts or give them anything for the Holidays. My Lady of Charity Sol and Anne Caruso would take us four boys out and let us see what living in a family home was like and on Christmas, Easter and other times of the year they would give us presents or an Easter Basket."

"So what kind of trouble did Tom get?" asked Korina bouncing the baby on her knee.

"If I recall right, we went to a movie to see '*Svengali and the Blonde'* I don't recall much about the movie but I felt bad for Tom having to go to bed early and not having to watch television, but what are big brothers for? They take the blame for everything that goes wrong."

"Hate to break up the reunion." states Brian finishing up his coffee, but it's getting late."

"And we have a kitchen to clean." implies Korina handing john Andrew to Sueanne, "You want to prepare john for bed?"

"Why don't you boys go find something to do." states Sueanne taking hold of John Andrew from Korina.

Brian shows Howard his guns and traps he uses for hunting and trapping "You ever go hunting"

Brian asks taking down some beaver traps. "If you want to go with me some morning, I'll show you how it's done."

"Sure I would love to go trapping." l*ies Howard, but not wanting to show it,* "What do you trap most?"

"Mostly beaver" states Brian taking down this wire rectangular box that shows how the beavers go in through a door that swings in and shuts the beaver or any other critter leaving him inside where he drowns.

As Brian was explaining his different traps and gun collection, Sueanne enters and disappear into the bathroom, and she begins bathing John Andrew.

That night, as they prepare for bed, they take turns using the tub, for there is no shower. The two spread a blanket on the living room floor for there was no extra bedroom in the house. Lying on the blanket on the floor, just earshot away from Brian and Korina's bedroom, Howard could hear them talking about him and Sueanne and Brian seemed uncomfortable that the two were living there.

As Howard tries blocking out the voices, he cuddles Sueanne into his elbow as he thinks back to the good times just a year earlier. How things have gone so bad in such a short time.

When Monday arrives, not wanting to waste any time, Brian asks Howard if he would like to go into work with him at Johns Manville. Upon arriving at work Brian goes into the office to talk with his boss. Brian had worked there before being drafted into the service, so he had a good rapport with the boss. Howard is invited into the office where he is handed some papers to fill out. He is informed that there was an opening in the house cleaning department, which consists of emptying containers of non usable fiberglass material and delivering the glass marbles to machines which shred the marbles into fibers. The job looked very hopeful as Howard is taken to the floor boss to show him what he had to do.

On his first day, Howard knew that he would like the work and explained to Sueanne upon his arrival home. Of just what the job consists of. "I really do think I can do this type of work. I pray that there will be no physical to foul this job up."

For the next three days, Howard would ride into work and back home again; each day feeling satisfied that he had gotten the job.

On the fourth day, Howard is told that he would have to report to the company's physician to undergo a complete physical.

"Oh no!" exclaimed Howard, "Not another physical."

"Why not?" asks the boss looking at him surprisingly, "Everyone here has to have a physical before listed as an employee and placed on the insurance program."

It is then, that Howard explains about what the other physicals had turned up about his heart condition.

"Don't worry; here you only lose your job if the Physician feels that the work would hurt you in any way. I believe you will keep your job, for I have watched you in the past three days and you show interest in your work."

"I hope you're right, I really need this job."

Giving Howard the address of the physician, he leaves by way of a ride from one of the other employee.

The physical takes all morning. He then is told to return to work and the results would be sent to his department boss.

Returning to his duties, he continues his job of delivering the containers to the machines. The whole time, he is keeping an eye out on the office watching the comings and goings of the boss. By the time the end of the work day arrived, the boss informs him to be ready to come in the morning.

Upon returning home, Sueanne asks him, "How did everything go?"

He tells her about the complete physical he had to go through.

"Well, I guess you can throw this job out the window." states Sueanne.

"Why do you say that?" questions Korina

"Howard has an enlarged heart, and it keeps him from landing a job."

"Maybe they might keep him on. They watched him work today, and everything looked good. You never know." remarks Brian.

"I sure hope so." replies Howard downheartedly, "But I know I don't have much of a chance."

Throughout the evening, the two couples kept talking on the same subject. But in his heart, Howard knew what was in store for him come morning. Just because he was informed to come to work in the morning, doesn't mean that he will be able to stay.

The following morning, Howard once again rides in with Brian with hopes of staying on the job. All that morning, he kept his eye on the office as he went about his work. Every time he heard the office phone ring he would freeze in his tracks, swallow hard and hope that it wasn't bad news.

As the day comes to a close, Howard breathed a sigh of relief thinking the worse was behind him.

Just five minutes before quitting time, the department boss approaches him, "Could you please come in my office?"

Entering, Howard didn't even wait to be told, "I know, I failed the physical. Now you don't want me to come back in the morning."

Looking at Howard, the boss shakes his head in affirmation saying, "I'm truly sorry Howard. I really am."

"It's an enlarged heart isn't it?"

"Yup you get it corrected and I'll see that you get hired again."

"Thanks." remarks Howard, "But how does one correct an enlarged heart?"

Without a good-bye, Howard storms out of the office, to await Brian for the ride back home.

"What did the boss say?"

"Put it this way, I won't be riding in with you in the morning. Damn it, why didn't the Army catch this when I was drafted?"

"You know the army during war time, they'll take anyone that can fire a rifle, and hope that no one discovers their ailments. That way they don't have to give you a disability for it when you ETS."

Arriving back home, Howard informs the girls about what the boss told him about his enlarged heart.

"I don't understand." states Korina, as she places John Andrew into the tub for his bath. "Didn't the army know about your condition when you went in?"

"I don't know." states Howard putting down his cup of tea.

Brian steps into the kitchen from the living room and asks, "With all the physical demands the army expects from you during basic training. It's a wonder you didn't drop dead if your condition is as serious as they say it is."

"Maybe, it developed after he was already in the army and they didn't want to take responsible for It." remarks Sueanne, getting up from the table to put away the dishes.

The conversation carries on throughout yet another evening until they become tired, and retire for the night.

Time has passed, it has been one month since Sueanne and Howard had moved in with the Westford's. During that time, Howard had made many an effort that was possible to land some sort of job. One afternoon, as Howard was going through the newspaper, he comes upon a certain number to call: if looking for employment. Howard calls the number; he finds he is connected to Mid-Central Industries in Harper, Indiana. Howard makes an appointment to go in for an interview. The job will take him fifteen miles west of Oneida, Ohio, but a job is a job, and he needed one as well as the next man.

During the interview, he found out that the work consists of grinding down fiberglass molds which would go into the finished product of the Hydrodyne boat. He would also be responsible for the painting of the inside of the unfinished boat and in helping with the assembling of the finished product.

While working here, Howard is thrown into some very interesting sect, known as Amish. Howard had never met anyone that was Amish before. This would be his indoctrination to a new type of people.

From what Howard has discovered while working there, the Amish people originated from the Anabaptist movement of the early 1500's in Switzerland. These people wished to conserve traditions and separation from the world more than the other Anabaptist. They arrive in Pennsylvania in the early 1700's part of William Penn's 'Holy Experiment'. These people are primarily farmers; some are carpenters and cabinet makers, while others are blacksmiths, buggy and harness makers.

Due to the farmlands being expensive and becoming increasingly scarce, some younger members have taken jobs in nearby factories, restaurants, and general stores which provide the Amish community with goods necessary to continue their lifestyle, that they could not produce themselves. Their neat farms are without electricity or telephone, but look much like any other farm around them. Their homes are built with numerous rooms to support typical large families. Their heat is usually by wood or coal. Cooking stoves are powered by propane, kerosene or wood. Kerosene or clear gas lamps provide the light needed. Amish people will not accept public welfare aid or retirement income. They do pay income and real estate taxes and are exempt from Social Security taxes if they farm or are self employed.

After a few weeks of steady work, Sueanne asked if she could go with him to see if she could get a job there as well. Howard tries talking her out of it thinking that it was no job for a woman of her caliber. "It would be just too dirty and hard for you to do."

Sueanne stands defiant saying, "After all, with both of us working, we could double our income. I'm going."

Without any further arguing, Howard drives into work with her, and a date for an interview. Sueanne is given a job in the paint shop, spraying the inside molds of the boat, but after the first day, she informs Howard that she would not be going into work with him in the morning that she found that the dust from the sanding and paint was bothering her even with the mask on.

"I tried telling you that."

"Don't push it."

The following morning upon arrival at work Howard informs his boss that Sueanne wasn't up to performing that type of manual labor.

As it is, Sueanne and Howard were receiving feelings from Brian, that they were overstaying their welcome in his home even though Howard was paying for their share of the food and Sueanne was performing the majority of the household chores and babysitting John Andrew.

Although things seemed to be going back to normal between Howard and Sueanne, they were still very much filled with remorse and discontent over the loss of their son. Those deep rooted feelings would occasionally surface from their inner emotions and blame one another as well as the Almighty.

To help them both overcome these feelings of guilt, the two decide on February 1stth, 1968 to be baptized unto the Lord at the Granville Church of Christ, in Granville Ohio, a short ten minute ride from Oneida. The pastor would come to the Westford home bi-weekly to give bible lessons, so it was then that Howard and Sueanne joined in the lessons which led them to be baptized.

Whether or not it was due to being baptized, within two weeks the two were able to purchase a second car, a 1960 Dodge push button automatic on the dash and rent a home on East Summer Street in Smithville, Ohio. Howard is told of a job opening closer to home. He goes in to see if he could get in. The job is in town, called Croons, philter Company, it is a lumber company. The job although a good one, paid less than his previous one. The pay just wasn't doing it for them. Their monthly rent alone is higher than his pay check. After two months of working there, Howard finds himself one month back in his rent with no sign of catching up.

One day while he was in the office talking to the receptionist about looking for another job that paid better, she informs him, "Don't let anyone know I told you this, But, there is a job opening at stokers, in Ft. Wayne, Indiana where my husband works." This job, would take him further than the one he had at the Hydrodyne Boat Factory. The job would have him traveling twenty-three miles from Smithville. She informs Howard that if he was to go there, he would have a very good chance to be hired right on the spot. Thanking her, Howard informs her that he would go out there in the morning, and that he would not be in to work.

The following day, Howard is on his way to check out the job. Driving in, he hopes that he hasn't just lost another job in his quest of finding one that will help both he and Sueanne to live a normal trouble-free life.

At stoker's, he fills out his application and is told that he was to report to the physician's office for a checkup and physical. Howard informs his manager about why he is so reluctant in having to go for his physical.

After listening whole heartedly to Howard's dilemma, the manager informs him, "Anyone who works here must go for a physical, and you do want to work here. Don't you?"

"Yes sir."

"Then go have your physical done, and bring the results back with you."

Howard goes and reports for his physical, while kicking himself for leaving the lumber company. At least he had a job and who knows probably could have worked him up to a good pay.

After going through the tight physical, the physician signs his results, folds the forms and places them in an envelope before sealing it and handing it to Howard, and tells him to give it to his manager upon arriving back at the plant.

When Howard arrives back, and turning the envelope over to the plant manager, he sits himself down and waits for the final verdict. Sitting there nervously, he notes the plant manager talking with the personnel manager going over his report.

The manager exits the personnel office and approaches Howard, "Could you come in to work in the morning?"

Surprised with the final results, Howard jumps to his feet and responds loudly "Yes sir. I can do that."

"Good. Now go into the personnel office and fill out some forms, and I'll see you in the morning."

"Thank you" responds Howard shaking his hand as he heads toward the personnel office, "Thank you very much."

Entering the office, the personnel officer turns over the report so that Howard could not read it. "Congratulations on being hired. Fill out these forms, and leave them on my desk when you are done, and we'll see you in the morning."

Returning home, Howard, winded, runs into the house and informs Sueanne about his new job. Hugging him, she asks, "What did they say about your enlarged heart?"

"They didn't say anything. They just looked at the results after I had handed it to them. Then the manager told me that I was hired and I would start work in morning."

"What does the job consist of?" she asks.

Taking a deep breath, Howard sits down and begins teller her, "I'll be working in the machine shop. Starting pay is two dollars and fifteen cents an hour; with a dime raise every two weeks that I show progress. And in three months span, jump to three dollars and eighty-six cents an hour."

Embracing him, she sighs and then states, "While you were out trying to get the job at stokers, I went down and applied for a job at the Klondyke Restaurant and got a job waitressing."

"Do you want to be a waitress?"

"I don't mind doing waitress work. Remember that was what I was doing when I met you. The pay isn't that much, but it does give us a little extra money so we can visit mommy this summer. And besides, I really don't mind working."

This good luck that enveloped the two only lasts through the first week. As luck would have it, bad luck comes just as well as the good, and the two were having their share of both.

Chapter 7

It begins on a Tuesday night, April twenty-third when Howard comes down with severe stomach cramping, which he believes to be gastroenteritis. All through the night, he kept vomiting. The pains had become unbearable enough that Sueanne decides to get him to the hospital. Getting him dressed, he notifies Korina that she was taking him to the nearest hospital, and that it was okay if Korina not go there, for she hoped that he would be given some medicine and return home.

Once at the hospital, the nurse informs them that the two would have to return in the morning, because there was no one on duty to look at him.

"No one on duty at a hospital?" questions Sueanne, "What kind of hospital is this?"

"We are not a big hospital; we don't have the staff to man it on weekends."

"What if there is an accident or someone need medical assistance? Say like my husband who is in severe pain."

"I'm sorry. You just have to go find a larger hospital or come back tomorrow morning when there will be someone here."

"Well, I never." States Sueanne turning her back on the duty person behind the glass enclosure."Come on Howard let's get out of here and go home."

Leaving the hospital, Sueanne turns to Howard and says to him, "Doesn't this hospital remind you of another hospital back in Baltimore?"

"It just can't be happening again." groans Howard holding his stomach wincing in pain.

Once at home, Sueanne runs hot water into the tub and helps Howard into it where he relaxes and allows the hot water to sooth his stomach. She leaves long enough to phone Korina and tell her about what she had accounted at the hospital before heading back into the bathroom to attend to Howard, who was relaxed in the hot water and seemed to be feeling a little better.

Once Sueanne had gotten Howard out of the tub, she helps him into bed where he groggily closes his eyes and falls asleep.

The following morning Howard had to miss work due to having to head out to Edgerton and see Dr. Davenport to have x-rays taken. Having given medication, Howard is told to go back home and rest, and to return the following Friday.

Once home, Sueanne prepares a sandwich and a bowl of soup for lunch. But, before he could finish it, the pains come back with vengeance. The two wait out two hours hoping that the pain would cease.

At this time, Sueanne could not stand by and watch him wincing in pain any longer. She tells him, "I'm going to find a doctor that will do something now."

Not having a telephone, Sueanne goes next door to see if she could use a phone. Arriving back, she informs Howard that she was able to get hold of a doctor and that she was to bring him up to the hospital.

Upon being checked out by the doctor, Howard was admitted immediately, placed into a room under the doctor's care, Howard is undressed by the nurse, placed into a 'Johnnie' and transferred to a room on the third floor where he is put in a bed.

Sueanne stays long enough to witness a nurse placing a tube up Howard's nose and down into his stomach. After Howard falls asleep she leaves and drives over to Korina's and Brian's, which is nine miles from the hospital to inform them of, what had just taken place. Sueanne asks if she could stay with them while Howard is hospitalized.

While lying in bed wincing in pain, thoughts go back to when he was living at the Derryfield Home for Orphans. The nuns thought he was just pretending to be sick. There were times that he did pretend to be ill whenever he was punished or did something wrong. This false illness allowed him not to face the other children.

It was during a time that Howard was presented to Mother Superior about his constant illness, that she had come across while examining him the stomach pains were what was known as 'gastroenteritis', an inflammation of the stomach lining. But it was the taste of the Cod Liver Oil that was worse than the pain itself. Then there was what the nuns did to him with the washcloth that helped ease his stomach pains. Maybe, he should ask Sueanne to touch there and help him to rid the pain.

The next day when Sueanne drops by for a visit, she asks what the doctor had found out. "Nothing as of yet." replies Howard cautiously moving her hand under the blankets and to his midsection area.

"What are you doing?" whispers Sueanne surprisingly

"I need you to help me get rid of these pains."

"How is this going to help you?"

"Please, just rub me. Make me feel better?"

"You are really crazy, but if you think it will help." She then takes hold of Howard and begins rubbing him while she tenderly bends over him and presses her lips to his.

Howard takes in a deep breath and with all he could muster, states, "You are so good to me, that I . . ." Before he could finish the sentence,

"Hush." replies Sueanne, "I would really hate to get caught by someone."

Lying there, Howard allows Sueanne to caress him until his stomach pains were just about gone. "Thank you, that feels so good."

"Hate to rush our time together but I have to leave early to get to work."

Suddenly Howard loses his desires and the good feelings he was having were gone. Sueanne in sensing what was happening to him, asks, "You okay?"

"Yes, I'm okay, I just was wondering about what you just said."

"Do you feel any better?

"No I don't."

"Why? Did I do something wrong?"

"It's what you said. You have to leave here early to get to work, when work is but a few miles away."

Sueanne's face goes red and as her head begins to lower, she states, the day you were admitted and I had gone to see Korina and Brian well, on the way I had to take the car to the service station because I smelled something burning." She goes on to tell him, as she inadvertently continues rubbing him under the blanket, "They found a large hole in the bottom of the radiator. And the car will be in the garage for several days. So, I have to walk in to work."

"Can't Korina or Brian take you in?"

"Brian is already gone to work, and Korina has no vehicle of her own."

"Oh yeah, I forgot, can you call my boss and inform him I'm in the hospital and won't be in for awhile?"

"Ok as soon as I get back home I'll call. You like what I'm doing?"

Noticing that Sueanne's hand was still under the blanket working him, Howard lets out a sigh and states, "If you keep that up, I'm never going to let you leave."

"It feels so cute when it is soft." Laughing, she pinches it and says, "It feels like rubber when it is like this."

"Ha ha." states Howard sarcastically, "I'll show you some rubber if I wasn't in this hospital bed."

"I'll wait until I get you in our own bed."

"Is that a date?" asks Howard pushing her hand down firmly into his midsection.

"It's a date." responds Sueanne patting his midsection area before removing her hand, "Are you feeling a little better?"

"I guess so for now."

Smiling, Sueanne bends down and plants him a kiss just as a nurse strolls into the room. "You all be going down for x-rays in the morning Mr. Walker."

Picking up the chart which hung at the foot of Howard's bed, the nurse begins to scribble upon it. "Did you move your bowels today Mr. Walker?"

"No ma'am. Not yet."

"So how do you feel right now Mr. Walker?"

Smiling Howard looks at Sueanne who is also trying to keep her composure, "Right now, I feel real good."

"That is real good." replies the nurse as she continues jotting something into his charts. "I guess we are on the right track."

After the nurse places the charts on the foot of the bed and leaves, Sueanne informs Howard that she had to get going or she would be late for work. Kissing him, she exits the room as Howard yells out. "Call a cab. I don't want you walking call my boss."

For the first five days, Howard is served nothing but a glass of milk every hour and Maalox every two hours. The x-rays show that he is suffering from a duodenal ulcer, and that he would be spending some time to come hospitalized. Sueanne would spend her Saturdays and Sundays visiting him up till 9pm.

By the end of the fifth day, the doctor tells him that he was going to try him on some solid foods. "Are you hungry?" asks the doctor pressing on his stomach.

"Yes sir. I am really hungry."

"Your stomach seems to be still very tender, but with a little food in it, it should feel a whole lot better."

As the doctor gets up to exit the room he is met with a nurse pushing a cart holding assorted medications and instruments. Approaching Howard, she speaks in an exuberant voice, "Good morning Mr. Walker and how are we today?"

"Good morning." snaps Howard right back, "We are feeling fine." Howard knew what was in store for him, "Not more of that junky Maalox?"

"You know that you must take this every two hours."

"But the doctor just told me that I can have some solid food."

"Maybe so, but until I get the orders in writing to the contrary, you will be continued in receiving the Maalox every two hours." The nurse then hands him the cup of Maalox.

As the nurse was about to exit his room, she turns back towards him and says, "I'll be back in two hours with another drink. See you later. Bye.

Watching the nurse leave his room, Howard folds his arms across his chest and pouting replies, "Good-bye."

That noon, Howard all set to receive his first solid food for dinner. Attentively he listens to the clatter of the dinner tray cart as it rolls down the hallway and ever so close to his room.

Sporting a smile that grows larger and larger as the sound of the cart grows nearer and nearer to his room. The smells of the food fill the air; there are visions of steak, potatoes, vegetables, chicken, veal, meat loaf and all sorts of deserts. The thought of actually biting into these foods make his mouth water then, there it is, the cart stops right outside of his room. A nurse carries a tray with metal coverings on it. She places the tray on his bedside table. She then bends down at the foot of his bed and begins to crank up his head so that he was in an upright position in order that he could reach and remove the cover of his dinner plate. Staring at what lies before him, Howard's eyes grow wide and his smile that was spread across his face, suddenly disappears as his mouth is now wide open.

Before him, is the biggest, the most heart-skipping meal any person would want after coming off five-days of nothing but milk and Maalox. With a shout that is heard all up and down the hallway, "Egg-on-toast and a glass of milk, Bllaaaakkk" This is a reminiscent of how he felt when the nuns at the Derryfield Home for Orphans made him take that terrible Cod Liver Oil.

A week later, Howard is feeling well enough to go home. "Now you go home." states the doctor, "and build you back up. And stick to the diet that I've prescribed."

Once at home, Howard remains home for another week before he reports back to work."What are you doing here? And where have you been? Didn't you quit?" asks his boss as he walks into the building.

"No, I didn't quit, I was hospitalized. Weren't you notified?"

Shaking his negatively, the boss replies, "No, we weren't and besides, we already have hired someone to fill your vacancy. Come into the office and I'll give you your check."

"But, I want my job, I need it." States Howard following the boss into the office, "It wasn't my fault I got so sick."

"I'm sorry." answers the boss, "We didn't hear from you in over a week so we had to hire someone else."

Howard accepts the check and turns to leave the office, when the boss notes, "I'm sorry, truly sorry, but I hope you understand?

All the way home, Howard tries to figure out a way to tell Sueanne. Arriving back in Smithville, he stops and enters the Klondyke restaurant. Finding a booth at a far corner, he sits and waits to be found by Sueanne. It wasn't long; Sueanne approaches him wiping her hands on a towel that is thrown over one of her shoulders. As she approaches him, she asks, "What are you doing here?"

"You're the second one that has asked me that same question. The first was my boss, and then he told me that I no longer work there. When I told him I was in the hospital for ten days, they had thought I had quit my job and hired a new man to do it."

"Oh no." states Sueanne bringing her hand up and slapping her forehead. "I was supposed to call them, but I completely forgot when I had that accident."

This time, it was Howard's turn to be surprised. Shocked by what he just heard, he asks "What accident?"

Realizing what she had just said, Sueanne tries to change the subject real quick, but Howard would not allow her to get away with it, so she explains.

"Remember when I told you that I had smelled something burning and had taken the car to the garage. Well, it didn't really happen that way. I was run off the road and into a ditch causing a rip in the radiator."

"How were you run off the road, and by whom? Was anyone hurt?"

"One question at a time "states Sueanne trying to finish telling the story. "I was run off the road by one of those Amish or Mennonites or whatever those people are called. This horse and buggy was coming straight at me on my side of the road. I swerved to avoid hitting the horse, and I landed in the ditch. The driver of the buggy never once looked back. I was afraid; you were in the hospital, so I lied to you. I was going to tell you when you got better, but I never found the right time. I'm so sorry"

Tears were beginning to fill her eyes and streak down her cheeks. She tries wiping them with her towel that was still draped over her shoulder, but it was Howard who had reached them first and with loving care, using his finger he wipes them off.

Reaching out his hand, Howard takes hold of her hand and begins to comfort her saying, "It's alright, and it's not your fault. I'm just as much to blame." He goes on to tell her that he would look for another job, but first, she should go get him a cup of tea and a sandwich before her boss notices her sitting too long and fires her.

Again, Sueanne wipes her eyes dry, smiles, gets up from her seat and goes to fetch him a tea and club sandwich.

One night when Sueanne and Howard were visited by the Westford's, the two were invited over to their home for a dinner party which was to be put on by a husband and wife team.

The couple goes to different homes and cooks a three course meal using their own materials. Then they feed all who have shown up for the party. While the meal is being prepared, the couple goes about describing how it is prepared. Once the meal is done cooking, they all sit down and enjoy the meal.

It is at this time, that the couple tries to enlist other couples in buying the cook set known as 'Miracle Maid'. Once someone buys the cookware, that couple invites other couples into their homes to prepare a meal and try to sell them the cookware. For every couple you get to purchase the cookware and put on meals, the first couple gets points where they could actually get trips to Bermuda.

Looking over towards Sueanne, Howard states, "Sure, why not. Sueanne needs a break from the kitchen anyway."

"Great," states Korina, "It's at four o'clock Friday. So far we have five couples coming, including you two."

At the dinner party, Howard and Sueanne were so pleased with the meal and the product, that they asked how it would be possible for them to get into the business. The two were told that they would make an appointment with the district manager and that the two would be contacted.

Sueanne joins Korina, while Howard joins with Brian in the living room. While conversing with the other guys that had come to the party, the women clean the kitchen up and go about looking over the cooking materials, before the two had left the party, Sueanne and Howard had purchased a set in hopes that this would be an easy job that both could do together.

The two did get an opportunity to try their sales pitch on selling this new product, but it did not last long when they found it was really difficult to find buyers once they got guests to come for a free meal. Without the sales, their standings in the district were going nowhere.

One would have to be born into something such as this, and they knew that it was not for them.

The demonstrations weren't so bad, it was getting those that showed up for the party interested in buying the product. Soon the district manager was beginning to put the pressure on them to make the sales in order for him to meet his quota of sales in his district.

"I believe that the district manager doesn't care about our welfare," states Howard one evening after returning home from one of their district meetings, "I think he's only interested in his own percentage of sales."

"I agree." replies Sueanne going about sorting out the demo set. "I'm not really interested in cooking for other families while we can't even get enough money to cook a decent meal for ourselves." Angrily, and with tears streaming down her face, she slams a pot that goes with the demonstration set into its box and pleads, "Let's just take this stuff back and tell them that we don't want to do this any longer."

"We will, but first we will have to do the bookings we have left. Then we will take the stuff back, okay?"

"Okay." Agrees Sueanne, "But we will take no more bookings."

"Right." agrees Howard, "We'll find something else."

In taking the demonstration product back, Howard has a guilt trip in having Sueanne quit her job at the Klondyke restaurant in order to follow him in this wild goose chase in getting rich scheme. Again, he feels as though he has failed her once more.

Here they are, Sueanne expecting again and once again way behind on their bills as well as their rent. The two have very little food in the house and no money to purchase gas for the car.

The days just seem to get bleaker and bleaker for the two, as Howard just cannot find a job, he is told the same old story, "You have an enlarged heart and our insurance cannot cover you."

Howard would lie in his bed and listen to Sueanne cry herself to sleep, and then continue to cry as she slept.

The two had become very angry with life as a whole, their heart had turned cold and shut off from one another, and as yet now they have received a note from their landlord that they were being evicted at the end of the month.

Howard and Sueanne do the only thing that they were able to do, and that was to call the pastor of the Church of Christ to seek help. The pastor, after hearing their plight, offers to rent them the old parsonage house. Jumping to the chance, they were informed that there may be an opening on the eleven to seven shifts at Suncor Corporation in Hicksville. Going to Suncor, Howard fills out an application and then goes in for an interview. During the interview, Howard informs the manager of his past history and that it was the pastor who had sent him to seek out a job there.

The manager listens tentatively as Howard goes about what his examinations have shown and how they had affected his ability in keeping a job. In the end, Howard is given a job.

By June's end Howard and Sueanne to go out to Baltimore and bring back her family for a visit. The trip started out fine until they get onto the Pennsylvania turnpike. Here they run into some real horrible weather, for the next one hundred and thirty-six miles. There is a hard downpour of rain and mixed with heavy fog. Plus to top it off they were traveling in the middle of the night at a speed of fifteen-miles-per-hour. This slow progress makes the two very annoyed and frustrated. With all that was going on, the two had come upon an accident in which a young woman and a child had been killed when their car had hit a slick spot in the road, causing them to spin and crash through the center divider before flipping over onto its top.

Howard and Sueanne begin to breathe a sigh of relief as the finally arrive in Baltimore and head towards Sueanne's' mother's house where they stay for two days, before heading back to Ohio.

Once the family has prepared for the ride back, they load up and stop at the market to purchase some food and snacks to take along with them. Once again the family leaves Baltimore and head to Ohio, Again they were hit with heavy rains and fog as well as gusty winds. But this time they were driving back in daylight.

They were half way home when this car with two teen-agers in it passed them at a very high rate of speed. Just as they were changing back into their lane, they hit an icy spot causing the car to go into an uncontrollable swerve and into a spin.

"Watch out." yells Sueanne as she brings her arms up to protect her face.

Howard gradually applies his brakes bringing the vehicle to a crawl. The car ahead of him begins to go into a spin before hitting the center divider, heading the vehicle strait towards Howard's vehicle.

Cutting his wheel to avoid from being hit, Howard was barely able to escape the oncoming vehicle as the two pass one another in opposite directions.

With the vehicle now behind him, Howard pulls off the side of the road as they all witness the vehicle again hit the center divider before coming to a stop.

"I'll be right back." states Howard opening his door and exiting the vehicle, "I want to make sure no one is injured."

Approaching the car, Howard asks if anyone was injured. Looking inside, he sees two badly shaken but uninjured youths who state that they were alright. The two exit the vehicle and join Howard in inspecting the damage to the vehicle. The engine is tilted in an almost thirty-nine degree angle, but is still operational. Howard helps the youths pull the fender free from the left front wheel.

After checking one more time on their health, Howard returns to his vehicle where the two children who had been watching from the rear window begin to ask all sorts of questions.

As the five sit out the pelting rain which the windshield wipers have very little effect, and the wind is blowing so hard that it is rocking the car like a cradle. For an hour they sit it out in hopes that the storm will die down a little so they could continue their journey.

When the rain finally did subside, Howard thought that it was safe enough to continue, as they headed out, Howard noticed that the car behind him continued to sit. Howard thought to himself that they would be taken care of by some emergency vehicle that is supposed to travel along the highway in case there is such an emergency.

Howard and the family had been back on the road for about a half-hour, when who do you think flies past them again? The same vehicle he had stopped to help in the accident. As the vehicle passes, it begins to swerve and slide back and forth and shows no sign of slowing down. Howard eases his foot up off the accelerators he allows the passing car to gain distance between them before he continues at a normal speed.

Before darkness falls, Howard pulls off the turnpike and into a rest area and into the garage where the mechanic tells him that the vehicle needs a new generator belt.

They decide to remain at the rest area overnight.

Sitting in the car, the five views a beautiful rainbow, "Have you ever seen anything so beautiful?" asks Sueanne placing her head onto Howard's shoulder.

"Yes I did but just once." Answers Howard looking at the rainbow, "Only what I saw wasn't a rainbow."

"What was it?"Asks a Joanne curiously.

"It was the Aurora Borealis, otherwise known as the Northern Lights."

"Tell me about it?" states Sueanne looking up into his deep blue eyes.

Howard begins by saying, "I was about thirteen years old and living with one of my foster families. I never really got along with this family, so one day I decided along with two other friends to run away from home. We had decided that we were going to walk to Rumford by way of the new turnpike that hadn't officially been opened to traffic yet. It was June of 1959; we had gotten some seven miles into our journey with another eleven miles to go when we saw these lights waving across the sky. Not knowing what the meanings of the lights were, we had become frightened. We looked at one another in hopes that someone was knowledgeable about what we were seeing. As for my belief, I thought it was GOD telling us to go back home. Slowly we turned around and we began running as fast as we could in order to get back home before it got too much later. It was already past seven by the time I walked into the house, and then did I ever get it. The punishment I received, did stop me from ever running away again.

"These lights, what were they?" asks Allen leaning into the back of the seat.

"The Aurora Borealis is the display of lights when charged particles from the Sun enter our atmosphere. This stream of light is carried away from the Sun by Solar winds; it becomes trapped in Earth's magnetic field, which is known as the Van Allen belt. It then ionizes the oxygen and nitrogen gas causing it to glow. You have Aurora Borealis for the Northern hemisphere and Aurora Australis for the southern hemisphere."

"Where did you learn all that?" asks Allen as he gets closer to Howard in order to hear every word.

"I read it in one of the MIT magazines, for I wanted to become an Astronaut."

"Where is MIT?"

"It's in Massachusetts, its Massachusetts Institute of Technology."

"I'm hungry." breaks in Joanne as she sits back into her seat, I don't know what he is talking about

"Me too, I'm starving" replies Sueanne, "Let's go into Howard Johnsons."

Once inside the restaurant, the five decide to use the bathroom facilities.

Once everyone was ready to order, the family enjoys what they had, "Those lights, that you said, will we see them?" asks Allen as he spoons his food into his mouth.

"I really don't know. I was young when I saw them and have never seen them again. If you lived up in Alaska you would seen them quite often."

After they had eaten and returned to the car, they prepared to get comfortable in the car in hopes to get some sleep.

Awakening around six-thirty AM they go into the restaurant, use the bathrooms, freshen up in Howard Johnson's and get a good breakfast before getting back on the road. They arrive at the Westford's house at eleven o'clock am.

From the moment that Marilyn and the two youngest children had arrived in Ohio, Things between Howard and Sueanne begins to disintegrate. The family is jumping down one another's throat for no reason at all. Though the visit of Marilyn and the two children were to be for a short time, Korina insists that they stay longer. This is not what Brian had wished for, for now with Howard and Sueanne out on their own, he was hoping to have his little family to himself. After all, Marilyn is not working, and this meant extra food would have to be bought and given out. So Brian refuses them. He tells Korina, "If you want them to live here, then they would have to stay with Sueanne and Howard. Or take them back to Baltimore."

Korina knew that if her mother and siblings were to return to Baltimore now, they would be physically abused by her husband. So with Howard and Sueanne, Marilyn and the two moved in with them.

Soon debts begin to mount as Howard has five to feed instead of two. He begins to feel as though his privacy has been invaded and he had to do something quick.

Marilyn knows that she and the kids presence is a load on all four and asks Howard if he would take them back to Baltimore due to the fact she misses being in her own home and seeing her mother.

"Are you just saying this? Or do you really wish to go back?" asks Howard

'Yes, we all want to go back. We don't belong out here."

Howard talks to Sueanne, Sueanne talks to Brian and Korina, and due to Brian having to work; it was up to Howard and Sueanne to take them back.

"I will give you gas money." insists Marilyn."

Brian and Korina pulled together to aid in Howard returning her mother and siblings back home.

Suddenly Sueanne changes her mind and asks her mother to stay. "I know you don't want to go back to the S.B. husband of yours. You know what he'll do to you and Allen and Joanne, How can I live with that?"

Marilyn takes Sueanne's hand as tears begin to stream down her cheeks. "We are going to be fine.

Howard informs Sueanne, "You know as well as I do that we can't afford to feed and care for five, although I wish I could get a job and keep them here with us."

"It's about you, and your heart, you can't do anything to help pay the bills. If I wasn't working we wouldn't even have this. I wish I had never married you and left Baltimore."

"You are upset and don't mean what you are saying." States Marilyn hugging Sueanne.

"You don't know. You haven't been here. Every job he has got, never keeps. He works two weeks here, a week there and since we have been married, I carried him. I want to go back with you."

Howard leaves the room and goes outside to get some air. His head aches with what is going on and being said he knows he is responsible for the marriage breaking up and he had to come up with a quick fix, but what?

Suddenly Howard enters the living room where Sueanne and Marilyn are still talking of having her and the two siblings staying with her. "Everyone, I have an idea, how about I call my brother tom and see if we could get a place and a job there."

"And where is, There" remarks Sueanne turning to look at Howard.

"Tom is a nurse at Ft. Dix, New Jersey, and his wife is also a nurse, so you'll be in good hands when the baby comes.'

"Without answering, Sueanne turns back to her mother and starts talking to her.

Howard turns his back knowing she would not answer him. So he does what he said he was going to do that was, Howard calling his older brother Tom who was stationed at Fort Dix, New Jersey, and informs him of his dilemma and asks if there were some way he could help.

"No Tom, it's not money I need. I need a job that pays well. With Sueanne's family to support, it is hard to get ahead."

"Why don't you and Sueanne come here and stay with us and in the meantime I'll see about what I can do about getting a job lined up for you, that's what brothers are for."

"But that's going to put you and your family in the same situation that I'm facing now and trying so hard to get out of."

"Not quite, we have the room and we are financially set so that we could help you out until you get settled into a job and find your own place."

"We'll come out as long as it doesn't affect your lifestyle."

"Don't worry," exclaims Tom, "If I felt that it would, then I wouldn't ask you to come out. So when do we expect seeing you?"

"I'll talk to Sueanne and the family would have to move back with the Westford's, store our belongings until we need them and if everything goes well, I should be ready to leave in a couple of weeks. If plans change before then, I'll call you, okay?"

Hanging up the phone in the telephone booth which was across but up the street from the house, he returns home to inform Sueanne as to what has just transpired.

"I'm not going." declares a reluctant Sueanne "This is my family and I'm not going to leave them."

"It's always your family, why did you marry me in the first place if you had no intentions in leaving your family to make one for ourselves?"

"They need me." shouts Sueanne loud enough to echo off the walls, "They are my family and I love them, that's why."

Following her from one room to another, he states, "I need you just as much as they do. Aren't you and I family? After all we are man and wife and you are pregnant with our baby."

Stopping suddenly, the two almost collide with one another. Turning to face him, pointing a finger into his face she states, "Tell you what, you go to New Jersey and set things up and we'll be out there within a month's time."

"What's this we'll bit?" asks Howard quizzically.

"If I go to New Jersey to meet you than so does my family, I'm not leaving here without them."

"Then let them go live with Brian and Korina."

"They said that they couldn't care for them." Shouts Sueanne.

Howard throws his arms up into the air and letting them fall he replies, "Well, neither can we. Why do you think I'm trying so desperately get us united again? No two families can live under the same roof without having troubles."

"I'm not going without my family." states Sueanne defiantly, "And that's that."

Howard wasn't getting anywhere arguing with her he knows now that the bond between her families was stronger than the two of theirs. Also he knows that he would have to bow to her defiance for soon she would deliver their child and they would have to be settled in by that time. But for now, Sueanne would be getting her way-again."

On July 13th, Howard and Sueanne move their belongings from their cozy home to Brian and Korina's. Sueanne would be staying there until Howard settled in and got a job before she would be going out to join him.

That afternoon, Howard calls his brother to tell him of his plans and of his departure the next day out of Fort Wayne, Indiana on the pm flight and that he would be arriving in Philadelphia around four pm. And that that he would wait for him at the United Airlines counter.

The following afternoon around twelve-fifteen pm, Howard is driven out to the airport by Brian, Korina and Sueanne.

While waiting for the flight, Howard continues to insist that Sueanne would change her mind and leave with him. But she remains unchangeable, but did say "If I should feel it's alright to travel then I will come out. First, I've got to make sure mommy is going to be taken care of."

"Promise me you'll write and keep me informed of your condition."Shaking her head in agreement, she answers, "I promise."

The loudspeakers announce Howard's flight number that it is ready for all passengers to begin boarding. Howard hugs Sueanne and tells her that he loves her. Then turning to hug Korina and shakes hands with Brian, he heads down the ramp and disappears into the tunnel.

The plane leaves much later than scheduled and when it lands in Cleveland, it was already three-fifteen pm and the plane that he was scheduled to exchange to be as well late due to inclement weather.

By the time he had arrived in Philadelphia, it was six forty-five pm, some two hours later than he had informed Tom. Quickly heading over to the United Airlines counter where he had told his brother that he would meet him upon arrival, he searches the area and unable to find him, he decides to head towards a phone booth to call him in case he was unable to make it.

When Tom answers, Howard explains the reason why the plane is so late and asks if he was going to come out to pick him up.

The airport is forty-five minutes from Burlington, New Jersey and Tom had just arrived home from going out there once already. But, Tom being the brother he is, states, "Okay little brother. See you soon."

While Howard waits for Tom, he goes into the cafeteria for something to eat. After, he goes over and sits down and puts a quarter into a pay machine to watch an hour of television.

When he had figured that it was enough time, he leaves the area and waits for Tom in front of the counter. But little did he realize it; his brother was already there and had snuck up behind him. Turning Howard recognizes Tom and gives one another a hug. "It's good to see you again I'm really sorry about the plane's delay."

"Don't worry about it. Little bro Planes are never on time. Do tell me what a Smithville is?"

Laughing, Howard tells him that it was the town he lived in, in Ohio. I was living with Sueanne's sister Korina and brother-in-law Brian. It just wasn't working out. It hasn't since I got out of the service." The two, head out to the parking lot toward a blue nineteen sixty-seven Dodge Charger where a woman was sitting inside. Tom introduces her to Howard as Laurie Adams, a neighbor of theirs. Howard shakes her hand and climbs into the back seat. Tom and Howard would talk of old times and try catching each other up on what was happening since they last met.

Arriving at Tom's apartment which was on the base, Howard notices that it seemed as though the whole court had turned out to welcome him. As Tom notes, this scene is an everyday occurrence. Everyone, especially on weekends, gather outside in the courtyard where they play games, records and eat a variety of cooked foods and deserts.

Tom, Laurie and Howard exit the car and make their way through the crowd to the door of the apartment. Entering, Howard is met by Charlene as she comes out of the kitchen, wiping her hands on an apron tied around her waist. Upon seeing Howard, she throws her arms around him and informs him that she is happy to see him. "How did your flight go? You want anything to eat or drink?

"The flight was just disastrous, and no thanks, maybe just a cup of tea if you have It.?"

For the rest of the evening, Tom stays inside and the brothers' reminisce about days gone by. It wasn't until the wee hours of the night when they decide to retire.

All that week, Tom would take Howard wherever there was an opening for a job. By Friday of that week, Tom had come home after his duty at the hospital where both he and Charlene worked; She a Lieutenant in the Nursing Corps and he a Specialist five. Tom had heard from one of his coworkers where Howard might get a job. This job, some seven miles from Burlington was 'All Star Dairy' in Delran, New Jersey.

Tom takes Howard down to check on the job. Howard is hired on the spot. The job consists of loading a delivery truck with five, ten and twenty-five gallon containers of different varieties of milk. After loading the outgoing truck, he would take the returnable containers and wash them clean in order to be refilled and reloaded onto a truck for the next day's delivery. The job pays him two dollars and sixty and one-half cents an hour.

In order to get to the job, Howard has been thumbing his way due that Tom had to be at duty by the time Howard was even ready to go to work, and Charlene had two children to care for so she couldn't make the trip. Tom or Charlene was there after work to pick him up every night.

The hitchhiking goes on for several weeks when one morning, as Howard was thumbing his way to work; many cars passed him by before this one red and white station wagon with two men stop and offers him a ride, Howard enters the back seat.

Howard notices that the driver looked to be about fifty with a balding head. From what he could view in the rear view mirror, he was also toothless and very thin.

The passenger looked rather young as though he could be the driver's son, somewhere in his twenties, with a short solid build, giving him the impression that he might lift weights. His hair is cut short to give that clean, neat, attractive young man look.

"Where are you heading?" asks the passenger turning in his seat to look at Howard.

"I'm going to Delran." replies Howard, "I work at 'All Star Dairy 'and I'm already late for work."

The young man places a cigarette in his mouth and asks, "Do you have a light?"

Howard was beginning to feel a little uneasy as he shakes his head negatively and says, "Sorry I don't smoke."

"You got any family here?"

"A brother, who lives in Burlington, I just arrived a few weeks ago from Ohio."

Though Howard had sensed that something was wrong, he couldn't put his finger on it until the car turns off the main road onto a dirt road and continues down it. "I think you are going the wrong way." states Howard nervously.

"Didn't you say you were late for work? Well this is a short cut."

"But, it's only a mile up the road pass the shopping center."

As the car travels down the dirt road, the passenger turns around towards Howard and flicks out a short switchblade, saying, ""Just sit back and shut your mouth if you know what's good for you."

The passenger then looks at the driver of the vehicle and states, "Want to pull up here? We can have some fun."

The driver looks in his rear view mirror at Howard, then at his passenger as he places his free right hand on his passenger's leg and begins to rub it up and down. As he continues the rubbing, the vehicle hits a large pothole thus jolting the contents of the vehicle. The driver releases his young friend's leg and slows the vehicle down in order to gain more control of it.

Howard sees his chance to make a run for it. Jumping out of the slowed vehicle, he rolls onto the ground before picking himself up and runs back down the road, knowing that the driver would have trouble turning the vehicle around to pursue him. As Howard runs, the vehicle comes to a full stop and the passenger exits the vehicle and begins the pursuit of Howard, while the driver tries desperately to turn the car around, being a station wagon, it is no easy task especially on the narrow dirt road he had driven on.

As the pursuer closes up on him, Howard heads off the dirt road and into the woods where he hoped he could lose him. Howard then finds himself out distancing him due to his long legs. Not knowing how much of a lead he did have, Howard begins to run faster than he had ever run before. His chest ached as though it would soon burst, but he had to get away and find a place he could hide. In giving it all he had, he jumps a fallen tree which was lying across his path and in doing so he stumbles over a second one. Fighting to regain his balance he falls and hits his head on yet another tree.

Upon rising to his feet, he looks around and sees that he was on top of a hill which sloped down into a gulley. The fall had enabled the young pursuer to catch up with him. "Why did you run?" asks the young man grabbing hold of Howard's shoulders "You shouldn't have run." The young man lands a blow to the side of Howard's head, causing him to slump to the ground unconsciously.

After some time, Howard awakens and groggily rises to his unsteady feet. His whole body ached and has trouble figuring out what just happened. His head was spinning and thumping from the beaten he has just taken. Once his equilibrium returns and he could stand upright it is then that he discovers just what the young man had done to him. He had been raped, how could this have happened? Men don't get raped, but his body tells him that it had gone through an ordeal that he had not ever witnessed before in his young age. That young man had stripped him of his clothes and had performed acts on his body that Howard was glad that he had been unconscious to know about.

Looking about the ground, he sees his clothes scattered about as well as some flung down the gulley. While the thunderous explosion in his head somewhat diminishes, he goes about recovering the items of clothing that were wearable. The young man had not been easy on his clothing. He had found only one shoe, no socks; his shirt was ripped of its buttons and its sleeves torn off. Looking down the gulley for his pants and his underwear, he notices his pants below in a somewhat ball, but as hard as he looked, he could not find his underwear anywhere. Howard proceeds to go down into the gulley to retrieve his pants. In doing so, he slips and slides down scrapping more of his body from the underbrush. Upon finding his pants, he notices that the button and zipper are unusable. The pants are ripped, but at least he can get them on. Still, he finds no underwear.

In trying to find his way out of the woods, he walks uneasy, for his whole body burns and itched from the scarring he had received. Soon, he exits the woods into a field that led to the rear of a Shopping Center. Howard recognizes it as the one he passed every day to and from work.

With blood flowing from his open wounds, dirty and exhausted, he limps his way into the crowd of shoppers who gaze at him in bewilderment as they try to stay out of his way.

Howard makes his way towards a phone booth and begs a passerby for change to make a call. One middle aged woman with a little boy at her side hands him change and asks if he needed help in dialing the number. Howard thanks her and proceeds to dial the number himself.

Howard felt as though he were naked as the people pass him by stare and begin to talk to one another of his appearance.

Howard waits by the phone booth as the passersby continue to try and avoid getting too close to him.

Several young girls pass by him and begin giggling and pointing to him. "Hush states the older woman" Who may have been the mother pushing the two girls closer to the side of the building, as Howard could only stay where he was and shed tears.

Soon Charlene arrives, stopping in front of him; she exits the vehicle with a blanket which she throws around him as a crowd gathers around them. With her arm around him, she turns toward the crowd and barks out, "What kind of people are you? You see someone in trouble and all you do is giggle and laugh at someone's plight. You should all be ashamed of yourself." She helps Howard into the front seat and goes around and enters the driver's side.

After telling the story to Charlene, she takes him to the police station where Tom is waiting. Charlene had called him at work and explained to him what Howard had told her.

At the police station, Howard again tells the story as he is examined for any evidence that would finger the person or persons that did this to him. Giving the police the description of the vehicle and the two people, the police take what information they could and inform them that when they hear anything on the case that they would inform them.

Leaving the police station, Charlene takes Howard back home while Tom had to return to duty at the hospital.

At home, Charlene helps Howard with a warm bath, cleans his wounds and helps him change into clean clothes. He then relaxes for the day.

Chapter 8

After many letter writings and telephone calls, Howard finally persuades Sueanne to come and join him in New Jersey. On August fourth, nineteen sixty-eight Tom, Charlene and Howard head out to the Philadelphia airport to pick her up.

They find her sitting on a bench next to the information desk. Howard runs and with arms outstretched to invite Sueanne into them, she stands and says, "I'm not staying." I want my baby to be born in Ohio not here in a hick state I know nothing about or even like."

Howard bends over with some shock in what Sueanne has just told him and picks up her luggage as his family go about introducing themselves to her.

"Then why did you come out?" asks Howard walking by her side as they head out the door and into the parking lot.

"Because you kept insisting that I come out here every time you called. Plus the calls kept upsetting mommy."

"So how long do you plan to stay? The baby will be born only three months from now and that isn't even long enough time to get use to New Jersey."

"Until I feel I've been here long enough."

"What about me?" asks Howard puzzled about where their relationship was going? "I am your husband and you should be thinking of our future and not putting potholes into the marriage."

Looking point blank at him, she replies, "What about you? And look whose putting potholes in the marriage. You can't even stay in one place long enough to be with me and my family."

"I have no family in Baltimore or Ohio. And there you go again, my family, yes it is your family it has resented me for taking you away from them, and from Baltimore."

Without looking at him, Sueanne didn't say a word but looked straight ahead catching Tom every now and then looking at them from the rear view mirror. Tom and Charlene carry on a conversation about the hospital that they were assigned to. Occasionally Sueanne and Howard would speak to one another. Howard asks that she try to see New Jersey for what it was and that she'd give it a try. I have a good job and I'm sure in no time at all we can find a place of our own and have the baby to make us a family."

Once the party had arrived at the apartment, Sueanne was met by the whole court inviting her to join them in their social family.

Inside the apartment, Sueanne is met with Laurie who had stayed to care for both Tom jr. and Dennis. As soon as Dennis sees his mother enter the room, he throws out his hands and cries out, "Mama" and Charlene takes him into her arms as Tom Jr. as well wraps his arms around his mothers' leg. "Ok now we have a visitor, this is Howard's wife from Baltimore, and her name is Sueanne. So be nice so Mommy can help her get relaxed from her long trip. Placing Dennis down he begins to cry, that's when Laurie takes the two children. So Charlene can put the tea kettle on.

Sueanne unpacks her luggage and she and Howard join Charlene Tom and Laurie along with the boys at the kitchen table.

"Want coffee or tea?" asks Charlene turning toward the two as they entered,

"Coffee cream and two sugars." responds Sueanne taking her place at the table.

"I'll have tea . . . ."

"I already know," cuts in Charlene, "milk and two sugars. I've got your number already."

"How long have you two been married?" asks Laurie to Charlene.

"August nineteenth will be two years."

"It's been Thirteen years for us." Adds Charlene, "It has been good, we are happy doing what we do, having housing and good friends and two beautiful children."

The remark causes Sueanne to put her coffee down and leave the table teary-eyed.

"What did I say?" asks Charlene with a puzzled look on her face.

Howard follows Sueanne into the living room and sits beside her, "Hon, I'm sorry. No one knows about what is eating at you but me, and I can't help you. If only you will let me in. I need you."

"Leave me alone; go back in there with your family."

"They could be yours as well if you just let it go and let me help you?"

"Get out! Leave me alone."

Howard leaves Sueanne stretched on the couch and joins the befuddled family at the kitchen table.

"She going to be alright?" asks Charlene.

"She'll be alright. We've had a loss back in December, 1968; we lost a baby and she has been taking very hard. She just won't let me in so I too can mourn the loss and help her."

"I'm very sorry." states Charlene.

"Don't worry about it. You didn't know. Maybe she might talk to you as the time goes by."

But as the time did go by, Sueanne never really got out of her shell, sure she would have good days and bad days, but there was that inner feeling that she didn't want to be there in New Jersey and the rift between she and Howard grew even wider.

On August fifteenth, Howard finds Sueanne crying the couch upon his return from work, asking her what the problem could be she tells him that she missed her mother and wanted to go back to Ohio.

"Okay. I'll see you get back in a couple of days. Don't get yourself upset as to where you may lose the baby."

When Tom arrived from work Howard asks if he minded in taking Sueanne back to the airport for her flight to Ohio. Tom offered to take her out that weekend. All that night, everyone tries talking her out of going back but to no avail.

Later that night, Howard is awakened to Sueanne's crying again, asking, "What is the problem, still missing your mom?"

Holding her stomach, Sueanne answers, "No, I've got pains in my stomach and they seem to be about five minutes apart."

Feeling her stomach, Howard asks if she is hurting where he touched. Upon getting a positive response, he decides to awaken Charlene because of her knowledge of being a nurse, but before he was able to get to her room, she had come out to shut down the air conditioning.

"Charlene "whispers Howard as not to waken Tom, "Could you come take a look at Sueanne, she's having pains about five minutes apart."

Checking Sueanne's stomach, Charlene begins asking her questions, then turns to tell Howard to go wake up Tom.

Tom is also a nurse at Kimberly Army Hospital at Fort Dix, New Jersey, and together, has done many pregnancies. Sueanne is in good hands.

Rubbing the sleep from his eyes as he enters the living room, he sleepily asks, "What's up Charlene?"

Without even looking up from Sueanne who was stretched out on the couch, she explains, "I think she is havening a premature."

Tom steps in next to Charlene and together they check her vitals and her stomach. "Charlene, call Rancocas Valley Hospital and tell the doctor on duty just what we expect and that we'll be bringing her right in."

As Tom rises and heads towards the bedroom to get dressed, he yells back, "Howard, get dressed and dress Sueanne. Pack her a travel case to take with her."

As Howard and Sueanne get dressed, the two didn't say a word, they both knew what each was thinking for they had gone through this before.

As time got closer to leaving for the hospital, fear swells up inside Sueanne and she begins to cry, Howard could only hold her and try comforting her the best way he could.

Arriving at the hospital, Sueanne is taken right in while Howard, Tom and Charlene wait in the waiting room.

Fifteen minutes later a doctor appears and calls out, "Mr. Walker, your wife's water bag has broken. She mentioned that this has happened before?"

"Yes, just last December. Tell me Doc why does she keep dropping her water bag?"

"Didn't the doctor tell you last time it happened?"

Shaking his head in a negative way, Howard replies, "No, they didn't tell us anything about why she lost the first one."

"Unless your wife has an operation, she will continue to lose the child as it reaches a certain weight."

"Operation!" exclaimed Howard, "what kind of an operation?"

Sitting down, the doctor goes on to explain as Tom and Charlene draw near in order to listen in. "An operation to tighten and strengthen her abdominal muscles in the womb. Her muscles are very loose and as the fetus develops, the muscles' being too weak to support it falls from the womb."

As tears flow down his cheeks, Howard asks, "Is she going to lose this one?"

"I'm afraid she is. There is very little I can do at this point in her pregnancy. But I will see that she is comfortable with no pain."

Howard thanks the doctor before he returns to head back into Sueanne's room. "I can't go back to Ohio and she can't stay out here. I have no choice but to send her back, for it would be wrong of me to force her to stay against her will."

"What will you do after sending her back?" asks Tom stretching his arm behind Charlene's shoulders.

"I'll probably try going back into the service, after all there's nothing for me in Ohio or Baltimore and I'm not going to mooch my life through."

It was around seven twenty-eight am when Sueanne delivers a baby boy. But his life is short lived; it lasts for about seven minutes. When Howard is told of the sad news his eyes fill with tears and he heads to the far side of the waiting room to be by himself.

Tom and Charlene leave him alone until they think that it was time for them to approach him, they convince Howard to go back home with them. First, stopping at the desk and asking if Sueanne was alright. The nurse informs them that Sueanne was under sedation and was sleeping soundly, and that she should be ready to go home tomorrow.

As promised, Sueanne does return home and because neither want to talk about it, the discussion on what to do with their deceased son was on their minds. When time did come, the two agree to let the hospital dispose of the child as they normally would others.

Howard informs her that he was to be sending her back to Ohio just as soon as she was able to travel.

"No!" interjects Sueanne, "I want to call mommy and have her meet me in Baltimore."

"Baltimore!" replies Howard as he is surprised by her request, "Why Baltimore?"

"I've decided I want to go back and live with grand mom."

"I thought you wanted to live with your family?"

"The winters are too cold in Ohio, we have to depend on Korina and Brian for everything, and Grand mom is getting older and can't do much for her, plus mommy misses her."

Sueanne asks Charlene if she could use the phone to call her family in Ohio, agreeing, Howard and Charlene join Tom outside on the steps while the rest of the families were enjoying each other's company, slip sliding on a watered down plastic mat or just enjoying each other's conversations. Looking up as the two exits the house Tom asks, "Is everything okay?"

"I guess so. She's going back to Baltimore to live with her grandmother." states Howard leaning back against the door.

"Are you going with her? Or are you planning to go back into the service again?"

"I'll go back, get her settled and probably join the navy. If not then I'll go back into the army."

"I have a cousin in the navy." remarks one of the neighbors who had been listening in on the conversation, "He's in the submarine service."

"I could never serve in the submarine service. I can't stand to be confined in such a small space."

When Sueanne arrives at the screen door, she tells Howard that her mother would be in Baltimore on the twenty ninth and if possible, if she could get a ride to the airport when the time arrives. Upon getting a positive answer from Tom, she retreats back inside.

Looking out among the gathered families, Howard notices that they all had heard and looked surprised as she had just come out. Looking at them, Howard remarks, "It must be the loss of the baby that makes her act this way."

On August twenty-second, Howard heads on down to the Burlington Federal Building and enlists in the navy. He is told to report to the main Receiving Station in Philadelphia, Pennsylvania on September second no later than twelve hundred hours.

On the morning of August twenty-ninth, Tom has driven Sueanne and Howard along with Charlene to the airport one more time. Upon arriving, Howard hugs his brother and thanks him for all he has done and that he was sorry that things had turned out the way it had.

Releasing Howard from the embrace, Tom states, "You just take it easy little brother and keep in touch you hear?"

"You bet." Answers Howard, "I'm sure everything will be alright and that Sueanne will feel better just as soon as she lets this loss leave her."

With outstretched arms, Charlene hugs him and states, "Bye Howard, take care, we'll miss you."

"Will miss you back, got to go." Yells back Howard as his flight number is announced over the loudspeakers, "Bye and thank you."

Sueanne thanks Tom and Charlene and turns to walk ahead and down the ramp, through the tunnel and onto the plane.

Tom and Charlene watches from the window as the plane taxies down the runway and lifts up into the sky. Once out of sight, Tom and Charlene turn away and head through the lobby to exit the terminal to the parking lot.

Once arriving back in Baltimore, Sueanne's cousin, Wanda had moved in with her grandmother justina. Howard helps Sueanne unpack and settle in with her mother and siblings. They all knew that to move back to the house would result in harm to all of them.

Knowing all is well with the family, and that Sueanne was content to be where she is, Howard takes a taxi to the bus station in downtown Baltimore where he boards a bus which is to take him to the naval receiving station in Philadelphia, Pennsylvania. The trip allows him time to think back on the times and the happenings since he first met Sueanne.

Howard arrives at the bus station in Philadelphia around five pm; he hails a cab that takes him to the naval receiving station. Upon exiting the cab and paying his fare, he turns and looks toward the main gate. Approaching him from behind the gate is a shore patrol marine that halts him in his tracks. "Halt, who goes there," shouts the marine manning the gate. "Have you any identification?"

"I'm here to report for duty." Replies Howard nervously.

The guard opens the gate, takes the manila envelope from Howard and proceeds to take him to the guard house. Once at the guard house, the marine opens the envelope that Howard was given at the receiving station and thumbs through them. He then, makes a phone call. Within a few minutes a shore patrol vehicle comes to a screeching stop outside the guard house. A rough looking third class petty officer enters the guard house and without looking at Howard who had stepped aside or get walked over, orders out, "Orders."

The petty officer is handed the paperwork and as he sits on the corner of a desk goes over the paperwork. Looking up at Howard who stood frozen in his tracks, he asks, "Prior service. Army, what made you come back into the service, and why the navy?"

Before he could get a word out of his mouth, the petty officer rises from the desk and looking at Howard with a grin states, "come with me."

Entering the vehicle, he is taken to a building where he is checked in and given a room. He is informed that he would be told when to report for clothing issue.

Once on his own, he looks around for the mess hall where he enters, goes through the chow line and sits down to end an exhausting day.

For the next two weeks Howard remains at the receiving station awaiting orders. While there, he gets his clothing issue, stands muster, goes on police calls, working in the mess hall, cleaning the billets and performing night watches. Whenever he had free time, he would call Sueanne and let her know what he was doing as he waited for orders to come down. Being prior service, he automatically is given the rank of SN or Seaman, equal to PFC in the army. It is one rank down from what he had when he left the army.

When Howard had entered the navy, he had hoped that he would get CN or Construction man, but in not looking over his orders very well, he is given SN and this meant that he was going to have to be given duty on a ship. He did not want to be out in the ocean on a ship. He wanted to remain on land where he could build bridges or harbors anything but go aboard a ship to be taken out to sea for long periods of time. But, it is too late he would have to make the best of it for the next two years.

On September twentieth, nineteen-sixty-eight, Howard's orders come down telling him to report to the U.S.S GAINARD—DD 706, a destroyer which is moored out of Newport, Rhode Island. Upon hearing the news, he calls Sueanne, not getting her, he leaves word with her family and that he would write her just as soon as he is settled aboard the ship.

Later that day, he is taken by bus to Philadelphia bus station only to board another bus that takes him to Newport, Rhode Island. Once getting off the bus in Newport, he boards a gray navy bus that takes him and other sailors to the pier where their ships are moored at the pier.

Exiting the bus, he notes ships tied up next to one another three or four ships on each side of the docks. Sailors and civilians are scurrying around each ship like ants.

Walking down the pier, he is enthralled as he gazes at the huge size of the destroyers on each side of him.

Stopping, he asks one of the sailors where the GAINARD was tied up. Howard is pointed to pier two and that he would have to board the first ship, go across it, and onto the GAINARD for she was the second of three ships tied there, and that all three were preparing to leave for a six month cruise to the Mediterranean.

Apprehensively, Howard boards the first destroyer, asks permission to board in order to cross over to the GAINARD. Once given permission, Howard is amazed at what he sees in crossing over to his ship.

After receiving permission to board the GAINARD, the officer of the day takes his orders and informs him that he was to report to first division, which consists of boatswain mates and new seamen better known as deck aides. These deck aides handle the ships lines, fenders, and raise and lower the anchor and whaleboat, they man the wheelhouse, do port and starboard watches, chip, scrap and red lead the ship before painting it haze gray. They as well go over the side of the ship on a boatswain chair painting the hull numbers. Then there is the gunnery practice, the coming alongside another destroyer or aircraft where we would have to handle the lines in order to bring over the refueling hoses in order to refuel while underway at sea.

The deck aides' work is very continuous, hard and dirty, but without the deck aides, the ship would rust and not last as long as some ships do because of the salt spray hitting the ship as it moves about the Atlantic Ocean and into the Mediterranean Ocean.

The US NAVY must keep their ships looking good and powerful as they enter many foreign ports.

On the morning of September twenty-third after only twenty days in the navy and three days aboard the U.S.S. GAINARD, he is now underway to begin a six month cruise to the Mediterranean.

The Gainard ; is a Sumner class destroyer which was first laid down on march twenty-ninth, nineteen forty-four, she was launched September seventeenth, nineteen forty-four and commissioned in new York on November twenty-third, nineteen forty-four. She is three hundred seventy-six feet six inches overall by forty feet ten inches across its beam. She is pushed along by its two shaft screws that take her to thirty six point five knots, or about forty-one statute miles per hour. She has a compliment of six five inch/thirty-eight caliber guns in twin mounts. In one that Howard is assigned to as a hot case man. In the aft of the ship, she holds twenty-four depth charges. Never in his short life had he ever thought about joining the Navy, for he was not comfortable with being in the water where he couldn't touch bottom.

Chapter 9

HOWARD IS AMAZED IN THE size of the ship and as he strolls its two hundred plus foot deck of this haze grey vessel, he finds himself in an unknowledgeable world. He has had no training, on what he is to do or even the language that is associated with seamanship. All he knows at this time, is that he was going out to sea for six months, where and what he was going to be going and doing is to be learned one day at a time. Because he had prior service, he did not have to go through naval boot camp as the other sailors had, so this made him less knowledgeable of what his job consists of.

Lined up in their dress blues as the ship pulls away from the pier, Howard feels lonesome watching the mass of people left behind waving to their loved ones. As the ship passes under the Newport Bridge which is under construction, Howard begins to really feel alone and wished he had gone back into the army instead of being shipped out into the Atlantic Ocean where there will be no land in sight. His thoughts are suddenly broken up as a Boatswain mates orders the men below decks to change into their work clothes and to report back topside for a muster before commencing with ship's work.

The long steel gray destroyer, home for Howard what is believed to be for the next two years makes her way up river and passes under the Newport Bridge which at this time is in the process of being constructed. Looking out into the beginning of nothing but water as the view of land behind him grows smaller and smaller, he begins to feel as though he had gone back into the army instead of the navy.

His thoughts are suddenly broken up as a boatswain barks out orders to" lie below and change into your work clothes and to report back topside for muster before commencing ships' work."

The destroyer makes her way up river as the crew lie below and change into their working dungarees and work shirt. Quickly locking up their personal items the crew scurries up the ladder onto the main deck and hurriedly meets in front of gun mount number one where they hastily fall into formation. As the Boatswain mate gives the crew their assignments, Howard who is fascinated but nervous witnesses the land passing the ship and in front of him was nothing but water. Howard hears his name being called off and he raises his hand. "You will be on port side watch alternating with the starboard side watch for the next six months. That means four hours on and eight hours off watch but doing ships' work."

The first day out into the Atlantic Ocean, Howard was having trouble learning the language of being a seaman. Since he had prior service, he did not go to boot camp thus he didn't get the first hand knowledge that everyone else did.

Breaking up the formation, the crew is told to report to the paint locker where they will draw scrappers, chipping hammers, paint: red lead, haze gray and deck gray and report to their assigned areas of the ship.

It was by the time the ship and company had reached its first port-of-call, that Howard is accustomed to some of the sailor's quick tongue-in-cheek vocabulary. As well as that the speed of a nautical mile is equivalent to 1.1516 statute miles per hour.

The first stop for Gainard and crew would be a short two day stay over in Malaga, Spain where the ship and others in its fleet would be taking over a six month sea duty from other ships who have performed their tasks and are now preparing to head back home.

This impressive city lies along the Costa del Sol, which is the coast where travelers use Malaga to get to their one of many fabulous hotels or apartments. Malaga is the capital of the province and with its lovely harbor worth a visit; it is famous for its pasas (raisins) and its superb wines. Since the ship and crew were going to be only two days in port, there was going to be no shore leave for the fleet.

When the fleet does leave Malaga, they sail out into the Atlantic for fleet operations. It is here that Howard really gets to understand the gun mounts as they practice every day firing at pulled targets. The crew practice rescue operations of downed airmen. The first division, kept the ship clean of rust, chipped of old paint, red leaded and repainted the areas.

Although the rough waters of the Atlantic Ocean tossed the ship side to side, thus making most of the new crew members seasick, just about all held through and performed their duty the best that they could. After several weeks on duty, the Gainard and a couple other ships enter the port of Rapallo, Italy to spend ten days getting replenished, refueled and time off.

Whenever his port duty had off he would go ashore and check out the city. If it had not been for being in the navy, he would never get to see such grandeur. Rapallo is in the province of Geneo, in Liguria, northern Italy and is located in between Portofino and Chiavari.

The climate is moderate and the main part of town is on fairly level land. Its villas are built in the hills that rise immediately from behind the city. To help in defending itself from barbarians in the sixteenth century, a castle was built on the seafront. This is the sight that first greets you as you enter the port, Howard just had to get one of these greeting cards and send it in to Sueanne. In his five shore leave visits, Howard is able to visit many famous places such as: The Castello sul Mare (Castle-on-the-Sea) erected 1551 in order to defend against pirate attacks. The historic tower of the Fieschi and the Torre Civica built in 1473. The church of St. Francis of Assisi built in 1519. And the ruined Monastery of Ville Christi built in thirteenth century and abandoned in 1568 after it was ravaged by pirates.

After leaving Rapallo, Italy, Gainard and crew spend fourteen days sailing the warm Mediterranean Ocean plane guarding for the Aircraft Carrier Independence as their pilots train take off and landings both in the day and the night. Gainard continues in its gunnery practice as the ship shell parts of Porto Scudo, Sardinia as the marines perform a mock amphibious landing.

Again, Howard's duty during this shelling is to catch the hot cases after each shell has been fired in the mount and pass them through an opening in the lower deck so they would not bounce around inside the mount causing damage to the crew inside.

The crew had been firing for about fifteen minutes; when word is passed down to stop all firing, while the marines make their landing onto the beach. Everyone inside the mount relaxed, and as they relaxed, the temperature inside the gun mount begins to rise, the crew soon fall asleep and did not hear word come down to reload, commence firing, It so happened that when Howard had relaxed, his right knee positioned itself just under the breach of the gun, and when the mount was reactivated, the breach comes down onto his knee and begins to pull his knee and leg under the breach and into the breach's well. This surprising and agonizing pain awakens him with sharp screams as he grabs hold of his leg fighting being pulled down into the well.

"STOP . . . HELP ME . . . MY LEG . . . STOP THE GUNS . . . IT'S GOT MY KNEE . . ." yells out Howard at the top of his voice unable to free his leg from the lowering breach. Soon, he reaches the point that he falls into unconsciousness.

When Howard does come to, he discovers that he is on a stretcher in a passageway leading to the Captain's quarters. The ship's medical doctor was addressing his knee which burned and throbbed. Gainard had pulled alongside the USS CHILTON-APA38 where his stretcher is hooked up and high lined aboard the Chilton. This ship is a Bayfield-class attack transport. Her dangerous task is to deliver troops to the battle front, and recover and care for the wounded. She was launched 29 December 1942 by the Western Pipe and Steel Company, San Francisco, California. Chilton served at Newport, Rhode Island, as a training ship for pre-commissioning crews of attack transports.

Howard spends several weeks in sick bay for he had torn several ligaments in his right knee. By the time he is able to walk on it, he found himself helping the pharmacist mate with the feeding of other wounded which had been picked up from Vietnam and is enroute back to their home ports. In the helping of others his job is the feeding of those unable to, and the taking those to the ship's movie. Howard listens intensively to the wounded as they speak about how hellish.

Vietnam is and how they doubt that the U.S. with all its modern weapons available to them will ever win the war due to the fact, the South Vietnamese who begged the U.S. to help them in the fight against the Communist North Vietnamese who is aided by the soviet Union and Communist China and besides, the Vietnamese have been fighting for thousands of years and have run every country out with a loss of thousands of fighters and billions of dollars in support of the war.

The aide that he attributes to the returning veterans gives him the awakening call that this would be a better suited job for him to perform rather the seaman duties that he is performing aboard the Gainard. While aboard the Chilton, Howard almost forgets that he was still in the navy. He wanted to remain aboard here and strike for pharmacist mate. But before he could do anything about it, he is told that his knee was healed enough for him to return to the Gainard and perform his duties.

The two ships, USS CHILTON and the USS GAINARD met up as they anchored in Taranto, Italy where Howard reluctantly reports back aboard Gainard to continue its Med cruise. During his time off, he approaches the pharmacists mate to question whether he has a chance to change his duty and get out of first division. He is told that he would have to take the test and pass then if he does he would be transferred to another ship. Howard is given the test booklet and is told to study hard for there are a lot of math formulas you will have to know. In between his duty of the day and his port lookouts day and night, Howard tries to study. The quietest place is on the fantail where out of one of hatches pops one of the machinist Mates wearing a headphone and mike where he converses with the Bridge.

Howard and the machinist mate, talk about what he was studying for and hoped to get out of being a deck aide.

Howard is informed that no matter how hard he studies, no one gets off deck aide unless you are uptight with one of the Boatswain mates or when the ship returns to home port.

With hopes diminished, Howard forgets the studying and attacks his aggressions on the ship.

The next port that Gainard pulls into is Naples, Italy, for tender availabilities. While in port the Gainard receives a new Commander onboard. It is during his shore leave that Howard visits the city which is known for its rich history, art, culture, architecture, music and gastronomy. It is some 2800 years old, and is situated halfway between two volcanic areas, Mount Vesuvius and the Phlegraean Fields, which is sitting on the coast by the Gulf of Naples.

It is one of the oldest cities in the world, founded by the Ancient Greeks as (New City), and held an important role as part of the Roman Republic in the central province of the Empire.

Howard enters the city only to be amazed at what he sees, before him the central and main open city square or Piazza of the city is the Piazza del Plebiscito. After picking up a postcard to send to Sueanne, Howard is Google-eyed as he wanders visiting one of the largest and oldest opera houses on the Italian peninsula. He stops by to visit one of Naples historic castles, Castel Nuovo built by the first king of Naples, Charles1. But the most memorable visit in Naples is when he travels to Mount Vesuvius which is located on the coast of the Bay of Naples, about six miles east. It is best known for its eruption in AD 79 that led to the destruction of Pompeii and Herculaneum. Mount Vesuvius was regarded by the Greeks and Romans as being sacred to their hero and demigod Heracles/Hercules, and the town of Herculaneum, built at its base was named after him.

Upon ascending the top of the volcano, the children of Naples gather around the visiting sailors and tell them that Vesuvius is a "humpbacked" mountain, consisting of a large cone, they call it, (Gran Cono) and is partially encircled by the steep rim of a summit caldera caused by the collapse of an earlier and originally much higher structure called Monte Somma. The Gran Cono was produced during the eruption of AD 79, for this reason, the volcano is called Somma-Vesuvius.

The height of the main cone has been constantly changing by eruptions but at this time is 4,202 feet high, separated from the main cone by the valley of Atrio di Cavallo, which is three miles long. The slopes of the mountain are scarred by lava flow but are heavily vegetated with scrub at higher altitudes and vineyards lower down. Vesuvius is still regarded as an active volcano. When Howard heard this, he begins to wonder if it could possibly erupt while he stood upon it looking down into the caldera. He becomes nervous and thinks he has seen and heard enough. He slips the boys a few bucks and joins the few that were retreating back down the slop.

Howard was really impressed about coming to view the volcano, for he had heard and read of it in school and the mighty eruption back in 79 AD that buried the city of Pompeii and Herculaneum drew him with his super eight movie camera to take pictures of the volcano and the two cities, where the stragglers who remained behind were engulfed, burned and asphyxiated.

These visions were etched into Howard's mind even after the Gainard had set sail once again to again rendezvous with the air craft carrier Independence Eva-62 for more practice with plane guarding the pilots leaving and returning to the flight deck.

Standing watch on the port side, Howard could not wipe out the countries he has visited and then sending his visits back home via the movie films, but no matter how many exciting countries he may get to visit, he was still lonely for the sight of Sueanne. Howard then brings his binoculars to his eyes and scans the view before him. For now all he sees are the running lights of the carrier and the takeoff and landing lights of the planes. There was no land anywhere between them. The sky and the waters have emerged into one blackened space.

Christmas is spent in Athens, Greece where he finds himself ashore to visit the Parthenon of Athens and the most supreme expression of the ancient Greeks architectural genius. Much of the structure remains intact; the Parthenon has suffered damage over the centuries. It is said that the beginning of the building of this structure goes back to four hundred thirty-eight BC where the initial construction of the temple of Athena. The rectangular building measured at the top step of its base to be 101.34 feet wide by 228.14 feet long and was constructed of white marble, surrounded by forty six great columns, roofed with tiles, and housed a nearly forty foot tall statue of the goddess Athena. It is told that it was known as Athena Promachos, Athena the Champion, was made of wood, gold and ivory and could be seen from a distance of many miles.

In two hundred ninety-six BC, the gold was removed to pay for tyrant Lachares' army; in the fifth century AD the temple was converted into a Christian church; in the fourteen sixty's it housed a Turkish mosque; in sixteen eighty-seven gunpowder stored by the Turks inside the temple exploded and destroyed the central area of the building; in the early eighteen-hundreds much of the remaining sculpture was sold by the Turks to an Englishman Lord Elgin, who removed the sculptures and sold them to the British Museum.

The name Parthenon refers to the worship of Athena Parthenos, the 'Virgin Athena' who issued fully grown from the head of her father 'Zeus'. The maiden goddess and patroness of Athens, She represents the highest order of spiritual development and the gifts of intellect and understanding.

Howard is amazed from what he learned in coming here. It's nothing like what little knowledge he had read about while in school. This is the real thing. Being there, actually touching history, and recording it on his super eight cameras for prosperity. He will send the film in to be developed and have it mailed to Sueanne so she can view it.

Before leaving Athens, Greece, Howard has another shore leave where he heads out towards Ramblas Boulevard to see how the people live. He notes that although there are taxi cabs all about the area, he sees people pulling donkeys hitched to carts filled with wood, grain and household goods. This is a much cheaper mode of transportation, for all they would need to do is stop in some green field and let them eat.

While window shopping, he goes into a clothing store where he searches through women's full skirts and dresses of all different festive colors. He purchases for Sueanne a green silk with silver stripes along the side hoping the size would fit her, spotting a medium size replica of the Parthenon, he buys this before leaving the store.

Upon leaving the door, he is accompanied by a fellow shipmate who walks with him to the 'New York bar' just off the Boulevard.

Upon sitting at a table where three crew members were sipping beers, Howard could just make them out in the dim light; one is Machinist Mate Fred Hanson who he had met on the fantail Howard orders a coke as a woman approaches to take their picture.

Smiling as the camera is clicked and then each pull out five drachmas to pay the woman.

The Gainard heads out to resume her duty as rescue destroyer for the USS INDEPENDENCE. One evening as he stands port lookout and watching the planes leaving and landing on the Aircraft Carrier, he hears word that one of their planes had a flame out and was unable to make it back to the Carrier, and that he was going to have to ditch the plane in the Ocean. Gainard is ordered to head out to the last known position and rescue the downed pilots. When Gainard arrives at the last known position, the crew begins to search the waters for any signs of life. Frogmen are sent into boats and criss cross the area in hopes of finding something. Fragments of the plane are found brought on the boat and lifted up to the destroyer, but there is no sign of any pilot or copilot.

The frogmen are given the order to leave their boats and search deeper to see if anything of the bodies could be found. It was some fifteen minutes later before the frogmen hoist up a body from the deep. Watching, Howard suddenly begins to feel ill and his hand goes to his mouth when the body is finally brought aboard. The crew quickly covers the remains. In the meantime, the other remaining frogmen continue their search for the other remaining member of the fatal crash. After some frantic searching, they were only able to recover the helmet with the name of the copilot on it and a large dent on the rear of it. Gainard continues its search until they are ordered to resume duty.

Seven days later, operations with the Independence comes to a close, and is Howard happy to see the Carrier steam away and out of sight. Gainard continues its Mediterranean cruise stopping at Ibiza, Spain, an island in the Balionic island chain where they replenish the ship and take on mail and movies for the crew.

After two days, they sailed off to visit Barcelona, Spain, which is the capital of Catalonia and the second largest city in Spain. It is located on the Mediterranean coast between the mouths of the rivers Liobregat and the Beros.

It is recognized as a global city because of its importance in finance, commercial, media entertainment, arts and international trade.

While in Barcelona, Howard visits the National Museum of Art of Catalonia which contains a collection of Roman art. He as well visits museums of history and archeology like the City History Museum and the Museum of the history of Catalonia. He visits the 'Gothic Quarters' the center of the old city of Barcelona. An outstanding view is of the Sangroda Familia, which has been under construction since eighteen eighty-two, and is still unfinished. Buying several postcards as well as several small replicas of the Statue of Columbus, Howard sends these and the film taken, back to Sueanne.

Before leaving port, the crew is invited to come ashore to the Servico de informacion Municipal telefonico, which is the telephone company and they can send a call to a loved one back home in a three minute conversation.

Rushing topside along with everyone that was not on duty, Howard wonders just what he would say to her, even if she was there since the two had not been on the best of standing on the day he left.

Once at the phone company, Howard notices that there were plenty of sailors ahead of him and that he had to fill out a form consisting of the name and phone number of the person that he had wished to be called.

Howard is instructed to wait in the big receiving room along with the others until his name is called.

As the group waits they are once again approached to be instructed that when their names are called, they would be talking to a ham operator and he would relay what you say to your partner on the other end. "In order to give the ham operator the hint that you have finished with what you have to say is when you state 'over'. Then he will pass on the message to the person on the other side and wait for when that person states 'over'."

Howard picks up a magazine and flips through it as he looks over the mass that has gathered hoping to get a call through to the states or wherever they call to. It had been some twenty minutes when Howards' name is finally called into a room having two rows of telephones on the table.

Howard is escorted to his phone and the lady points to where he was to sit. Looking around and hearing the mumbling of the other callers, he sits and picks up the phone where in a nervous voice says, "Hello hon. how are you doing? Over"

The reply comes back from the ham operator's voice saying, "I'm fine the family is fine. How are you doing? I haven't received many letters from you? Over"

"I will write just as soon as I can. Over"

"I miss your letters. I hope you are getting ashore? Over"

"I'm getting to visit many countries did you receive post cards and gifts I sent you? Over."

"Yes and they are beautiful. Over"

"Will you be able to meet me on the pier when we arrive in Newport, Rhode Island on February 14th? Over."

"Don't know for sure, but will try. I love and miss you very much. Over"

"Okay hon. I love and miss my North Star. Bye. Over"

At that moment, the line goes dead. Rising up from his seat, Howard heads back to where his ship is anchored, hoping things had become better between the two and her family. In his mind he goes over their problem, and he is convinced if only her family would let them live their own life, everything would be great. Several times he had to retrieve the map he had tucked in his blouse pocket which he had tucked away since he left the ship.

Howard had no idea if he would be accompanied by any of his ship mates, due to the fact that most of them would head out to the closest bar and spend the day drinking and carousing with the native girls who invite the sailors to her room or have them buy drinks until the sailor man is broke.

Howard would not and could not lower himself to that degree, for he is married and loves his wife very much. He did not want to be one of the returning sailors that had come down with any disease that would keep him from leaving the ship on arrival back at port.

After these two port calls, Gainard is ordered to rescue destroyer for the aircraft carrier; USS SHAGRI-LA,CVA 38 and the USS FORESTAL,CVA59 for more plane guarding, watches, chipping, scrapping, red leading, deck painting, gunnery practicing, and firing of the depth charges. After ten days of this duty, the Gainard pulls into Syracuse, Sicily. This city is over 2700 years old and is located in the south east corner of the island in Sicily, right by the Gulf of Syracuse which is next to the Ionian Sea. It was founded in 734BC by Greek settlers from Corinth and Tenea. It is famous for its rich Greek history, culture, amphitheaters, architecture. The Patron saint of the city is Saint Lucy; she was born in Syracuse and her feast day; Saint Lucy's Day is celebrated on December 13th.

While here, Howard visits many of its main sights especially, the theater which is one of the largest ever built by the ancient Greeks. It has sixty-seven rows divided into nine sections with eight aisles. Although only traces of this magnificent theater remain, it was modified by the Romans who used for different spectacles including circus games.

Nearby he could see the stone quarries that were used as prisons in ancient times.

Howard is really amazed what he has seen and learned on this cruise, he never imagined that it would turn out the way it has. Even though he still didn't like the duty, he did enjoy the ports-of-call. No history class could tell the story like what he had witnessed. He couldn't wait to get back home and tell Sueanne everything he has seen, and to see how the films turned out.

Upon leaving Syracuse, Sicily, the destroyer Gainard is about to come to the end of its Med cruise. Howard just couldn't wait for the return, although the countries he had visited were something for him to remember, and the warm waters of the Mediterranean was enjoyable, they would now have to travel back to Newport Rhode Island through the cold, rough North Atlantic and he was not looking forward for this.

Howard had still not acclimated himself to the vibrations of the ship, the heavy listing from port to starboard, the washing of the decks from the high waves, the handling of lines that almost take you overboard if you are not careful. Then there is the time down in his rack, as he tries to sleep, there is the shudder of the large twin screws below him that shake the entire ship to a point that Howard feels as though the ship would split in two, after all, the destroyer is twenty-seven years old and has made quite a few of these wave pounding cruises during her lifetime. While enroute back home the Gainard makes a stop at Rota, Spain, on February 4th, where the ship is replaced by another destroyer which will begin her six month cruise. From Rota, Spain, the ship and crew heads back out into the Atlantic stopping at Ponta Delgado, an isle of San Miguel in the Azores for refueling, and one more time in Bermuda for receiving stores and refueling. From here, the ship and crew heads up the east coast of the United States and into even more colder water. Regardless of how cold it was as he and other crew mates worked on the decks chipping off the ice that had appeared as they sailed further and further north, Howard is kept warm with the thoughts that Sueanne was going to be there waiting for him upon arrival.

Chapter 10

SUEANNE HAD PROMISED HIM DURING that Christmas Day phone call and letters mailed stating that she would be there on the pier waiting for him when the ship comes in Valentine's Day.

Gainard sails into Newport harbor on February 15th, one day late and covered from bow to stern with ice, looking as though she had just come back from the North Pole. Howard notes as he looks up at the Newport Bridge that it was just about three-quarters finished. As the ship and her crew pull up to a pier and is tied, he sees the people on the pier that had gathered to see them and the other destroyers in. Scanning the masses, Howard hopes to lock onto his Valentine present.

While he continues to scan the masses, the Navy band strikes up some welcome home music. Gainard is fourth ship out from the pier, and already family members are showing up on the third ship out.

Howard and crew wait patiently as the Commander takes his leave first, then word comes down to welcome the families and guests aboard. The guests flow across the brow carrying babies or pulling their children along crying as they find their loved one and run into their arms.

As the guests continue to come onboard, Howard thought he had seen Sueanne, but wasn't quite sure. "Sueanne, is it really you?" asks Howard running towards her with outstretched arms, "Oh am I glad to see you. I'm glad that you came."

"They told us that you were going to be in yesterday. What held your ship up?"

"We ran into a little rough water, see" pointing to the ice covered ships that lie along the side of the pier, "When can we leave the ship?" asks Sueanne following him down the ladder to the mess hall where the cooks had set up some cookies and coffee.

Of course, she happens to be wearing a dress, and down the bottom of the ladder were sailors looking up.

"Just as soon as they make out my leave papers, I'm getting a ten day leave so we can go search for an apartment."

"I have a room in Newport, at the Stone Tower Hotel; we can go there as soon as you get the leave papers."

"So tell me, how is the family doing?"

"They're all fine. They didn't want me to make the trip out, especially alone."

"Your family is always worried about this and about that. Why don't they just allow you to grow up and do what you want?"

"If I did that, than I'd still be there and not here."

"You mean you didn't want to come out here to meet me?"

"I thought it was a waste of money we don't have, but I do love you and missed you and I can't wait to get you back at the hotel."

"Mmmm, wonder what you got on your mind."

Looking down, Sueanne remarks, "They just put too many buttons on those navy bluer trousers. It's a good thing I can sew, if I need too."

Howard gulped his coffee as he thought of just what is in store for him when he arrives at the hotel. His mind begins to reflect on the time that she had him pull over onto a dirt road after he had given her an engagement ring. She had taken command of a certain situation and he was satisfied by the way she had accepted his ring.

Once permission to leave the ship is announced, the two follow the other personnel and families up the ladder with Howard behind her, protecting her from the others eyeballing her. Once on the main deck, the two cross the ramp to the other ships, on the way Howard salutes the Officer of the Day and the flag before stepping onto the pier where they board a shuttle bus that takes them through Newport and stopping in front of the hotel that Sueanne was renting.

Once the two enter the apartment, Howard finds it a little small; it has a bed, a full size dresser with two end tables on either side of the bed. There is a small bathroom, providing sink toilet and shower. Dropping his sea bag and looking around, Howard says, "Yup! We definitely are going to have to find a bigger and better apartment."

"This room will do for now." remarks Sueanne reaching her arms up and around his neck where she plants a hard kiss upon his lips before running them across the hollow of his throat in which she was thrilled to feel that his body has tensed under the surprise of her affections.

"You like this?" she asked pushing her body into his.

"Oh yes." Howard replies as he gasps for breath which Sueanne is taking from him.

Sueanne continues kissing down from his neck to his jaw line. In doing so, she now felt as she has him in her control. Tugging at his shirt, she raises it over his arms and then removes his t-shirt where she casts them onto the floor before pushing him backwards onto the bed. Looking down deep into his blue eyes she goes about unfastening those thirteen buttons on his blue trousers as she bends over and nibbles on his earlobe.

Drawing a deep breath, she stretches out on top of him feeling his body coming to life. She then continues working on the buttons until the flap of his trousers fall free. Sliding them down his body, she pulls the trousers from him before tugging down his boxer shorts and has them join the clothes on the floor. Howard is at her mercy.

Watching his actions she teases and taunts him while playing and seducing him until she was sure that he was going to get what she was after.

Sueanne looks up and as both their eyes meet the two smiles at one another. Sliding her body up to get nose to nose and she asks, "Are you ready for me? Do you want me?"

"Oohhh yes, I want you so much I ache everywhere for you."

"Are you really, really sure you want me?"

"Yes I really do. I love you and want you right now.

Sliding down and back up on his naked body she cups his face in both her hands and again they both kiss. His mouth opens to hers and for a long moment the two kiss and taste one another as she inhales his manly smell which makes her that much more excited.

She lies on top of him just feeling his hardened body press into her through her clothing, she presses even harder against his lips as her body pressed into his. Howard finds himself pinned on the bed as her weight pushes his body into the mattress. All he could do was to wrap his arms around her, pull her tighter to him as his tongue found hers and electricity begins to surge through both bodies.

Freeing his hands, he cups her breast before unbuttoning the top of her dress. He reaches down to pull it upward until the backs of her legs became bare. His hands found bare skin and his digits teased up and down her legs and proceed to go higher until he cupped her buttocks in his hands. Yet still their lips remain locked.

Finally she pulls her mouth from his and sits up, straddling his hips, his arousal hard beneath her.

"Now what?" he asks in a labored breath.

"My dress, I think that it should finally come off." Sueanne pulls the dress up over her head as Howard still remaining flat on his back, helps remove her dress, bra and tosses them aside

"Excellent." She gasps as his hands grasp her breasts. Moaning, her head falls back. His hands slowly move over her breasts, and his thumbs toy with her hardened nipples. Sueanne wondered just how much she could take before she was ready to take him.

Without warning, Howard surprises her while she was in her thoughts, he comes to a sitting position and shifts his body and rolls her over so that he now was on top of her and his legs are now between hers while his lean, hard body pressed tight against her.

His hands and mouth roamed over her as if she were another far off country that needed to be explored. The two could not touch one another enough. Slowly he slides down and along the way grabs a hold of her panties which was the only item left to be discarded and he tosses them with the other pieces of clothing.

On his knees he could feel the searing heat of her body as he explores her with his hands and mouth. He kisses her from her feet up to her midsection and continuing up until he was back on top of her. She struggled for breath and clutched at him as he swept her into a spiral of increasing sensation, the feel of his lips, and the reality of his body pressing against hers.

His hand, as if on automatic pilot glides over her body until he innocently begins to touch that part of her that gave her a shock of pleasure so intense she has arched her back to meet her pleasures. She felt his digits slowly and deliberately glide into her as she marveled at what she really had missed about him being away for six months at a time. She throbbed against his exploration of her body and yearningly burned for more,

Removing his hand, Howard positions himself between her far spread legs and begins to guide himself into her with a slow, gentle pressure. She was so ready and enveloped him in heat and sensation. Her eyes were closed, her mouth slightly open, while an expression of exquisite tension shadowed her face.

Holding him tightly against her body, she gave the command that she could hold out no longer, she arched upward and wrapped her legs around his hips. He thrust into her and she met his increasing demands with her own. He could feel her throb all about him, feel his pulse within her. They were joined together as one, faster and faster and harder and harder the two rocked the bed until her body seemed to soar mindlessly and ecstatically, before bursting into a series of brilliant explosions.

"Oh Howard" stammers Sueanne trying to catch her breath.

Howard groans as he slides down the length of her, cups her buttocks in his hands and lifts her to him. He inhales the sweet, wet love nest and then begins to search through her pink folds with his tongue. She gasps and shudders, arching herself at his seeking mouth. Again she climaxes so quickly it takes him by surprise. She lay there in full view of his face open and wet.

As Howard kisses his way back up to lay atop of her once more, she rolls him onto his back and drops her hand down until it reaches his hardened love stick which she encircles with her warm hand. Slowly she begins to expertly bring him to full erection. She increased her playful touching; he begins to shudder, arching his body to meet her hand. Sueanne watches him withering, until with no warning he climaxes in her hand. He lay very still as she goes about cleaning him off and then herself before laying her cheek against his thigh as she playfully continues to rub and slide her hand over his exhausted sweaty body.

"Wow!" exclaimed Sueanne, "That was some welcome home."

"You sure pooped me out, I'm exhausted."

"I sure did miss you when you were out to sea."

"I missed you something terrible as well."

"I bet you missed me less than I missed you."

"I thought of you the whole time I was out to sea."

"Did you see any pretty woman in those foreign countries?"

"Sure! I saw plenty of pretty women, but I never gave them a second look."

"You wouldn't lie to me, would you?"

"Honest, hon. I'm not lying to you, though I wouldn't have minded being relieved by one or two."

Sueanne gives him a little love tap on his chest saying, "You had better not have brought anything home and given it to me."

"Oh! I thought maybe you wanted a gift from abroad." smiles Howard trying to get the joke from a broad over to her.

"Oh! Ha-ha, I get and I don't want it."

"Did you get the movies I had sent to you from the various port-of-calls?"

"We saw a couple of them until our storage stall was broken into and the movies screen and projector was stolen."

Howard raised himself up on his elbows and asks, "Do you know who did it?"

"No, there were several other stalls broken into as well."

"That's a shame, hon. there were some interesting shots on the films. Something we'll never see again in our lifetime."

"It's okay; I still have the post cards you sent from each of the countries you visited."

"Boy." states Howard, "This love scene reminds me of the story my dad told me how he met my mother."

"Tell me as I pick up the clothes."

"There is this Island in Penville and during the summer weekends everyone from town would meet there to buy the single ladies baskets of goodies. My dad bought this woman's basket and gathered under a tree to eat and get acquainted. Of course my dad loved to drink whiskey which he quickly consumed. Soon dad had fallen asleep, and when he had awakened he found himself lying on the blanket without a stitch on. Miriam: which happens to be her name, tells him that they are the only ones on the island for the last trolley has left for the day."

"Was your dad upset with her?"

"He couldn't do anything about it so he enjoyed the evening with her.

"Sounds like a nice place to be right now."

Placing the soiled clothes into a plastic clothes basket and heading towards the bathroom to start the shower. "Alone and away from everyone." states Sueanne.

"Come on let's get cleaned up and go out for supper. I could use a good hot shower."

"I'll go prepare the shower while you pick out the clothes you want to wear. We can take our shower together to get done early." Winks Sueanne as Howard heads back to the bedroom in order to retrieve some clothes from his sea bag.

The two get into the shower and help one another in washing their backs amongst other areas of the body, but not to the point where they were to too much water.

After getting dressed, the two head out the door and walk down the road hand in hand until they spot a restaurant. The two enter and are escorted to a table where a waiter takes their order. As the two sit and Howard tells her of the ports-of-calls that he had visited. The most impressive was when he climbed to the top of Mount Vesuvius. She in turn talked of her family and how the old man was being the same in tormenting Marilyn at the drop of a hat.

After eating their meals the two head up to the cashier where Howard pays the tab before heading out the door and back to their apartment and a place of refuge where the two undress and climb back into their love nest where the two converse awhile before holding each other as they drift slowly into the peaceful world of sleep and dreams.

The following day as they sit about talking of world affairs, Sueanne remarks, "I'm declaring that I side with the hippie movement, But I don't agree greeting our returning soldiers with jeers and taunts, spitting on the troops in the airports or when on main street."

"I agree," Declares Howard, "It is sure hard to believe that this is what we all thought would be a quick and decisive war to keep Communism from spreading to smaller countries."

"One can read any paper, watch any TV channel and see the war raging and the death of innocence everywhere." remarks Sueanne.

"But the U.S. is over there to help the South Vietnamese gain their freedom from the Communist North Vietnamese."

states Howard showing his side in the defense why the U.S. is fighting in a far off land.

"It's not working," replies Sueanne, "Every day and night it shows the war and our young boys including you some day dying for what? It's a political war that no one can win."

"We don't see much television while we are out at sea, only movies." Bewildered by the conversation they were having" he asks, "Can we stop talking about the war and enjoy our leave time?"

The two decide that they would take their dirty clothes to the laundry mat at the far corner of the motel where they place them into the washers and sit around to wait on the long folding tables. While waiting Howard reads a magazine showing scenes of hippies and drugs and clashes with the establishments. Howard begins to see what Sueanne is talking about and places his arm over her shoulders and draws her near. Later they dry and fold the clothes before heading back to the motel. As the two head back, they cite a takeout for Crispy Chicken, Mashed potatoes, gravy and Cole slaw and take it back with them.

The following day, as they go about refreshing and sipping on coffee, Howard remarks, "What would you like to do?"

"Let's take the bus and go site seeing around Newport and see what it has to offer." replies Sueanne excitedly

"Sounds good, we'll pick up a guide book from the motel office."

After picking up the rooms, the two get the guide showing all the interesting spots that they could visit.

The two settle on a visit to 'CLIFF WALK' which is a 3.5 mile walk along beautiful views of the sea and exotic mansions of the rich and famous. The trail begins at Easton Beach and continues to First Beach. Walking along taking in the view, the two stop at areas and rests in the grass to catch their breath.

They as well stop at an area known as the 40 steps. Here they could step down to the waters' edge, but the climb back up is for the ones in shape, and Howard nor Sueanne at the moment were in any good shape but go down ten or so take one another's picture. The only trouble about reaching the end of the trail was a more challenging continuation of an unpaved stretch where though some rocks were easily maneuverable, others a bit more challenging. The two found that this was a great way to spend a few hours and get closer to one another for they depended on each to get them through this walk.

During their excursion along "CLIFF WALK" the two would go into the back of the mansions, sit on the grass and pretend to be the owners. One such mansion is known as 'THE BREAKERS' built for Cornelius Vanderbilt the second. It is said the seventy room mansion had cost over seven million dollars to build which in today's amount would be about one hundred fifty million dollars."

Though Howard and Sueanne were unable to go inside, the two would join others peering into through the windows.

"Sure is beautiful." notes Sueanne peering deeper and deeper through the glass.

"It is magnificent." replies Howard." Wonder how anyone can make so much money, while others have to go without?"

"Some people are luckier than others." says Sueanne shading her eyes with her arm to keep the glare off from the noon day sun.

"Some are born into it and others are lucky to know what they want in life and go after it. Then there are those of us who don't know what they want and we wind up always wishing we had something else than what we have. It's known as,' it's always greener on the other side of the fence.' "

Are you insinuating that I, we-"

"Don't start and ruin a perfectly good day. I wasn't talking about anyone in general, if I did I would be talking about more of myself."

"Alright if you say so, let's continue on." Huffed, Sueanne leaving the window and headed out of the back yard and toward the next mansion.

"Wait a minute will you? Don't get huffy, I didn't mean anything that was towards you."

Sueanne pays no attention to him as she enters the back yard of yet another exquisite mansion known as 'ROSECLIFF'. This mansion boasts of having the biggest ballroom in Newport, it is measured to be forty feet by eighty feet in diameter.

ROSECLIFF mansion was built between the years 1898-1902 and is opened as a museum to the public. It was built by Theresa Fair Oelrichs who happened to be married to James Graham Fair one of the four partners in the Comstock Lode. She also married Herman Oelrichs, American agent of the Norddeutscher Lloyd steamship line.

After looking at the mansions, the two stroll back to Easton Beach where they board a bus that takes them to another attraction known as the Newport Tower, The Old Stone Mill and the Mystery Tower. Or whatever different people call it. It is made with shell lime, sand and gravel. Its diameter is twenty feet and its height is twenty eight feet. The tower lies on eight stone columns. The walls are three feet thick and have four windows below and three windows at the top. Though there is still no certainty as to its origin, some believe that it was built in the 16th century by the English, while others claim it was built by the Vikings.

"Just amazing what type of people could have built something like this and wonder what was its purpose?" says

Howard turning to Sueanne who had no impression about her on the Mystery Tower before her.

As the day comes to a close, the two walk the streets of Newport looking into the stores windows, sometimes going in and looking around.

"You getting hungry?" asks Howard holding Sueanne's arm.

"Sure. Where do you want to eat?"

Looking up and down the street, Howard spots a restaurant and together, they cross the street and enter the restaurant where they enjoy a good meal drinks and mild conversation before leaving the restaurant, catching a bus to the motel where they get into their evening clothes and prepare for another night cuddled into each other's arms.

One afternoon as the two go through the newspaper in the hotel, they come across an ad for an apartment to rent at thirty-eight Howard street which is located just off the famous Thames street where each year is the start of the famous Americas Cup yacht races. In checking out the apartment, the two find that they could afford it and that it was just perfect for them.

Howard and Sueanne go about fixing up the apartment and making it into a home for them, when a neighbor, Gunners mate 2nd class Norman Gleason who happens to be a crew member on the Gainard as well, informs him that his presence is requested at the Executive Officers Stateroom.

Upon arriving, Howard is escorted to the XO's stateroom where he is informed of the passing of his father. This message had been forwarded to the Gainard by his brother Tom, who was still serving his duty at Fort Dix, New Jersey. Howard is given enough time to take leave and attend the funeral in New Hampshire. It is March 27th, 1969, a day to remember.

Howard and Sueanne take a bus out of Newport, Rhode Island and arrive at his mother's trailer in Gossville and wait for his brothers to arrive. March twenty-seventh, nineteen hundred six nine, all four boys are home for the first time and all in uniform, Tom is in his army uniform, Howard in his naval uniform, Jr. in his army uniform and Seth in his marine uniform. What a sight they make. They each carried their father's casket to his final resting place at Calvary Cemetery in Rumford, New Hampshire. Each family member drops a rose on the casket of Edward John Walker Sr. age 59.

It is here, that the boys were able to see their sister for the first time in years; she had been lost in the shuffle of foster homes that the boys were never told of her whereabouts.

Anna Marie is a good looking blonde eighteen year old young lady. As she runs into the arms of her four brothers, she had all sorts of questions to ask them, but at the moment the priest speaks of their father. He notes that, "Edward John Walker was a good catholic man and went to mass quite often. That he loved his children very much, and although he had a problem it was no Worse than that of any normal man has. Though he was divorced from his wife Miriam, he spoke many times that he still loved her. You children who are young adults now know what your father had gone through to leave us at such an early age, but he is in good hands now and lives in one of the mansions that the Lord has prepared for each and every one of us. Let us say a prayer."

As the prayer is said, the boys stand tall as their fathers' casket is lowered into the ground. It is a lot harder on Anna Marie for her father visited her quite often in her foster homes as he did when the boys were in the Orphans Home.

After the service, the boys and Anna Marie returned to their Aunts house where they really got to know one another by telling how and where they had lived. In one of her foster homes, she discovers that she was but five miles from where Tom was living.

Howard told her he's sorry for not staying in touch with her due to even his father didn't tell the boys were she was.

"You sure look great all four of you." says Anna Marie going up and hugging each of her brothers who she hasn't seen since she was twelve weeks old and then she only knew them from what her father had told them.

"Are you boys all married?"

"I'm married." states Howard as he points toward Sueanne, "This is my wife Sueanne Walker walker of Baltimore, Maryland."

"Walker Walker?" questions Anna Marie.

"Her maiden name is Walker before I married her."

"Wow'" replies Anna Marie going up to her and hugging her. "Hope you two are happy.

'We are very happy I'm expecting in November."

"I'm going to be an aunt?"

"You already are." replies Tom this is my wife: Charlene she is from Connecticut and we are stationed at Fort Dix, New Jersey and we have two boys. They were left with a baby sitter.

"Their names are: Tom Jr. and Dennis."

"I have two nephews, and one on the way?"

"And two Nieces," replies Seth as he introduces his wife Yvonne from Long Island, "Their names are Lorelei and Sabrina.

Amazed, Anna Marie becomes speechless as she turns toward Edward Jr. to find out her next surprise.

"This is my wife Brenda and we have a boy Edward the 3rd and a girl Sheila."

'Let me see." ponders Anna Marie trying to remember how many nephews and nieces she can add to her family besides the ones she had met through Aunt Sarah of Rumford, "three nephews and three nieces and one on the way, wow."

After the funeral the five spend a few days with their mother and step-dad: Jeffrey Collingswood, at their mothers' trailer in Gossville, their mother begins to put the real father down by calling him a drunk that had broken up the family.

Tom steps in immediately to prevent her from saying anymore about their real father, "It wasn't dad's fault alone mom, you were just as guilty by bringing all those men home with you and kicking us out of the house so that you could enjoy each other's company."

At that remark, tom was slapped across the face by Miriam as she replies, "What do you know about what had went been going on, you were only seven?"

"Mom I'm not seven anymore I still have the memories and they don't ever go away. And don't you or Jeffrey ever lay another hand on me or my brothers again."

Without waiting for their leave to extent, the four brothers said goodbye to their sister and headed back to their duty station. Outside the trailer, the five hugged one another before departing on separate ways once again. Again Howard felt as though he was grasping for life.

Upon reporting back aboard the Gainard, Howard discovers that they are about to get underway in a couple of days for a fifteen day cruise in the Atlantic operating with the Aircraft carrier JOHN F. KENNEDY-CV 67. The Kennedy was a former CVA designated as an air combat ship; however, it was changed to CV to denote that it had anti-submarine warfare, making her an all-purpose carrier. She was named after the late 35th President who was assassinated in Dallas on November 22, 1963. She was just commissioned on 7 September 1968.

On April 3rd, Gainard sails out again to plane guard for the new pilots flying on and off this new aircraft carrier. She has been upgraded to handle the F-14 Tomcats and the S-3 Viking aircraft. Compared to the Gainard, the Kennedy is 192 feet from top of the mast to the waterline, and she could hold speeds up to 34 knots (63km/h).

This impressive ship took Howard's breath away as the Gainard would pull along side of her during maneuvers as well as refueling. Howard's ship looked so small compared to the Aircraft Carrier. For the next fifteen days out at sea, all he got to do was: chipping, scrapping, painting the ship over and over again. The lookout watches were cold He would try to get as close to the heater vents just to stay warm as he scoured the horizon and inform the Officer of the watch what he was viewing and in which direction the ship was heading. Green light meant it was going left to right, red meant the ship was heading right to left and if one sees green and red the ship was coming right at them. Then there were the gunnery practices which had him thinking of the time when his knee was pulled under the gun mount. Just the thought of the injured knee kept him on his toes and he made sure his knee was never again under the breach.

Just the thought that would be only a fifteen day cruise and not six months makes it a lot easier. He knew that Sueanne was waiting for him in their new apartment and that she would be setting up home while he is at sea.

After the fifteen day cruise ends, Gainard sails back into Newport, where upon tying up to a pier Howard could see Sueanne waiting for him on the pier. It was just before disembarking that an announcement is made that Gainard would be making a sudden departure within the next ten days.

For those ten days, Howard and Sueanne enjoy one another's company as they go about buying furniture for their apartment and enjoying the sights that Newport had to offer.

Ten days goes fast when one is enjoying it, so the day comes when once again Howard kisses Sueanne and boards the Gainard for operations in Key West, Florida for two weeks. This tour consists of acting as a training ship for new officers that had arrived aboard While in Newport. The ship and crew zigged zagged around as the new officers became familiar with the ship's operations. Howard hated being away from Sueanne, but he did enjoy the warmth that the Florida Keys brought them on this deployment.

Key West is roughly 129 miles southwest of Miami, Florida, and 106 miles northeast of Havana, Cuba. Key West is a seaport that attracts many cruise ships. It was once known as President Harry S. Truman's Winter White House.

Key West is as well known as the "Gibraltar of the West" due to its strategic location on the 90-mile wide shipping lane, the Straits of Florida, between the Atlantic Ocean and the Gulf of Mexico.

The battleship USS MAINE sailed from Key West on its fateful visit to Havana, Cuba, where it blew up, thus igniting the 1898 Spanish—American War. Crewmen from the ship are buried in Key West, and the Navy investigation into the blast occurred at the Key West Custom House. It is believed at that time, the Spanish had mined the ship but today, it is said that there was an explosion onboard that was the result of negligence and the Spanish were not responsible for the destruction. Thus the Spanish-American War and Teddy Roosevelt leading the Rough Riders up San Juan Hill could have been avoided.

The whole time that Howard and the Crew were sailing around Key West, the crew was not given time to go ashore. The cruise is like taking children to a candy store and not allowing them to have any. What a dreadful two week cruise.

GAINARD arrives back in Newport, Rhode Island on May seventh. The following week she is sent twenty-five miles upriver for three days in dry-dock to have her bottom sandblasted of all the incrustations formed while the ship is underway and to have the ship's hull inspected for any damage.

All this inspection and sandblasting meant only one thing, Gainard and her crew were about to ship out again. Nosing around to see what he might find out makes his head spin and his heart throb a little faster than it had. He understands that on July sixteenth, Gainard will be heading for operations off the coast of Virginia before heading to Cape Canaveral (Kennedy) to act as rescue destroyer for the Apollo 11 moon shot. Being his lifelong hobby, Howard really looks forward to this cruise, and each day that draws nearer, Sueanne, who is happy for him, does not want him to go.

But as Howard's luck would have it, he was not to be aboard this historical event in Man's Conquest of landing a man on another celestial body.

His mother, through the help of the American Red Cross had contacted the Gainard's captain who had handed the message down to his executive officer to inform that the message to get Seaman Walker to his stateroom in order to receive an emergency leave because his step-dad has been hospitalized for cancer in the roots of his lungs.

Upon arriving once again in Capital City, New Hampshire at one thirty am by bus, the city had been shut down; they couldn't even get a cab to take them to their Uncle Fred and

Aunt Eunice. So calling his Uncle on a pay phone and letting him know where they were, Howard asks if they could come and pick them up. Soon his uncle and Aunt Robinson pick Howard and Sueanne up outside the taxi station on Main Street, Capital City to take them home to Rumford where his mother Miriam is staying. Entering the car, Howard asks, "How's dad?"

"He's resting peacefully, but it doesn't look too good." replies Aunt Mary.

"How is mom taking it?"

"She's been staying with us since he was admitted."

Now Howard's aunt Mary is the step sister to his mother and although there were seven family members, Howard never got too close to them, after all where were they when he and his brothers and sister were placed into an orphanage and scooted about in different foster homes.

Though he didn't along with his step dad, for the way he would talk about his real father, he is showing his respect for it is his mothers' husband and he needed his family at this time. Then Howard's eyes meet those of his half-cousin Tamara and Danielle who were seated in the living room when he and Sueanne enter. Shyly he approaches them and though the girls say nothing, it's the eyes that tell all. They are very polite when they are introduced to Sueanne.

From the seventh of July to the nineteenth of July, the family, to include Howard's cousins, Fred Jr., Joanna; Steve; John; Katrina; Karen and Phillip would spend the day visiting and praying that he would battle back from this dreaded disease.

While at his aunt and uncles' house the family, got together to catch up on getting to know one another again.

"Do you remember when you dumped that bucket of tar over your head?" asked Tom

"Yea I remember that. The other kids called me tar baby."

The rest of the family cracked up laughing, as their Aunt states, "Your mother was furious at you. You could have suffocated."

"You boys always did frighten me in one way or another. There never was time to sit down and relax with you boys around."

"It was the neighbor's Randy and what's her face Clark." states Tom.

"Mom it wasn't just us boys, you and dad got into some real down fist-a-cuffs when we were young." remarks Howard looking over to his mother.

"You're father was a drunkard. He would spend his money on booze before he even got home from work."

"Mom, you were no saint yourself." States Tom trying to protect his dad

"I did much more for all you kids than he ever did."

"We're not here to put anyone down; we are here for your mothers' husband who is sick."

"I know that we are." states Tom, but I just can't get the feeling out of my system that we kids were not wanted."

"We loved you the best way we knew. The state took you guys away from us. There was nothing we could do."

"Maybe not, but you could have at least come visited us when we were in the orphan home rather than me having to run away to find you." says Howard reflecting on the time that he ran away from the orphan's home in search of his mother and dad.

"I just couldn't bring myself to come to the orphan's home to visit knowing I would have to leave you there when I left."

"You know" says Tom, "That is exactly what dad would say about you whenever he came to visit. After all, you were a very long time in the hospital, when you told us it was going to be only twelve weeks. It turned out to be three years and then some."

"Are you still upset with me about that?" asks his mother.

"I'm a lot older now, I'm getting over it."

"Can we talk about something else instead of this." asks Fred Jr.;

"Why does this conversation bother you?" asks Tom looking over at Fred jr. who was seated on the couch.

"Yes it does. That's my Aunt you're talking about."

"Well excuse me, but that is supposed to be our mother, but she never acted as one as your mother had, and she had seven kids to us five. So tell me who fought harder at being a mother and giving love."

"Alright stop it right now" demanded Uncle Fred, "we are all family here. No one is better than another."

"Oh really!" remarks Tom, look around you, who is seated on soft chairs, and couch, and who is seated on the floor. We are. Is this coincidental?"

"Yea," asks Howard," how come we are never treated like family if you say we are family? I never had felt like family since the Caruso's took us in from the orphan's home and brought us to Waterford."

"We never found the time to get up to the Orphans Home to visit." states his mother, while rocking herself in a large soft chair.

"Funny dad was always visiting us whether we were in the Orphans Home or in another Foster home." said Howard looking crossly over at his mother.

"The trouble with your father was that he was always drunk, he didn't know where he was going." replies his Aunt Mary.

"Drunk or sober, he loved us enough to keep contact with us." butted in Jr.

Just then the television begins showing the separation of the Eagle Lunar Landing from the mother craft and heads to rendezvous with the moon it is July 19th 1968, and the astronauts will not exit the Lander until early in the morning.

"Sorry it isn't a better visit, maybe next time." states Fred.

Tamara and Danielle were still in the dining room looking over at Howard as they thought that he had grown into a very handsome young man.

"Not a very enjoyable visit is it?" asked Tamara as she crosses one leg over the other just high enough so that Howard caught the sight of her creamy thigh. Averting his eyes towards Danielle, he notes that she had an even shorter dress; she crosses her legs so that her white underwear showed.

Howard looks over to Sueanne who was looking around the dining room, noticing all sorts of pictures of the family but none of the boys. "I don't see any pictures of you or your brothers."

"We are a separate family. There are two, one is my mother's family and the second one is my father's family and neither the two shall be one."

As he talked, no matter how hard he tried, he could not keep from bringing his eyes to rest upon Tamara's legs. They just kept bringing back those memories of when she and Danielle made that pact in the salt shed of never discussing with anyone about when they had played with him and straddled his little body. Just the thought of that action, now brings his body to life. His loins ached and his muscles hardened wishing he could get away with his wife and take the horniness out on her.

The girls knew what they were doing and Howard became very uneasy. Tamara and Danielle both noticed that they indeed frustrated Howard, and there was no hiding it.

"Want to go out and see the new ducklings?" asks Tamara getting up off the sofa.

"No thanks." remarks everyone.

"Oh come on" states Tamara "they are so cute." Grabbing Danielle's hand and pleading with the others to follow them. By grabbing Danielle's arm, she wouldn't give any display that she and Danielle wanted Howard to follow them.

"No thanks I really don't want to go, insists Howard.

"Me neither," replies the rest of the boys getting involved in the television show and still talking to their mother and cousins.

'I already saw them. States Anne Marie, "they stink. Plus I want to stay and talk to my brothers; I haven't seen them in a very long time."

Tamara and Danielle both grab the arms of Howard and Sueanne hoping that only Howard would come with them.

"No I really don't want to see the ducklings, Howard, you like farm animals, you go see them."

Though Howard really did want to go with the girls, he had to show resistance in front of everyone.

"I'd rather not, I'm comfortable sitting here and talking."

"Oh go and make peace here, satisfy the girls in going out to see the ducklings. There are about a dozen or so." remarks Uncle Fred.

Both girls now grab hold of each arm and pull him up off the floor. Aunt Mary goes into the kitchen to get some duck food so they could feed the ducklings.

Walking out to the back yard, Tamara and Danielle hold tightly to his arms as they ask, "Do you still remember us from being kids?" asks Tamara.

"Yes I do I'll never forget it, but I was too young to know what we were doing."

"Well now that you are older, do you like what you learned?"

"Yes very much."

"I thought I was going to marry you. I still wish I could, after all we are only half cousins."

"But I'm already married and I love her very much."

"Who says you have to love someone to make love with them?"

"I think it is wrong to make love unless you are in love with that person."

"Well, we were only children and you didn't love me then did you? But you liked what we did to you on the salt bags, didn't you?"

"I guess I did, I didn't know what you girls wanted from me. You were older and wiser than I, and I just didn't get the feeling until I got older."

"Oh Howard . . . you've got so much to learn, and we'll teach you."

Once in the duck coop, Danielle stood guard at the door looking out across the field while Tamara begins to rub her hands between his legs to stroke that automatic bulge that seemed to appear whenever a female began to touch him.

"Please! I'm too weak to resist this, I just can't do this I'm married and my wife is in the house."

"Are you hot?" asks Tamara.

"Yeah I'm hot." at the same time she tugs up her dress to rub between her legs. "Please! Please, don't let me do this?"

Tamara unbuttons his trousers and lets them fall to the floor, she then goes to her knees, pulls his shorts down so as to see and grab hold of him. Danielle pleases herself as she watches Tamara caring for Howard and then to make him even weaker she places him to her lips and engulfs him into her mouth." You like this don't you?" she asks as she looks up at his pulsating body.

"Yes I do. But we shouldn't be doing this." Squirms Howard as he knows what they were doing was wrong.

"Hurry Tamara I want some of that too. "States Danielle watching Tamara pleasing Howard by kissing his squirming body from bottom to top.

Tamara rises to her feet and hikes her dress up to her neck as she proceeds to take his hand and places it along her belly.

"Boy Howard you really have grown."

Danielle, who was pleasing herself as she watched, couldn't stand it anymore and she goes over and begins to kiss him as she rubs the palm of her hand softly over his body She also goes to her knees and begins probing until she acquires what she was after. She as well gets Howard panting so much that the girls thought that he was going to have a heart attack.

"I remember when you were so small, you were my first boy. But now wow have you grown in more ways than one."

Together they kissed and played until he couldn't hold his actions and he excretes into one or both of the hands that were preventing him from soiling anyone of them.

"Wow did you like that?" asks Danielle wiping her hands on the bottom of the ducks cage, as she cleans him up.

"Sure did. But I'm afraid my wife will notice the smell."

"You're not stingy are? Are you going to please us?"

Howard takes his hands and together he turns the girls so that their backs are against the wall and he proceeds to touch both at the same time.

Knowing time was running out, Danielle takes Howards hand and gently uses one of his digits to help, as does Tamara.

Howard spreads both girls' legs apart to freely feel and see the evidence from both their areas of wanting love.

Rising up from his squatting position to his feet, Tamara grabs him one more time and milks him as though she had been around a few cows in her days. Exhausted, Howard knew that there was not much left to his weary body.

After kissing him from his sweet thighs to his sweet lips, Tamara pulls his short back up and pats him while Danielle gives him one last kiss before pulling up his trousers and buttoning them. Howard wipes his digits between both their legs before helping to pull up their underwear and straightening out their dresses.

"Is this still our little secret?" asks Tamara pressing her body against his.

"Yes it is still our secret. Wow that was enjoyable."

"Glad you liked it. Hope you come home again soon." replies Tamara

"But don't you have husbands or boyfriends you can satisfy?"

"Sure we do. In fact, Danielle is engaged to a guy that's in the Air Force. They are planning on a wedding next year. As for me I've been married and divorced. He was a dud."

Before going back into the house, they decide to pick up the ducklings and get as much of the smell onto their hands in order to mask the smell of their love making. The three run around a few circles before sprinting windless back.

Within a couple of days, their mother's husband was ready to return home from the hospital, so the boys say goodbye to their half cousins and their Aunt Luella. As Uncle Fred drives

Miriam, Howard and Sueanne back to her place, Tom, Jr. and Seth decide to head back to their duty stations. Though Howard and Sueanne wanted to return home to Newport, they couldn't due to the lack of inadequate funds. He was just too proud to ask his family for it.

Once back at the trailer with his mother and step-father, Howard asks a neighbor if they could give him a ride into Capital City to visit the American Red Cross. Here, he is given twenty-five dollars.

The next day, Howard and Sueanne board a bus that takes them to Newport, Rhode Island, where Howard leaves Sueanne at the apartment and quickly scurries to the naval base in order to report aboard the Gainard before he is listed as AWOL, absent without official leave.

Out of breathe, he runs down to the pier and searches for his ship. Not finding it tied up at any one of the piers, he takes in a deep breath and tries to calm his heart down to a normal pace.

Turning about face, he catches a bus heads back home where he informs Sueanne that the ship wasn't in port and that he was hungry. After eating soup and sandwiches, the two unpack their suitcases from the exhausting trip.

While sorting through their mail, the landlord stops by and requested that Howard pay his rent which was already overdue. Not getting it, the landlord informs them that he would return on the twenty-seventh for the rent, and again on the third of August for that month's rent.

After the landlord had gone, they quickly put their remains of the month's pay together and discover that they are short for this months' rent not to include for next month.

That night the two go to bed early for they both were tired and exhausted.

Howard awakens around ten pm with severe stomach pains and vomiting. This was the same that had acted up on him when he was in Ohio, just four months prior.

"What's the matter?" asks Sueanne awakening to his groans, and turning on the light.

"My stomach, it hurts just like before." remarks Howard in between gags.

Quickly dressing, Sueanne helps Howard to dress before running next door to a neighbor to ask if they could call the Newport naval hospital, and if they could give them a ride up, for she was too shook up to drive herself. The neighbor, Gunners mates' second class Norm Gleason has been befriended by Sueanne while Howard had been having week end duty on the ship.

Norms' wife had left and gone home to be with an ailing mother. Norm drives Howard and Sueanne up to the naval hospital where a naval corpsman helps place Howard on a gurney and begins probing his stomach and asking him all sorts of questions, which he finds difficult to answer due to his pain.

Rolling him down the corridor, they are stopped by Sueanne to ask what he knew about what his problem could be she is quickly ignored as he is continued to be pushed into the x-ray room where he undergoes x-rays of his chest and abdomen. When a nurse returns from looking at the pictures with the doctor, she pushes him into a room containing a dozen beds, six on each side of the wall.

As Howard lay there, another nurse comes over, draws the drapes and begins finishing undressing him. Once the clothes have been removed, she places a Johnny on him. Placing his clothes into a plastic bag, she leaves the room and delivers them to Sueanne who is waiting in the waiting room with Norm.

"Any word on how long I'll be hearing anything?" requests Sueanne accepting the plastic bag.

"It could be hours. He's under a series of tests and the doctor is with him now. I suggest that you go home and rest and come back tomorrow. Maybe we'll know more by then."

"But I can't leave him here alone. I would like to say good night to him."

"I'll tell him if he is still awake when I look on him."

The doctor had entered the ward and proceeded to place a tube up into his nostrils which go down into his stomach. This begins to draw the gastric juices up out of his stomach and into a pump. Once this process is started, the nurse hooks him up to an intravenous. It is now closer to midnight. And Howard is beginning to fall asleep.

Howard's neighbor is the same Gunners mate that had befriended Sueanne when he had told Howard to report to the executive officers stateroom. With his arm around Sueanne, Norm tells her."The nurse is right, you need to get some rest and visit him tomorrow."

"I can't sleep. I'm wide awake now."

"Then let's go home have some coffee and unwind until you get sleepy."

Chapter 11

As the vehicle stops in front of her apartment, Norm asks, "Would you like coffee at my place or yours?"

"Let's go up to my place."

Before exiting the vehicle, Norman throws an arm around the back of Sueanne's shoulders and bends to kiss her. She knew where this was going as a slow burning excitement swelled deep inside her. His gaze lowered to set upon the heavy swelling of her breast as she tries to contain the situation.

Brushing his fingertips lightly over one of her nipples, he feels the response as she lets out a lowly moan and presses her body backward into his elbow.

Though she knew that what she was doing was wrong, her husband is in the hospital and very sick, she should have spent the night there, plus she was very tired from the long day, but again here she was the two of them, he was doing things to her that made her release the fires that kindled deep inside her loins. As he plants a deep passionate kiss, her lips parted without thought. Her body moves to a state that gives Norman the invitation that she wanted him to touch her.

Pulling her closer while one arm is around her neck and the other hand moving up along her leg under her skirt and tickling her thigh she in return brings her hand to rest between his legs until she is not mistaken he definitely was aroused. Filling her hand and with a whimper of complete and utter surrender she squeezes him to let him know that she was ready for him.

As their licking tongues delved into one another's mouth, Sueanne begins to forget everything. She forgets that Howard is in the hospital, she forgets where she is, what is happening, her mind begins to swirl due to the action taking place, but one thing she did recall through all this, was that being with Norman was not her first time.

The first time she met Norman was right after when Howard and she moved into their apartment. Howard would sometimes ride into the naval base together each car pooling. It was on the days that Howard would get weekend duty and Norman was home alone while his wife worked downtown Newport.

That one day was when Norman was home alone and ran next door to tell Howard that he was wanted to report to the executive officer's stateroom, to be informed that he was requested to go home on Emergency Leave.

Howard had dressed and driven himself to the base alone because he had no idea why he was being called, or how long he would be gone. This situation will leave Sueanne alone at home and Norman had been left home alone due to his wife being in town at work.

"Are you alright? You look sad." asks Norm to Sueanne going about picking up the apartment.

"I'm okay. It's! It's just that I feel I have no life."

"Why do you say you have no life?"

"In every way, Howard can't hold a job in civilian life, I hate being home while he's constantly at sea all the time, I hate Newport, I hate the Navy, and I hate my life."

"Tsk tsk, come here let me help you settle down."

Then before she knows it, she allows Norman to kiss her unknowingly while brushing her own body towards him instead of pulling away from him.

"We shouldn't be doing this. You have a wife and I have a husband."

"Do you want me to stop, asks Norm softly caressing her shoulders and back.

"No, no, no, states Sueanne shaking her head, "We've come too far to stop now."

Knowing the two didn't have much time to make the most out of the situation that they have embraced before Howard would be coming back; the two decide to touch one another so that they could get some relief in order to come down from that cloud they were on.

"Are you alright?" asks Norman retrieving his hand from under her skirt.

"I am, for now, how about you. You still feel hard, you okay?"

"I'm okay, but before we depart, let's get together again and finish where we left off?"

"I'm sure there will be times we can get together when Howard has duty or when your wife isn't home."

Suddenly without warning, Sueanne felt Norman pull away from her, "Where were you? It's as though you were caught up in some erotic activity."

"I was, I was just thinking of our first time together, and we promised to make up where we left off. Well here we are."

"Let's not finish it here, let's go inside where we can really get into it."

Before she can agree, Norman was exiting the vehicle as Sueanne straightens out her skirt and fluffs up her hair.

Norman follows her into the apartment where she invites him to sit on the couch while she goes makes coffee.

"Do you really want coffee now?" he asks wrapping her around the waist from behind and pushing him forward into her rear.

"No! I guess we can skip the coffee and just go to bed." states Sueanne twirling around in his arms and cupping his face and kissing him smartly on the mouth.

Sueanne leads Norman into her bedroom, pulls the covers down and the two proceed to undress, when both were completely naked, they lay down in the bed as Sueanne rolled on top of him covering him with kisses from head to toe. That night, they made love and when the fires died from their bodies, they fall into a deep restful sleep.

For the next seven days Howard had gone through extensive x-rays, blood tests, upper G.I. series and still everything coming up negative. After noticing an incision on Howard's left side of his abdomen, the doctor writes to the hospital back in Capital City where Howard believes the incision was performed. The results, also proves negative due to the fact the original hospital no longer exists and the records were unknown. The hospital then informs Howard that he would be released the following day.

When Sueanne is told of this information, she makes her visit short by telling him that she would have to go shopping and get the apartment in order for his coming home. What she and Norman really did was to make their last rendezvous that much more heightened in satisfying each other's lustful needs.

The day that Howard and Sueanne return home, attached to their apartment door is a note from their landlord informing them that as of September first, his rent would be going up another fifteen dollars. Howard informs Sueanne that he was going to be riding in with Norman to report aboard Gainard while it was still in dry dock.

After reporting aboard, Howard gets himself squared away and returns to his duties.

That evening after his duties were complete, he rides back with Norman who informs him that he would be having the weekend duty and would have to drive himself in to Darnellville. When Howard leaves in the morning, Norman is just getting home and his wife was just preparing to go off to work thus leaving Norman and Sueanne having coffee before she gets out of her housecoat. Norm makes sure that he would help her out of her housecoat and he nightgown as they take a shower together before heading into the bedroom to enjoy one another's company before getting a couple hours of rest.

On the day Gainard is due to leave Darnellville and return back to Newport, Howard has duty and asks a friend who was off duty if he could drive his car back to Newport for him.

Once back in Newport and tied to the pier Howard finishes up his duties he goes about looking for Machinist Mate 2 Class John Morrison.

When he is located, Howard is informed that his car was in an accident and he would take him out to the parking lot to show him the damage. Looking over the damage he discovers the right front quarter of fender and bumper had been pulled away from the car. Being behind on his insurance premiums, Howard knew that he would have to pay this repair out of his own pocket.

Taking it to a repair shop, he is given an estimate repair value off One hundred twenty-five dollars. Feeling responsible, MM2 Morrison hands Howard Eighty dollars to help in covering the cost of repairs. But being behind in bills and mortgage, Howard has to settle on dividing it between the two the repairs of the car would just have to wait.

Life was just becoming too much for both of them to handle, pressures were mounting in everything they did, and the only release valve they had was to blow up at one another sometimes for no reason at all, or other times when Sueanne is kept from joining Norman in their coffee rendezvous.

The final blow comes when one morning while reading the paper, Howard comes across headlines of a friend that he had made while stationed at Fort Holliman, Baltimore, Maryland, It was Jim Thompson, he was the one that insisted Howard in going over to the Service club the night he met Sueanne. Jim had been killed in a fire fight in South Vietnam. He died as he tried saving a wounded buddy that had fallen from an early morning attack of rocket fire from the VC (Viet Cong) who had invaded the south to make it all Communist.

With all that is going on, Sueanne informs Howard that she wanted to return and stay with her sister in Oneida, Ohio in order to save some money and to help get out of dept. Besides Sueanne is seven months pregnant. With Howard remaining aboard the ship at nights he could send her the money from his pay each month or have an allotment made out to her so that she receives it automatically.

It was a good thing that they had agreed on her return to Ohio by bus when they did, for on September first, Gainard and crew set out once again on a six-month cruise to the North Atlantic, where they would get to visit such ports as Brest, France, England and Ireland. Howard is excited about the fact of seeing Ireland, since his family comes from Ireland.

But again fate has its day as Gainard nears Breast, France; orders come down for the destroyer to transfer down to the

Mediterranean in order to replace one of the ships in the area which had to report back to its home port for deactivation.

From September first until the thirty-first, Gainard is underway, traveling across the North Atlantic turning south to the 'Med' which turns out to be one long hard treacherous and lonely trip, for Howard is constantly sea sick, and those long cold four hour watches in the blackness of the cold nights dig deep into his soul as he tries reaching across those many long sea miles between he and Sueanne wondering what she was doing as he tries to ease the lonely nights spent without her. It was during this month, that Gainard saw no land, no visits of ports, and if things couldn't get worse the ship's washing machines had broken down and the crew had to tie their clothes to a line and let them wash in the wake of the ship. The salt in the Ocean only caused their clothes to shred or fade out faster than normal.

As the destroyer limps her way into the port of Naples, Italy, she is running on only one of her two boilers. Ship and crew tie up for five days but it is more for repair duty than going ashore to see the country. After the five day repairs, the ship and her crew set out once again for gunnery practice with the ship's three inchers. What seems to be a couple of weeks of gunnery practice, invasion practices as well as search and rescue missions, the ship's crew is in dire need of a port-of-call. The captain requests shore leave in Naples since they are that close.

The ship and crew is given ten days to refit the ship and energize the crew, she pulls into port and ties alongside the Destroyer Tender GRAND CANYON AD-28.

Howard takes advantage of his shore leave by going back to Mt. Vesuvius and Pompeii for there was a lot that he had missed on his first visit. This time he takes more pictures and purchases postcards of all that he sees. He was going to take no chance that these would be lost.

Following Naples, the next port-of-call is Barcelona, Spain where the ship opens its radio room for the crew in order to make personal calls to their families back in the states. Howard waits several hours before he was able to get his chance. First he would say what he wanted to say to an unknown person on the other end of the short wave radio, after saying over; the individual would relay the message to the person whom you are speaking to. For instance in this case it was Sueanne that the unknown person is relaying the message that you had just said.

Sueanne in returns says to the unidentified person her response, which was relayed back to Howard. The only thing troubling about communicating this way is telling Sueanne "I love you and miss you." And have it be spoken to a gentleman on the short wave who forwards it for you.

This is the same procedure that he had gone through once before.

"Have you had the baby yet? Over"

"I'm overdue, expecting any day. Wish you were here. Over"

"I wish I was home with you, but it won't be long before we return. Over"

"You're going to be a daddy before you get back. You're going to miss his birth. Over"

"I'll make up for it when I get back. I've got to go now others are waiting their turn. I love you. Over"

"Love you. See you when you get back."

On November thirtieth in the year of our Lord nineteen sixty-nine Howard is notified that a message had been received by the captain of the aircraft carrier USS SARATOGA CVA-60 in that he had a son born Howard D. Walker Jr. in Defiance, Ohio weighing in at eight pounds ten and one-half ounces twenty-one inches long. It finishes with the note "both mother and son are doing fine.

With this message, Howard takes a deep sigh and looking skyward, states "Thank you Jesus."

He then goes about spreading the news around the ship about him being a daddy and all thank him and wish him well. But when he comes to inform Norman about little Jr. being born, he shakes his hand and remarks, "Are you really sure it is your kid?"

"Sure I'm sure. Why shouldn't I be? She's my wife and I'm the only one she's been with."

"You know women." remarks Norman leaning up against the bulkhead just outside the head.

"What is it you're trying to tell me?" asks Howard quizzically.

"When the cat is away, the mice will play."

"Are you saying my wife is unfair to me?"

"I think all women are. They need it just as much as we do when we are on these cruises."

"Not Sueanne she wouldn't do that."

"Even my wife has affairs when I'm gone to sea, and I have affairs when I'm in port. Don't you?"

"No I've never touched another girl when I'm in port; I always go to the historical places and learn of the country, I don't want to go astray looking at the women."

"I don't know who you're kidding, but I don't believe you one bit."

"You know Sueanne; you know she wouldn't cheat on me. We have our arguments, but deep down we love one another.

"Can you honestly say that you have never cheated on Sueanne, never ever?"

Before he could answer, Howard begins to reflect back on the time with Tamara and Danielle while the three were out in the duck pen at his Aunt and Uncle's house.

"Oh my GOD I have cheated on her without realizing it."

"You see married or not we just can't stay away from the girls."

"So you think Sueanne is having an affair while we are out cruising around?"

"Yup at least up until the time she couldn't have an affair due to the baby coming along.

"So do you think little Jr. could be someone else's?"

"You'll know when you get to see it. Look for some identification marks on his body."

"It's got to be mine. It just has to be." remarks Howard turning away from Norman and proceeding to walk down the ladder to his compartment.

For the remainder of the cruise, he didn't allow any more cold to bother him from his night port watches. He stood gallantly into the winds, ice, snow and sea sickness for in ten days he would be home and able to visit his wife and son.

Howard is given a ten day leave in order to get to Ohio and see his wife and new born son who is already four months old. Also visiting the Westford's, the house is filled with family for Sueanne, little Jr., Marilyn, Joanne, Allen all have arrived to visit with Sueanne and the newborn.

Howard looks little Jr. over and over, but all he sees is himself looking back at him there is no doubt about it, little Jr. is definitely his child. Giving Sueanne a big hug, he states, "Honey, you gave us a beautiful son. I love him as much as I love you."

"I love you too. You seem awfully doubtful that he is yours"

"Forgive me hon. it was just something that someone had mentioned to me, but forget it."

Howard had no intentions in talking to Sueanne about what he and Norman had talked about before they returned from the cruise. He was going to let by-gone be by-gone whatever she may have done could not have been half as bad as what he had done.

The family stayed up late talking of what took place while Howard was out to sea and what the family had gone through getting to Defiance when it was ready for Sueanne to deliver.

When they did retire for the night, Sueanne and Howard stood around little Jr's crib and admired him before leaning over and kissing him good night. The two lay out upon the floor and whispered before falling asleep.

Early the next morning, Brian awakens Howard to ask him if he would care to go trapping with him. Not really wanting to go, he chose to leave the warmth of Sueanne's arms for the frigid outdoor winds and cold. Brian teaches him how to lay out traps to capture weasel, mink, and muskrat. The two would drill down into the ice and drop a line to do some ice fishing.

By the time the two return home, breakfast would be ready, Brian and Howard would have to wait their turn to get their shower in.

Sueanne and Marilyn would get little Jr. dressed while Joanne helped Korina with John Andrew there was a lot of conversation going on, but no one really knew who was speaking to whom.

Life was confusing but everyone had a task to do and it got accomplished. The rest of the day, the family sits around the kitchen table and play board games or just converse and laugh at jokes. When Sueanne does bring the baby out to join the family, Howard gets to hold him and to bond with him as he gets to know him.

The evening before he was to return to base, Howard asks Sueanne, "Would you come back to Newport If I was able to find us a cheaper apartment?"

"Yes I would." She says readying little Jr. for bed Korina has a houseful as it is, and I and the baby would only be in the way."

"Good I'll start looking for one just as soon as I get back."

Sueanne covers little Jr. and walks towards Howard where she wraps her arms around his waist and plants a kiss on his lips.

"I love you so much I can't bear to see you leave tomorrow. Ten days went too fast."

"And I love you right back." states Howard holding her close, I don't want to leave either, but if I don't get back in time I'll be AWOL. And we don't want that do we?"

"I guess not. But that doesn't make it any easier."

Running his hand through her long hair Howard tries to console her by saying, "I'm sure little Jr. will be keeping you occupied enough to keep you from worrying about me."

"I'm sure he will, but we'll make up for it when we come out."

"OOOOOhhh can't wait."

Arm in arm the two steps back to admire Howard Jr. who is lying in his crib on his back smiling, kicking his little feet about and cooing as if he knew what was going on between his mother and father. That night as the two lay upon the floor, they quietly made love to ease the pain in the separation which they are about to feel as they await their reunion once again in Newport, Rhode Island.

The following morning Howard says his good-byes to the family and kisses Sueanne and little Jr. just as she states, "Why can't you stay for Christmas? It's only two weeks away and besides It'll be little Jr's first."

"I can't stay." replies Howard trying to fight back the tears swelling up in his eyes, "It's not fair of you to ask me I've got my duty time to do and I must do it."

Holding him closer and harder, Sueanne begins to sob as she cannot hold back any longer. Howard holds her as she gets it out of her system before pushing her back from him saying, "Look hon. I've got to go. I love you and I'm going to miss you and little Jr. very much, but come Christmas Day, I'll be thinking of you both and my heart will be here with you."

After kissing her, Howard plants a kiss on his son's forehead and says, "You be good my son take care of mommy, help keep her safe. I love you. See you soon."

Howard then proceeds out the door where Brian had already cleaned off the snow and scrapped the ice from the windshield. Howard blows everyone a kiss as he enters a warm car and Brian waves as he heads out the driveway and heads to the bus station.

Once arriving at the bus station, Howard exits the car, turns to Brian shaking his hand and states, "Take care of them, and thanks for everything." He boards the bus that takes him to the airport in Ft. Wayne, Indiana where he catches a flight out of Cleveland to Newport, Rhode Island.

Chapter 12

Christmas day finds Howard on duty on the mess decks as he serves the crew and their guests Christmas dinner. He finds the duty difficult as he is thinking of his family.

Upon finishing his duty, he leaves the ship to go onto the pier and phones Sueanne to wish her and the family a very merry Christmas. The sound of her voice and the cooing of his son help him through the rest of the day.

One day while out about Newport he comes across an apartment where he feels would be just right for the three of them plus it was located just outside the naval base known as Willow Rose Motor Court. Upon notifying Sueanne of the apartment he as well informs her of the scuttlebutt that is going around the ship of an early out for certain personnel. This meant that he could be discharged from the navy three months early.

Not wanting to take the chance that Howard would not be on the list, she tells him to take the apartment and she and little jr. would be out as soon as they could.

The night Sueanne was due into Newport; Howard had walked the three miles to the bus station because he couldn't afford cab fare for both ways. The bus was due to arrive at four pm. By five-fifteen pm, he found himself still waiting. Becoming worried he phones Korina to ask if Sueanne had left yet, Korina replies "The snow in Cleveland is so severe that they closed the airport and she had to wait four hours before it reopened to get the planes airborne again."

"So she is now on her way?"

"Yes. She is on her way. She had called me from Cleveland just before she was about to board the flight."

"Alright I'll wait right here until she arrives, we'll call you when she arrives." claims Howard wiping a tear from his cheek. After saying his goodbyes, he returns to the waiting area where he sits upon the wooden bench and waits for Sueanne's bus to come in.

It was eight-fifteen pm when the bus finally arrives and as Sueanne steps from the bus clutching little Jr. who happened to be asleep, Howard runs up to meet them, kisses Sueanne and takes the little bundle of joy from her tired arms. Sueanne describes her journey as he escorts her to a waiting car. As they settle into the back seat, the cab driver places her luggage into the trunk of the cab.

"Willow Rose Motor Court" replies Howard when the driver entered the vehicle.

Once they had arrived at their destination, they enter their apartment, First thing that Sueanne spots is the large 'Welcome Home 'which Howard had made from one of the paper bathroom mats.

The two go about settling down and unpacking. There is no crib for Howard Jr., so Sueanne places him in the middle of the bed and surrounds him with pillows as he lies there so innocently asleep.

Once settled down and unpacked, Howard orders some food from a fast food service which is delivered.

For the remainder of the night they talked and called Korina to let them know everyone was safe and that they were settling into their apartment.

After catching up with the gossip from back home, Howard informs Sueanne that he has to go to bed early, for he had to get up early to walk to the ship because he had mess cooking duty.

This duty: requires him to be onboard at five am in order to prepare for the morning breakfast. This meant Howard had to rise at four am, get cleaned up, dressed and because he has no vehicle, he has to walk from the motor court down to the pier which was about a little over a mile. But at four am it seemed as though it was about ten miles, especially when it was really snowing and the winds blowing so hard that it seems to blow right through him as he fights desperately to remain on his feet. At times it seemed as though the winds would win out, but he found that walking backwards into the wind helped to protect him.

Sometimes the early morning would get the best of him and he would want to give up and go back to bed and let the navy declare him AWOL. But because he felt so positive about what he was doing and in what he believed in, he stayed and battled the cold winds and snow because it wasn't half as bad as the times he spent without his wife, the loss of his two sons, the loneliness spent on the cruises, the frustrations of finding a job, the irritations of the landlords and doctors, the upsetness of their union of marriage, the problems with his health, the debtedness of their bills, the lack of having enough money, the inability to provide a home, the constant dependency on others.

Even doing their laundry turns out to be another hassle for them. The two would bundle up and with little Jr. placed into a stroller with bags of laundry in the back of the stroller and push it down about a half-mile to the nearest shopping center and the laundry mat. This journey was a hard struggle as the wheels of the stroller kept getting stuck in the snow while little Jr. would be tossed and turned about and whine at the top of his lungs. But yet they endured, so was the life at Willow Rose Motor Court, so is the life of a sailor.

Was the ship's grapevine predicted? The President did come out with early outs and Howard was on the list. So with the three month early out, he and Sueanne prepare for her return to Baltimore so she could lock up the apartment there set up housekeeping before he gets out of the navy. Sueanne is ready to return to stay with her grandmother until she finds herself an apartment.

The two go about cleaning up any debt they had incurred. But as the two worked on preparations for getting out, Gainard is given orders to report to get underway for Charleston, South Carolina for replacement in the reserve status thus leaving Sueanne alone at the Motor Court to do everything herself. She receives Howard's checks and pays off the bills, then takes a bus and heads to Baltimore, MD to stay with her grandmother until she is able to find her own apartment and a job.

Howard remains with the rest of the USS GAINARD 'S crew in Charleston, South Carolina until new orders are made up sending the crew in different directions and duty stations. After a month in Charleston, Howard returns back to Newport onboard the USS MOALE DD-693, an even older destroyer than the Gainard.

Aboard with him were the only other crewmembers which were getting their three month early out. Among the crew is Gunner's Mate Second class Norman Gleason. They both remain with the Moale until their discharge on May twelfth nineteen seventy.

Although Howard did not like the navy life, he feared going back into civilian life, where it meant he would have trouble finding and keeping a job.

Howard joins Sueanne at their apartment: sixty-five twenty Brown Avenue Apt. 1 which Sueanne had found as she knew a lot about the area and where to look for the good buys, the apartment is down the road and across from Ft. Holliman.

Howard just sensed that he would be back in the army if given the opportunity even though he had promised her that he would try to make it go in civilian life, for she had stated, "If you go back into the service, I will remain here in Baltimore and not go with you. I want no more of the service."

Sueanne and Little Jr. are all Howard has, his father died of pneumonia, his step-father dead of cancer and his mother who he knows very little of and being so far away in New Hampshire that there was no one he could confide in.

Civilian life: oh how it has changed in the short two years he has been away from it. The people were not of his caliber, what with their quick defiance against the Vietnam War, the youth begin looking for something to believe in and this leads them to usage of hard drugs and free speech.

Multi-colored flashing lights known as strobe lights like those Howard had experienced when he first went to the Service Club at Ft. Holliman where he first met Sueanne some four years ago, light up the dance halls, the youth find inspiration in one another thus showing their lack of trust in adults. They gather in masses to become part of its Music, Marijuana, and LSD, nakedness, nature lovers and free love.

Though he believes everyone has that right to express their own feelings and although there was a lot out there that didn't have any idea what they were expressing or searching for, Howard knew they only wanted something or someone to belong to. They reached for what they could call their own, something that no adult could touch or destroy.

The one thing that Howard did find out that did not change was how hard a descent paying job was to get. Unless one is experienced in one particular field, getting that job is next to impossible, especially a good one.

After some hunting, Howard is able to get a job at Lockmere & Whitehead: a company that canned food products. His job consists of working three-thirty pm to midnight shift working in the sanitation department cleaning and washing floors, rest rooms and locker rooms. The pay is low to standards and the work is dirty with no chance of advancement. There is no security in this type of work and he was able to get this job because no one else would take the job. But to him, he is happy just to have a job.

For two months Howard worked the job hoping that something better would come along. The pay is so low that it just is never enough to keep up with the rent and bills or to keep food on the table. Even with him working, the two had to go to the American Red Cross again to seek aid.

Fed up with what he had to do in order to keep food on the table and milk for Little Jr., Howard informs Sueanne, "I'm quitting my job and going back into the army if they will take me."

"No, no more service. I'm tired of the separation."

"We are not making it in civilian life. I need to regain my respect."

"Then I'll get a job."

"You have enough to do in keeping the apartment up and caring for Little Jr. who needs your attention."

"Please don't do this Howard?"

"I've got to. I'm just not making it. I've got to go back in so we can get a good monthly pay and get insurance."

Going against Sueanne's wishes, Howard on July 7th re-enlists into the army at Ft. Holliman. Returning home he informs her of what he had done. This infuriates her to no end.

"Why? Howard Why?" screams Sueanne throwing her arms up in disgust?"

"It's the only thing I'm able to do and take pride in. I should have stayed in the army right from the beginning." remarks Howard as he heads into the bedroom to pack a suitcase.

"You realize you are going to lose another stripe for breaking service, don't you." replies Sueanne following him around the room.

Turning to face her, Howard implies, "Do you plan on coming with me to my next duty station?"

Shaking her head in a negative way, she replies stomping her foot, "No way."

"Then the loss of a stripe will be worth it to me, seeing I'm the one pulling the duty."

"What if you get sent to 'NAM' what will happen to us?" continues Sueanne trying to persuade Howard in what he has done.

"Don't worry about me going into combat or off to Vietnam for that matter, after all if my heart is really as bad as they claim it is then they wouldn't send me over there."

"Well, we need you here."

Putting his arms around her he states, "I believe that I can help you more in the service than I ever could in civilian life. Besides, you see what we have to do in order to get anything to eat. Well, I can't live like that anymore. I have more potential in me than I'll ever get to use as long as I remain a civilian."

Sueanne begins to cry as she places her hand against his chest and she begins to softly pound on it stating, "I'm pregnant, and I want you with us during this pregnancy. Then after, if you still want to go into the army, I'll follow you."

Pulling away from her, Howard states surprised, "Pregnant, why that's terrific, but why didn't you say something sooner. It's too late to get out of it now, even if I wanted to, I'm right now under orders to report to Ft. Dix, new jersey the day after tomorrow."

Holding her closer, Howard states, "By the time its born we'll be together at a permanent duty station and by then we should be able to give it everything it needs. Besides, the army insurance will pay for it."

Chapter 13

LEAVING HIS FAMILY BEHIND ONCE again, Howard reports to Ft. Dix as an E-2 and is placed into the 1387th Replacement Company to wait for further orders which finally did arrive on the sixteen of August informing him to report to the five hundred third replacement company in Frankfurt, Germany.

While here, he again waits for his permanent orders for his new duty station.

The orders come two days later ordering him to report to 2nd Battalion, 73rd Artillery, 3rd Armored Division (Spearhead) in Hanau, Germany just twenty miles from Frankfurt. Howard is assigned to the Francois Kaserne just one of five in the area.

The Kaserne is a post which once was Hitler's horse stables. When Howard enters the area, he sees GI's sitting in their windows with boom boxes playing loud music. The first song that Howard hears is "This Diamond Ring" sung by Gary Lewis and the Playboys. From the windows you could see over the brick wall to the German civilians going about their lives. They must have been thinking that the Americans were really a rowdy bunch. But this happens when another country is conquered in a war. After all they started the war along with Japan and Italy against England and the United States as well as the Soviet Union. It is only their fault that they had listened to an evil dictator with a forked tongue such as Adolph Hitler.

Once settled, he looks around for quarters in case he could talk Sueanne into coming out and staying with him. His duty consists of keeping his M35 2 ½ ton cargo truck ready for use whenever the time comes to start up her engines, pick up its cargo and go to a determined area anywhere in Germany. This vehicle could carry some 5000 pounds across country or 10'000 pounds over roads; they have been known to haul twice as much. This truck has been in service since 1951 and is used by all US Armed Forces as well as various Allies. Operational mileage is from 400-500 miles traveling at fifty-five miles/hour. Howard was getting to know his truck and as the driver felt as if he is finally responsible for something. He was in charge of his own truck.

However, he wasn't over there more than a few months when he receives a message from the American Red Cross informing his Company Commander that it would be in the best interest to Sueanne if Howard was able to get home due to her being hospitalized and that his presence is needed.

With the Commander's help, Howard is able to board a plane out of Frankfurt/Maine and arrive in Baltimore. Taking a cab to the apartment, he meets up with his brother-in-law at the door. "How's Sueanne?" asks Howard as soon as Allen opens the door.

Rubbing his eyes, for it was after one am, Allen answers sleepily, "She has toxemia, but the doctor says that she has gone through all stages and right up to convulsions. Now she is full of toxemia and he says that she will be hospitalized until the baby is born in December."

"Why that's almost three months." exclaimed Howard taking a seat at the kitchen table while Allen gets up and puts the kettle on for hot water. "Care for some instant coffee?"

"I'd rather have a cup of tea if you have any?"

After pouring the hot water into his cup, Allen sits down looks at Howard and remarks, "That's not all Howard she has a very bad kidney infection and the doctors are having trouble clearing it up. That's one of the reasons they want her to remain in the hospital. Once they get to clear it up then she can come home."

"God, that poor woman, she has gone through hell, when will it end?"

Korina and Marilyn enter, seeing them Howard rises and goes over and gives each a big hug. "I hope I didn't awaken you?"

"It's alright. I can't sleep too soundly anyway." replies Marilyn with a big yawn.

"What about the baby? Is she going to lose this one as well?"

"I don't know answers Marilyn; the doctors are doing all they can."

"How is Little Jr.?"

"He's fine. He's sound asleep."

Getting up from the table, Howard goes down the hallway and enters the room where Little Jr. is sleeping soundly. Leaning into the crib Howard pulls the blanket up across his shoulders and kisses him on the forehead and whispers, "I love you son."

Returning to the kitchen he finds the family seated around the table, joining them, they spend the rest of the early morning talking of Sueanne, Little Jr. and Howard's duty in Germany. But the forces were on how the separation has taken its affect on Sueanne. The family thought Howard was being selfish as to not think of Sueanne's health.

"But I did and I still do think of her. I needed to do this to keep our marriage together . . ."

"We don't see it that way. You abandoned her when she needed you. You should have remained with her. You know she has difficulty pregnancies."

"When I enlisted, I didn't know she was pregnant. I couldn't keep a good paying job, and she had to work long hours just in order to help pay the rent. And besides who is paying the insurance?"

"The army But that still doesn't make it right that you up and left her as you have always done."

"I never just up and left her. You and your family never gave her time to breathe. All of you try to live her life for her and she loves you so much that she sides with you against me."

"She is our family and we want her to have the best life. Like she had before—"

"Before she married me Right? Go ahead say it. You've been thinking that all along. Your whole family blames me for keeping her pregnant and losing the babies. But you know something Marilyn in case you have forgotten, it takes two to have a baby, and never have once did I force her. So excuse me while I go up to see Sueanne, and as far as I'm concerned, go home where you belong."

Howard spends the entire day visiting with Sueanne at the hospital in hopes to comfort her. He is there to help her through the pain, and tells her stories of what he had seen when he was in the 3rd Armored Division in Germany. He helps feed her and together they seem as one.

He notifies the pentagon telling them of his wife's illness and asks for a compassionate reassignment to Fort Holliman in order to continue his military duties and still be near her when she needs him.

One day the doctor comes into Sueanne's room and tells them "Sueanne could go home only if she remains bedridden and that there should be someone would be with her at all times".

Korina was called back home to Ohio by her husband and Marilyn returned home to care for Joanne but Alan, if she wished to remain with Sueanne, she could. But Marilyn would not want to be around Howard when he was home, and Howard did not want to upset Sueanne with what took place between he and her Mother.

While awaiting word from the Pentagon about his compassionate reassignment, Howard got Sueanne home and did all he could to keep her off her feet. He found out just how tiring and tedious the job of mothering is. It seemed no matter what he did there was never enough time in a day to get to everything that needed to be done, but he had no intentions in allowing Marilyn and the rest of the family that he couldn't do the care for Sueanne.

By November, Howard is notified to report to the US Army Garrison, Fort Holliman where he is to inform them that a copy of his orders would be on the way and that he was to return to duty as soon as the orders come in.

One morning, as Howard goes about picking up the living room he hears Sueanne calling from the bedroom. Upon entering she informs him that she was having severe pains and for him to call the doctor. Howard is informed by the doctor to give her three (3) Phenobarbital tablets every four (4) hours. By five (5) pm Sueanne states that her pains were quite constant with no let up at all. After finding little Jr. Howard calls the doctor. While he was on the phone Sueanne, who was at this time lying on the couch, let out a wicked scream and runs to the bathroom leaving a trail of blood behind her. "Oh my God her water bag just broke and she is leaving a trail of blood" yells Howard into the phone.

"Bring her right up to the hospital just as soon as you can. I'm on my way there just as soon as I hang up" states the doctor.

Unable to get hold of a county ambulance, Howard calls the city ambulance which responds very quickly. While in route, the driver states that they would have to go to the nearest hospital which happens to be city hospital.

While there, Howard calls the doctor to inform him of why he was at the wrong hospital. He then goes back and waits, he starts thinking of the same situation they had encountered once before.

As he sits looking around the drab colored walls a doctor approaches him and with one hand outstretched. He introduces himself to Howard and states that he has been in touch with the doctor at the Hospital and that everything that could possibly be done will be done. Then the doctor informs him "your wife is in good hands, the placenta that is: the umbilical cord has detached itself from the fetus thus denying the baby the blood, food, and oxygen needed to keep it alive".

"Then the baby is dead" interrupts Howard.

"I'm sorry. But your wife is as well in danger and will drown in her own blood if we don't do a cesarean immediately".

"By all means" states Howard, "You have my permission to do whatever you must. Just save her please."

The two doctors keep in touch with one another about what was happening and both agree that a cesarean was necessary.

An hour and one half later, the doctor returns to the waiting room and approaches Howard. He states, "We didn't have to do the cesarean after all. For some unknown reason the body rejected the foreign object and just as we were about to put her under the knife, she delivered. I'm sorry the baby didn't make it, but your wife is doing real fine and will probably be ready to go home in a few days."

The loss of the baby comes as no surprise to Howard for he had anticipated all along that there was no chance in Sueanne carrying it through full term, especially from what Sueanne has been going through.

The day Sueanne comes home, Howard receives word from the Veterans Administration to report to Fort Holliman and that his orders were on the way from Germany.

Having reported to Ft. Holliman, he is assigned as Post Commander Colonel Charles D. Ekberg's driver. Within three weeks he is promoted once again to Private First Class. His orders arrive along with his 201 file, finance records, health and dental records, thus confirming his Compassionate Reassignment.

One day, when Howard returns home, he is confronted with an angry Sueanne as she informs him of the argument between him and Marilyn. Looking at Marilyn and the kids who were standing around Sueanne, comments "I didn't want to burden you with that. You had enough problems to attend to."

"Don't ever put yourself ahead of my family again. They have as much right to be here as anyone."

Hon. you have a lot of your old man in you and you should be lucky I'm in the service or you would have to pay the hospital bill and the burial of our son yourself."

"His name is Jeffrey Lewis. Don't forget it."

'Nice name. Who named him, your mother?"

"In fact it was? He was named after her father and Uncle Lewis."

"That's what I mean. We have no life of our own. You let your family in everything that should be between us."

'You have got to learn an awful lot if you want me and Howard Jr. stay with you."

"Of course I want you and Howard Jr. But I want us not all of the family poking in on our lives."

Turning her back on Howard, Sueanne comments to her mother, "You can't talk to him, He's a Yankee from New Hampshire"

"You people still fighting a war that happened over one hundred years ago. That's silly."

Howard knew that he could not talk to her as long as her family was around, but when she was alone he would talk to her and hopefully get her to understand.

Christmas of nineteen seventy is the first that Howard and Sueanne have spent together since Christmas of sixty-seven. As the family gather around the tree, there is a mixed feeling of love, joy and family unity.

As Howard sits on the floor watching little Jr he tears into a package revealing a World War air battle game called "Dog Fight" which he lays aside along with a white shirt received by his Mother-In-Law, a tie from Allen, three pairs of socks from Little Jr.

After all presents had been opened, Sueanne mentions "I didn't get a present from you. Howard!"

He responds, saying, "I was too occupied to get out doing Christmas shopping. I apologize."

Although somewhat disappointed and hurt inside, Sueanne remarks, "I understand. It really doesn't matter as long as my family is home to be with us this Christmas."

Watching her, Howard begins to feel that she has really been expecting something from him since it was the first time they had gotten together. Getting up he goes into the bedroom and returns, handing her one of his tall model rocket which he had put together in his collection over a period of time.

"I'm sorry hon." states Howard as Sueanne reaches to accept the model, "All I have to offer you is this model of mine, please say that you will accept as my Christmas gift to you?"

Accepting the model, Sueanne thanks him and places it aside, as Marilyn and the kids give a perplexing look toward Howard.

"You don't like it, do you?" asks Howard watching her placing it carelessly aside her."I like it." Huffed Sueanne, "I just don't know what to do with it."

Howard raises to his feet goes over towards Sueanne. Picking up the model rocket he places it into her hands stating, "Look it over good, If then you don't like it I'll exchange it for a new one."

Somewhat reluctant, Sueanne takes the model and begins looking it over. As she turns it around in her hands, looking at the bottom, she twists the two halves and peers inside. A large smile crosses her face as she looks up at Howard who couldn't contain his smile either. "You put something in it, didn't you?"

"I did." remarks Howard pretending to be surprised. "I must have forgotten about that. Take it out and let's see what it is."

As Sueanne pulls her hand out from the inside, she sees that it is money. Counting it, she has fifty dollars along with a note which she reads out loud: 'Merry Christmas, I love you, spend in good health on yourself.' The two embrace and kiss as the rest of the family look on.

In the meanwhile, Little Jr. has unwrapped a little red wagon, a large size cement truck, a pocket radio, a purple truck containing a carousel attached to the back, a snoopy dog(from

Col. Ekberg: Post Commander,) a musical television, a Roly Poly ball(from Kitty Ekberg).

Allen receives a Russian fur hat, pair of gloves, white shirt, pants, socks, record album, two dollars, a jacket, key chain, wallet, three more pair of socks.

Marilyn receives a new pocketbook, box of chocolates, some new clothes.

Later that day, visitors arrive from West Virginia; they are Suanne's uncle Eddie and Aunt Nettie, Aunt Nellie and three of her cousins.

As the day progresses, it becomes even more enjoyable. There is no time for anyone to reflect on the past few weeks, there is only joy and happiness in being together and celebrating as a family that has gathered on the Lord's Day.

On December thirtieth, Korina and Brian arrive with their two boys for a holiday visit, along with them comes a snow storm that just happened to fall on Howard's snow removal duty weekend which is from six am until eleven thirty pm shoveling snow around headquarters.

Then he had to wait as the snow continued to fall to see if they would have to remain throughout the night.

As it looked, it had let up so the snow removal detail is dismissed. Howard arrives home just after midnight tired, cold, wet and completely exhausted.

As soon as he had freshened up and changed into his pajamas, he goes and sits on the couch joining the others watching 'Guy Lombardo' bring in the New Year. As they watched the show, Korina leaves the room and returns with some belated gifts which they ravoushly attack.

The following morning Howard returns to duty in order to finish up shoveling the remains of the accumulated fallen snow that had fallen during the night. All together some eight inches of snow had fallen. This seemed an awful lot here in Baltimore, but at home in New Hampshire, eight inches is nothing. It's not uncommon to see twelve to fourteen inches fall in one storm with many more storms to follow in the winter season. Howard would love to see the snow fall for the more the state received the better conditions it was for running the sled dogs.

When Howard was first introduced to sled dog racing, it was due to the fact that the original musher was unable to rise. They had asked Howard to fill in, all he had to do was to hang onto the back of the sled and the dogs would do what they are trained to do. Agreeing, Howard, steps onto the runners of the sled, the dogs sensed that there was a rookie running the team. Howard stood, hands frozen to the handle of the sled, his feet, pressed down hard onto the runners, he was ready to make his inaugural entrance into the world of Mushing.

Looking around at the other mushers, he could see that they were a lot more relaxed than he felt. Turning to look at the starter, He notices the starter sending out one team after another; soon he was due up the handlers set the dogs on the starting line and gave the starter that dogs and musher were ready. The starter gives the signal and the dogs bolt to life quicker than Howard had anticipated, as the sled lurched forward, Howard's hands were jolted from the handle and tumbled backwards into the snow bank only to watch his team running down the trail without him. Somewhat embarrassed that he had lost the team and the other mushers were laughing at him, he did the only thing that he could think of: which was to lie back in the snow and laugh along with the others.

The runaway team was later retrieved and returned to the owners who did not give up on Howard for the way he reacted to the inability to handle the dogs, the owners continued to be use him in other races during the rest of the week until

Howard learns from experience on how to interact with the dogs so that he was used in other races to win third prize in a few of them.

After the holidays, Brian returns to Ohio due to having to go back to work, he allowed Korina and the boys stay and visit. One day Korina's oldest boy: John Andrew is rushed to the hospital for what is described as "blood points" a virus which he had at fifteen months earlier which almost killed him. Howard and Allen visit in the waiting room while Korina is with the doctor. The nurse informs Howard that there was a phone call for him from his wife.

Picking up the phone from the desk, Howard states "Hello"

"I just called the police to report that a burglar just tried breaking into the apartment." screams Sueanne into Howard's ear as she tries catching her breath.

"Be calm honey, I'm going to send Allen back in a cab. Are the police there now?"

"They are outside looking around."

"Stay inside and Allen will be right there. He's a big boy. They wouldn't want to mess with him. We'll be home soon. I love you."

"I too, how's John Andrew?"

"Korina is in the room with the doctor. I haven't heard anything yet."

"Okay. Hurry home."

Hanging up, he goes and continues his wait in the waiting room. What Howard doesn't know, is that Allen, while in the cab, had wrapped a length of chain around his knuckles. Upon exiting the cab he pulled the chain loose expecting to meet up with the burglar. But, as it turns out the police had caught the burglar and was in the squad car getting ready to be taken into town.

While Allen whips the chain from his knuckles and wrist he injures it but never says a word about it until the following day. After taking him to see a doctor Allen is told that his wrist is badly sprained but would heal if he kept it in a sling.

The following week, Sueanne had to return to the hospital for a tubulargation. But, as she lay there on the table she begins to start thinking, which leads her to get up off the table and walk out of the room frightened and unable to go through the operation, and returns to her room. The following morning, the doctor releases her to go home.

That weekend, Brian returns and stays through the week before taking Korina and the boys back to Ohio with him.

The following week, Howard gets word from housing that they could move into Cummins Apartments which is cheaper than the apartment they were in, plus it consists of two bedrooms, kitchen, full bath and a full basement with washer and dryer which is much more convenient for them. It as well contains a large storage locker which they badly need.

As they go about settling into their new apartment, the old man started in his abusing and throwing Marilyn and Joanne out of the house and onto the street. Sueanne hears of their plight and has them come live with them until Marilyn can find a place that she and Joanne can live, or are able to go back home.

For the next couple of months all goes well outside a few expected family quarrels. It is during one of these "so called" family quarrels that Joanne decided that she wanted to go back home to live with her dad because she felt there were too many restrictions on her living with Howard and Sueanne. She had packed her bag and started cussing at her mother. Calling her father, she persuaded him to come and pick her up.

On July first, Little Jr. is taken to the post hospital because he is having a temperature of one hundred degrees. The corpsman in the dispensary refused to look at him, saying that his temperature is normal for children his age. Discouraged with the findings, Howard and Sueanne take him to the Army post Hospital where they find that Little Jr. is suffering from a strep throat.

Upon being treated with the right medication, a few days later, Little Jr. is himself all over again.

While Little Jr. is recovering, the government seems to be dissatisfied with the days that the holidays fall on, so they quickly change it so that each holiday would fall on a Monday thus giving a three day weekend.

On July 5th, Howard, Suanne and Little Jr. were sitting on the grass next to Marilyn and Allen at the Francis Scott Key Junior High School watching the fireworks and celebrating the Fourth of July Holiday weekend. The evening was pleasant with a gentle breeze and spectacular fireworks.

After the fireworks were over, they proceed down the Avenue to where there was a carnival that had been set up in the parking lot of a large Department store.

There, Little Jr. rode the rides while Howard played the games in order to win prizes for all of them. There is much to eat and drink and did they eat and drink. By the time they were ready to leave the carnival, Little Jr. is sound asleep in Howard's arms, while continuing to make their way up the road to catch a bus home they each take turns carrying Little Jr.

In all, it turned out to be a very enjoyable holiday and a day to remember.

Near the middle of the month, Howard finds himself having difficulty with his vision. In calling the Army Hospital to get an appointment, they tell him to come in the following morning, which he does.

"I want you to go to Walter Reed Hospital and see what they have to say." states the doctor.

This back and forth seeing one hospital and then another continues throughout the month. Finally they admit him into Walter Reed to have his right eye operated on. While hospitalized, Sueanne would come to visit him by bus for the next four days. After, he is released and placed on a week of convalescence before returning to duty as Post Commander's driver.

The month of July not only brings happiness and joy into their lives but it brings dissatisfaction and its arguments which always seem to be one-sided. Whenever there was an argument or disagreement in the family, Sueanne would always be on the side of her mother regardless who was right.

It seemed that all through the marriage there is always someone interfering or making it impossible for Howard to be alone with Sueanne. When one member of the family leaves to go somewhere, another member would show up.

Howard is beginning to feel the toll this has on him, and tries to talk to Sueanne about it, but she doesn't back down and informs him that, "she will have her family around anytime they wish to visit. Her family came first before her and Howard's life."

Even Little Jr. could sense that with his mother he is able to get away with a lot more than he could with his father. When Little Jr. didn't feel like doing something that he didn't want to do he would get his father hollering at him until his mother or grandmother comes to the rescue and takes Little Jr. from his father. This common practice bothered Howard to no end, he feels that the family is interfering in his rights of parenthood and this denied him in being the father to his own son.

One evening, as the women were in the kitchen talking and having supper, Howard and his son were in the bedroom eating and watching the ballgame on the television. Soon the women hear Howard's voice getting louder and louder, trying to get his son to stop acting up and eat his supper.

Entering the bedroom, the women see why Howard was hollering at his son. As soon as Little Jr. notices his mother and grandmother Little Jr. puts on his little act that he is choking and throws his spoon at his father and refuses to eat altogether.

Scolding him in a loud tone, Howard picks up the spoon, cleans the supper off his shirt and with an open hand slaps his son on the back of his hand. Seeing this, Sueanne gets up and runs over to grab her son. As she approaches, Howard steps in front of her. "Stay away or he'll never learn to eat his supper."

Suanne turns to sit on the bed with Marilyn and Joanne, just waiting their chance to take the child out of the bedroom. Seeing his mother and Grandmother still there in the room, Little Jr. begins to play in his supper and soon grabs handful of food and rubbing it onto his face throwing it and laughing along with his mother and grandmother.

Getting angrier, Howard yells "Stop playing in your food, and eat."

While Howard yells at his son, Sueanne begins yelling at Howard. Soon it becomes a bitter argument.

"Let him play. Stop yelling at him."

Reaching behind his sons' head, Howard remarks, "You like your face in your supper. Well let me accommodate you." and proceeds to push his face down into his supper. In anger Howard had cussed his son not realizing it until it was said.

By now both Sueanne and Marilyn spring to their feet, while Marilyn grabs Little Jr., Sueanne picks up the rest of the supper and heaves it at Howard, he ducks and the dish and supper splatters on the wall covering a picture. Running toward her, he bumps her against the wall. She then begins to lash out at him tooth and nail as he tries to cover and protect himself while trying to explain how he had come about bumping her on accident. Howard tries to pull her head up in order for him to explain, but, without his knowing it all he was doing was pulling her hair. There was no reasoning with her.

Marilyn was holding Little Jr by the bedroom door as he could see his mother and father wrestling. The whole time she was yelling at Howard to leave Sueanne alone. "Bad daddy Bad daddy" Marilyn kept saying as Little Jr. watched.

When it looked as though Sueanne had quieted down in order for Howard could explain what really happened, he let loose of his hold on her. Suddenly she bolts from the bed knocking him backwards onto the floor. She runs into the bathroom where Marilyn had taken Little Jr. to get cleaned up. Howard remains in the bedroom contemplating over just what had happened. He now feels alienated from the rest of the family. He had cussed his son, bumped his wife possibly several times and he has lost respect from the rest of the family.

Cleaning up the bedroom, he now knows he stands alone; there is no one around that could come to his aid. He knows he has done wrong, but he had to get Sueanne aside to talk this over before they all would regret it.

While he continues cleaning up the bedroom, the women exit the bathroom without saying a word leave the apartment and head up the road.

When the room was in somewhat normal order, he looks outside to see if he could see them. Not finding them, he sits down to wait for their return. When they do return, Howard asks, "Can we talk about this?"

Without a word, they head off into his son's room where they prepare him for bed, and there they remain. Knocking on the door, Howard doesn't get a response, so he leaves the apartment to go for a walk. He finds himself walking into Dunwalk where he sits on the bench in the park and looks up into the "Spook Tree" that had once brought them together. Tears stream from his eyes and blur his vision as he recalls his thoughts which are ready to cause his head to spin.

The sun's last rays were beginning to disappear over the horizon when he returns back to the apartment where he sits down on the front steps too embarrassed to go back in.

Looking toward the living room window, his eyes meet those of Marilyn, they both quickly look away.

As the chill of the night drives Howard to enter the apartment he finds Marilyn sitting on the couch watching television. Without a word he enters the bedroom and prepares for bed. Suanne, who was lying there, suddenly looks up at him, grabs her pillow and heads out to the living room.

"Can't we even talk about this?" question Howard sitting on the side of the bed.

Without a word returned, Howard lies down turn to one side sniffs back the hurt and rejection and soon falls asleep as Sueanne spends the night on the couch while Marilyn and Joanne sleep in the child's bedroom.

The following morning, Howard dresses and goes into the kitchen to get some breakfast, only to find the others eating do-nuts and drinking coffee as they talked amongst themselves. They all looked up at him as he stops and decides to go into the bathroom where he washes up, walks past the kitchen, and out the door.

Howard had no idea where he was heading he just had to be out of the atmosphere of the apartment. He walked and walked, again ending up in Dunwalk, down Triesk Avenue, to Combs Avenue and onto Summerland then onto Patterson where he comes to a park where the two had sat under the spook tree and at one time had gotten to know one another, and they found love.

Getting hungry, he enters a drug store and orders a coke trying to kill as much time as he could while thinking of what he could do. Being a proud man, he stays away from the family in hopes they will forgive or forget.

Finishing up his coke he heads through town past the movie theater and walks until he arrives across the apartment building. Hesitantly he looks over toward the apartment hoping to see someone. But there was no one outside. Figuring they were still inside, he continues walking past a brewery and onto a dirt road where he climbs over a barricade which prevents automobiles from using the road. He then crosses over a railroad track behind some apartment buildings.

Continuing, he strolls down a pathway that crosses the same railroad line that he had crossed earlier. Climbing up a steep embankment, he sees below him down in the alleyway, several kids racing go-carts. Watching them laughing and playing, Howard sits down on the hill to watch them for some time.

Rising to his feet, Howard strolls around the field to find his bearings. Noticing the vehicles he was seeing were traveling down Donaldson Avenue and Triesk Avenue, he now knows that he is near where the family watched the fireworks at Francis Scott Key Junior High School. Looking at his watch he notices that it was after one-thirty pm. He crosses the field, down an embankment, across a set of tracks, follows the alleyway to Nightingale Rd. He heads back onto Triesk Avenue and down Cannes Avenue and back onto Summerland.

Around the corner he spots a YMCA. Stepping inside to look around, he notices it is now three-thirty and he was getting tired of walking, sitting down in one of the chairs in the television room. Howard Picks up a few magazines and browses through them. Spotting an article on Apollo XV he quietly rips it from the magazine while looking around to see if he is being spotted.

Once freeing the article, he folds it into quarters and places it into his shirt pocket. He proceeds with the same plan in obtaining the cover of the magazine.

Upon leaving the building, he goes around the other side where he sees a large swimming pool, sitting on the steps he listens to a "Hopalong Cassidy" radio show. It is six pm by the time it had ended. Getting up from the steps he heads into the square where he looks into the store windows as he continues his way back to the apartment. Entering, he immediately goes into the bedroom retrieves his space articles from his shirt pocket and files it with the rest of his space collection.

When Howard goes into the kitchen to get something to eat the women having finished their dinner get up and goes outside. Going to the window to see where they were heading, he spots them boarding the city bus. Sitting down, he watches television as he eats a tomato and cucumber sandwich. The family arrives back around eight-thirty, at which time they enter Little Jr's; room to prepare him for bed. After, they sit down in the family room to join Howard watching television.

Acting as though nothing had happened they talked of everything and anyone, ignoring Howard as though he weren't there. The laughing, joking and talking got to be too much for him so around eleven o'clock he gets up and goes into the bedroom and prepares for bed. As he was about to climb into bed, Sueanne comes in the room, grabs a pillow off the bed and heads back out to the living room where she settles down for another night on the couch.

Alone once again Howard buries his face into his pillow as he turned to one side and begins to cry for being so weak. He then falls asleep.

The following morning Howard had left early to catch a bus in order to keep his appointment with the eye doctor at the Army hospital. The doctor states, "In order for your eyes to heal, you will have to wear a special type of lens in your glasses."

Upon returning home, Howard remains with his son as Sueanne who now is alone due to the fact that her family had to return home due to the fact that the old man called and told them to return, and Sueanne had an appointment with the Public Health. The day was pretty quiet as his son slept most of the day. When Sueanne returned home, she had her mother with her once again. The two women go into the kitchen where they prepare something to eat, and Howard is once again left out by himself in the living room.

For three days Sueanne and Marilyn act as Howard doesn't exist. As they make him pay for hitting her. Then when Howard could stand no more of what was going on, he stomps out of the bedroom and into the living room where Sueanne was preparing to spend another night. "No more." yells Howard turning the television off, and turning to face Sueanne. "This ends here and now. You are my wife and like it or not you are not going to spend another night out here and me alone in the bedroom."

Startled, Sueanne gazes over at him from the couch with her mouth open and frozen in suspended animation.

"Good or bad, I am your husband. If you don't want me, divorce me, and if you're not going to divorce me, than please come with me into the bedroom so we can clear this matter up tonight."

Sueanne regains herself, looks at Howard and then over towards her mother who had come out of Little Jr's room.

"Don't look at your mother for any more answers, I can send her back home just as fast as you brought her here."

Marilyn looks at both but never sounded a word as Sueanne follows Howard into the bedroom, where the door is slammed shut.

Listening, Marilyn can hear loud voices and yelling followed by accusations and counter accusations throughout the night. Soon the yelling subsides to just loud talking. Soon the talking turns to apologizing which lead to more crying. Then comes the sounds of rustling and then silence for the rest of the night.

Chapter 14

A month later Korina, Brian, Allen and the two boys visit from Ohio. Howard at this time is on duty in the Transportation Warehouse until his eyes are corrected. While there, he helps in the packing of household goods for personnel who are being shipped out to their new duty stations.

One day he asks Allen if he would like to join him to help clean one of the officer's quarters who had received his orders for overseas duty, and he asked Howard if he would mind coming over and help give him a hand cleaning up the quarters before the new tenants move in.

Going along with Howard, helps with the windows, painting, yard work and the cleaning up of the cellar. The day has been very hot and since they had moved everything out, they had nothing in the house to offer but beer which Howard gives permission for Allen to have a half glass to keep cool him off. Howard didn't really think there was anything into giving him a half glass to drink as long as he drank it slowly. But, when they arrived home tired and sweaty, little did Howard know what that one half glass of beer will do. As Allen tells Korina what he did for work, she sniffed the beer coming from his breath. She goes into a holy rage swinging at Allen tooth and nail. She then bursts into the bedroom, grabs her sons and tells them, "I want you to stay away from the drunks," then slams the door.

Getting up from the floor where he was playing with the toys and his nephews, he opens the door and remarks, "Keep this door open. And if you want to yell your foolish bible head off for nothing, then go outside and yell or keep your mouth shut."

Korina approaches Howard with both arms waving in the air like wings and begins to cuss him out for getting Allen drunk. One word leads to another, soon Brian gets into it and Korina and Brian were all over Howard as he tries to defend himself in giving Allen that one half glass of beer in order to escape the heat. As names are crossed between the three of them, Howard finally tells them, "Get yourselves packed immediately and get out tonight or I'll take your stuff and throw it out myself."

Howard is now at wits end, he cannot take anymore of being pushed around. When Brian clenches his fists, Howard states, "You either unclench them or start throwing them and if you decide to throw them, I'll guarantee you that you or your family won't be leaving for Ohio tonight, because the MP's will be here to take you to jail or the hospital, your move?"

Suanne, who has been quiet through it all speaks up and tells her family, "I think you had better leave we don't need the neighbors to know our business." Shocked Howard just looks at her not understanding why she had remained quiet all through the argument and now she is suddenly speaking up for his side.

After packing, Korina, Brian, Allen and the two boys say bye to Sueanne before heading over to Marilyn's to inform her that Howard had kicked them out and that they were headed back to Ohio. Of course, Marilyn believed anything her children said about Howard, after all it was Korina first then Sueanne.

Instead of going back to stay with Howard and Sueanne, Marilyn decides to go stay with her mother, Justina Rose in Dunwalk.

As long as Korina is in Ohio, Sueanne would be the one which Marilyn depended on, but when Korina is around she would be the one their mother would believe in.

This time Howard and Sueanne didn't mind it one bit for this is the first time they actually were alone and they could count on one hand how many times this has happened.

One night when Howard arrives home from duty, Sueanne informs him, "I would like to go out tonight and we must be in Dunwalk by five-thirty."

Quickly Howard and Sueanne prepare by showering, eating their supper, feeding Little Jr. and dressing him in his best clothes. They exit the apartment, cross the street and take a bus to Dunwalk.

"Where are we going?" asks Howard curiously.

"It's a surprise for Little Jr." replies Sueanne bouncing the child in her lap.

Arriving in Dunwalk, Sueanne points to the marquee above the regal theater. Reading it, Howard states aloud, "Pinocchio. I remember this movie when I was a kid. Little Jr. will really love it. It is his first movie.

When the movie started his eyes showed that he was amused. Only twice during the movie did he show any kind of a fit. The first was when the theater lights went off and the darkness scared him and the second when he found out he couldn't get up from his seat whenever he wanted. But he shortly settled down and the three enjoyed the movie as well as the popcorn.

Not once since the two married had they really gone out and enjoyed themselves.

As Howard's eyes improved, he goes from duty in the Transportation warehouse to night duty as the Ft. Holliman Motor Pool night dispatcher from four-thirty pm until six am. His job consists of making sure that all vehicles that had been logged out that day had been returned in good shape, gassed and cleaned for the next day's usage.

For Howard's birthday on September 28th, and his twenty-sixth, Sueanne surprises him with a homemade birthday cake which she places on the top, a miniature model of a space capsule of the Mercury series, an astronaut, a moon buggy and several other space exploration items.

In October, for Halloween, Howard dressed up his son in an astronaut costume and both he and Sueanne take him out Trick or Treating within the other apartments. The weather is a little brisk, but all in all the three have a very enjoyable evening.

In November, Joanne is hospitalized to have her appendix removed. She remains there for about a week. It is during this period, that Howard once again responds to Marilyn's wish for transportation from work to the hospital to visit her daughter. The day Joanne comes home, Sueanne goes in for her tubulargation, which she once walked out of the hospital during the past year.

Sueanne is operated on the day before Thanksgiving. Joanne and Marilyn remain back in the apartment to watch Howard Jr. Before heading up to visit Sueanne, The mailman delivers a shocking letter. Howard receives orders for Vietnam. He doesn't say anything to Sueanne for he waits for her to come home.

Once Sueanne comes out of the surgical unit and to her room, Howard remains with her through the hours until he is forced to leave by the nurse in charge of the floor.

That evening Howard goes home, He informs Marilyn that Sueanne had come out of the operation and was doing fine. He then grabs a quick snack before taking a shower and heads off to bed, leaving Marilyn watching television while Joanne had already gone to bed earlier.

The following day, Thanksgiving, Howard stays the entire day with Sueanne while there; Howard is introduced to one of her room mates: Regina Stephanotis the wife of a Greek businessman named Alexandros.

Regina informs Sueanne that she had met her husband in Piraeus, Greece when she was stationed there with her first husband Nickolas who was serving in the Navy. Just after the two were married in Philadelphia, Nickolas was ordered to Turkey and then to Greece.

It was while in Greece her husband is killed in an automobile accident. After taking his body back to Philadelphia for burial, she returns to Greece where she and Alexandros begin to see more and more of one another until they married. Moving to the United States, they open a Travel business where Regina would book flights and accompany them on tours to Greece.

While hospitalized, Sueanne and Regina become friends. "Would you like to work with me in the office?"

"I would like to think about it. And talk it over with my husband before making up my mind. But it sure sounds good."

On December first, Howard picks Sueanne up at the hospital and before leaving Sueanne informs Regina." I'll stop in the office for a visit and let you know about the invite." After shaking hands and hugging one another, Sueanne is wheeled out of the room with Howard tagging behind.

Arriving home, Sueanne is met by her son as he makes a running dash at her and hugs her until she is about to turn blue. Then they go about giving little Jr a birthday party which happened to be back on November thirtieth. Everyone decided that they would wait until Sueanne had gotten home. Howard picks up the cake from a bakery, stops into a department store and picks up a few presents. They call Colonel Ekberg to see if their daughter Kitty could come to the party. Joanne comes with her cousins, Aunts and Uncles, among all the balloons and noise makers.

Little Jr receives a play telephone, creative blocks and some new clothes. The day is filled with fun and excitement as everyone has a good time and no one yells at anyone.

By the time Howard returns from dropping off the last of the family and guests, both are exhausted. They settle down for some peace of mind as Marilyn and Joanne were in little Jr. Room asleep. It is at this time that he thinks it would be the best time to inform her of his orders.

"No!" yells Sueanne bringing Marilyn and Joanne out of the bedroom.

"What day do you have to leave?"

"I have to report to Ft. Lewis, Washington on January nineteenth. Nineteen-seventy two"

"What is it?" asks Marilyn, "You ok?"

"Howard has orders for Vietnam."

"I don't want you to go. Can't you speak to Colonel Ekberg?

"I don't want to go either. And besides, Colonel Ekberg couldn't stop me from going. He has his orders too. Besides he has already served his time in Vietnam."

"Why do you have to go?"

"I knew that when I was drafted and returned to the service that I possibly could get orders to go besides everyone in uniform has to follow their orders."

"But your heart, they can't send you if you have a bad heart, can they?"

"I don't think the people who write the orders check into every minor detail of the individual they send to Vietnam once they are in uniform."

The four gather together and talk about his orders and upon his leaving to Ft. Lewis before going off to fight in Vietnam. As the night grows shorter, Marilyn and Joanne head back to the bedroom and Howard and Sueanne talk about going to New Hampshire to visit his family. The two then go into the bedroom wrap one another's arms around each other and fall asleep.

Chapter 15

On December fifteenth, Howard signs out of Ft. Holliman to go on leave until he has to report to Ft. Lewis, Washington. After packing some clothes, the three leave to head north to New Hampshire.

Upon arriving, they stop off at his mother's to spend the night and introduce his mother to her grandson.

"What fine looking lad. He has your blue eyes and blonde hair. Can I hold him?"

"Sure!" replies Sueanne reluctantly handing Howard Jr. over to Miriam."

"Boy, are you heavy. How old are you?"

"He's just turned two on November 30th."

"He sure is going to be a big boy." responds Jeffrey looking at Jr. in Miriam's arms.

Handing Howard Jr., back to his mother, Miriam asks, "Anyone want coffee or anything?"

"Sure, we would love some," Answers Howard, looking over at Sueanne, heading over towards the table, as Jeffrey pulls out a chair for her.

"Thank you." states Sueanne, sitting down and placing Howard Jr. on her lap.

"Any news from the other boys?" asks Howard trying to make conversation as the teapot whistles and Miriam brings the pot to the table and begins filling the cups.

"Seth wrote us telling us he just arrived in Vietnam along with Billy Joy. You do remember him don't you?

"Yes? I remember him. He is Seth's best friend and the son of Sid and Barbara Anne."

"As for Edward Jr. he is finally out of the army and in Maine."

"We heard that he was living in Maine, in Clinton, we plan on stopping to visit him before heading back to Baltimore."

"How long you plan on staying?"

"Just overnight." responds Sueanne rocking Howard Jr. on her lap. "I think he's getting a little tired. Is there a room I can put him in? "

Rising up Miriam leads Sueanne down the hallway and into a second bedroom where Sueanne places Jr. onto the bed.

Later that day, the family eats supper; the girls have put a cold meat plate together and made a pot of vegetable soup. All during the meal, nothing is said about the last time they had gotten together.

The following day they take Miriam and head to visit her half-sister Mary and her husband Fred Bakersfield. Howard's half cousins: Tamara and Danielle Robinson were away, but in place of them were Howard's Aunt Sarah and Lloyd Carpenter, their children: Lloyd Jr., Steve, Katrina. Uncle Brian and Alice Brown and their children: Joanne and Philip. Aunt Gloria and Arnold Bakersfield with their children: John and Karen.

This is the first time the entire family has gotten together. The missing one is his uncle Andrew who is stationed in the Navy on the Pacific Coast . . . There is so much conversation going on that you could not distinguish one word from another even if it is directed to you. The women are rushing around in the preparation of the meal and setting the tables in separate rooms in order to accommodate everyone.

It is a fun family time and all Howard's cousins were taking turns in caring and playing with Little Jr.

After a day filled with laughter, joking, talking and getting everyone brought up with what was going on with their lives, the gathering breaks up and begins clearing off the tables.

The men washed and wiped the dishes before heading off back to their homes. When all had left, Howard and Sueanne sit down with his mother, uncle and aunt and relax with a cup of coffee.

After a good night sleep Howard takes Miriam, leaves his aunt and uncle's house to head up into Maine to visit with his brother Edward Jr. who had recently married a local girl and is residing in Clinton, Maine.

While in Maine, the family has a Christmas dinner before exchanging Christmas presents and enjoyed one another's company. Edward was doing very well for himself, he bought rundown homes and had them refurbished and resold them for twice what he put into them.

After spending the night there, they headed back to New Hampshire. The snow is falling and the winds were just howling, but Howard knew that he and the family had to leave or they would be set back in their itinerary. After being given a few blankets in case they were needed, they say their good-byes and head out to New Hampshire.

The traveling south has become very treacherous as the snow continues falling and the roads are very slippery. Howard could just barely see the road due to snow but continues at a slower pace.

At one time he had slid off the road and had gotten stuck. Trying to rock the car in order to get out was to no avail.

"Hon you get behind the wheel and I will go out and try pushing as you hit the gas."

Howard exits the car and trudges through the deep snow to the rear where he places his back toward the rear of the car and yells to Sueanne, "hit the gas!" as he pushes with all he has. But little did the car move from its stuck position.

After several pushes and gunning of the gas, the car begins to spin snow at Howard as Sueanne guns the gas pedal to the max, "Easy! Easy not too much gas you'll blow the motor."

Sueanne couldn't hear him for the roar of the engine, but as she steered the car, it begins to slip and slid out of the stuck snow and is now back on the road.

Howard returns back to the car, brushing Himself off. Just as he enters the car, it stalls out. Sueanne moves over so that Howard could once again take the wheel.

As Howard turns the ignition, the engine spits and sputters before coming alive. They then continue toward Kittery.

"I'm surprised we haven't seen one vehicle go by since we started on the trip? "States Marilyn, continuing to hold Jr. Snuggly in the warm blanket.

"Nobody is safe in this weather; we should have stayed an extra day." remarks Sueanne looking towards Howard.

'Any of you could have said that they wished to wait, but I didn't expect this much snow."

As they continue, Howard notices that the engine was reading hot, but he knew he could not stop or they would be stranded. The car begins to sputter and the women look at Howard who looks back at them.

"Will we make it home?" asks Sueanne.

"I hope so. But the car sounds as though it wants to conk out, the engine is running hot."

Upon entering Kittery, the car breaks down, so in the middle of the night with snow blowing and the wind howling, they sit along the side of the road trying to keep warm.

"What are going to do now?" asks Sueanne holding the bundled up Jr. Tightly against her bosom.

"We'll just have to wait until someone comes by and get help for us." Implies Howard, making sure his lights and hazard warning lights were on

"We haven't seen anyone since we left. What makes you so sure someone will be coming by in this weather?" barks Sueanne.

"We are closer to a town, I'm sure there must be emergency crews out cleaning the roads, police out looking for vehicles stuck in this weather."

They must have waited for about one-hour before Howard sees these red and blue lights coming up behind them over the horizon.

"I see rescue lights coming up over the hill behind us. We are going to get help." gleams Howard looking into his rear view mirror.

A police car stops and asks if he could offer assistance.

"The car broke down and we have no heat to keep our baby or ourselves warm."

The police officer offers to call a tow truck, and proceeds to invite the women and the baby into his cruiser to get warm, while Howard remains with the car.

Within about twenty minutes the tow truck arrives and with Howard in the cab of the truck, heads towards Kittery with the police car guiding them in front of the tow truck.

Arriving at the garage in Kittery, The cruiser unloads his guests and after he is thanked, the officer leaves knowing the garage would help them.

At the garage they discover that the coil has gone and the starter has gone bad, so it would have to remain overnight to be repaired. Leaving the car at the garage for repairs, the tow truck operator volunteers to drive them to a nearby restaurant where the family could be warm and call someone to fetch them. But who in their right mind would come all the way to Kittery, Maine to rescue them.

The tow truck driver brings them to a restaurant that was about to close. After explaining to the owner about what had taken place, the owner serves up hot drinks and sandwiches to the family.

"How we going to pay for this?" asks Sueanne

"Now you don't worry about anything just drink and eat and get warm. The tow truck operator, Jonesie paid for everything."

"Call Uncle Fred and explains the situation." Says Miriam, he'll come and get us."

As the storm intensifies, and nothing could reasonably be out in it, no one but, Uncle Fred is, and he arrives, where the owner offers him something warm.

"I didn't think even you would come out in this weather?" questions Howard sitting next to him, as everyone takes their turn going to the bathroom and freshen up Howard Jr.

After thanking the proprietor for staying open until help arrived, they all find room in the vehicle where they are all comfortable for the next fifty mile trip back to the Bakersfield's.

And with Uncle Fred cautiously handling the vehicle the family arrives safely home.

For the next fifteen days Howard and his family stay with his mother, Aunt Eunice and Uncle Fred Robinson along with visits from Tamara and Danielle as they once again gather for Christmas dinner at Uncle Fred's and Aunt Mary's.

Howard, Sueanne and Jr., Are all welcomed again as they settled in. The women go about preparing the Holiday meal and setting the table. The men gather in the living room to watch the football game. There was a lot of chatter throughout the house as the atmosphere became more festive. Tamara sets the table so that she and Danielle were able to sit next to Howard while his wife sits opposite to him.

As the men were into the game, Aunt Mary calls them into the dining area to take their places around the table.

Once seated, and Tamara smiling as she sits by his side, they all hold hands, while Uncle Fred begins to say grace. Tamara glances sideways while bowing his head. Her hands are locked securely onto his at the end of the prayer; Howard had to pry his hand from Tamara's squeeze.

She then places one hand down onto his thigh and rubs the inside of his leg. Without giving it away, he asks her to pass the bowl of mashed potatoes. Patting his inner thigh, she raising her hand and reaches for the bowl and passes it to him rubbing his digits as he accepts the bowl.

"So Howard where are you going in Vietnam?" asks Steve spooning out the squash.

"I believe it's going to be somewhere in the northern section maybe Quang Tri or someplace near there."

"Is Quang tri a hot spot?" asks Katrina looking puzzled.

"It's almost on the Southern border of North Vietnam, but you hear a lot of fighting in the far south, like around Saigon I'll probably be safe."

"Are you scared? I hear a lot about the war on television." asks Philip picking at his turkey.

"Yes I am a little scared, but I have to go, although I wish I could stay at Ft. Holliman, I really enjoy my duty there."

"Okay" states Uncle Fred, "change the subject, I'm sure Howard doesn't want to think of it while he is on leave."

The rest of the conversation is centered on the children as the mothers help feed them and wipe them up their drooling.

Tamara tries getting Howard's attention by looking sideways at him, but he looks at Sueanne and Jr., thinking to himself that maybe he should have chosen a different seat.

While they continue in their own conversations, Aunt Sarah gets up from the table and gathers the pie from the kitchen table while Aunt Gloria goes to the refrigerator for the ice cream.

Once the pie and ice cream is seen by John, Karen and the other children, they were quickly shushed by Aunt Mary before they got too loud.

The dinner went on with a lot of conversation, noise and family pleasure. This was the first time in a long time that Sueanne had actually been at a large family gathering.

After the dinner was finished, everyone picked up the table and once cleared, the women sat around the table enjoying coffee while the men did the dishes. Tamara thought she would try to get next to Howard as he dried the dishes so that she could put them away but was called back by Aunt Sarah to return to the table and leave the men alone.

Howard joins the family in the living room where he gets into a game of 'monopoly' with Tamara, Danielle, Lloyd Jr. and Philip, while the other younger children play 'chutes and ladders'.

Sueanne joins Miriam, Aunt Mary, Aunt Sarah, and Aunt Gloria as they talk of the holiday and getting to know one another as a family.

"So where is Andrew? "Asks Sueanne

"He's on the West Coast, in the navy. He is serving on, U.S.S. Enterprise."

"I hear it is the largest warship in the world, besides it is nuclear powered and can travel some 400,000 miles at the speed of 20 knots per hour." says Uncle Fred.

"Did you know that there are fifty-five hundred people on that ship?" includes Katrina as she looks up from her game."

"Those carriers are big," I remember when we were touring the Mediterranean, we would pull up alongside the Independence for refueling and mail, I was sure surprised at the height and length of the carrier."

"What type of ship were you on?" asks Karen looking up from the 'Chutes and Ladders' game.

"A Sumner class destroyer, whose main function is to protect the Aircraft Carriers from the enemy, My duties were to swab down the deck and when practicing firing from the gun mounts, I would have to catch the hot shell cases and throw them out of the mount or they would bounce around a hurt someone if not kill them."

The family had a good time conversing about what Howard did, how he and Sueanne got together, they had their turns holding and feeding Howard Jr. And before they realized, it was time to take Miriam back before Jeffrey thinks she abandoned him.

Howard was glad the family had accepted Sueanne, maybe now there will be peace in both families.

Tamara and Danielle tried standing close to Howard as he went about picking up the living room and packing Howard's clothing and accessories bag, while Aunt Mary placed the dirty diapers and clothes in a bag for the ride to the nearest laundry.

On December thirteenth, Howard and family give their hugs and kisses and enter the car to begin their journey back to Baltimore where they will stay for two days in order to unpack their luggage and refresh it with other clothes which they will take with them on their next leg of their vacation. Before heading out to Ohio, to visit with Sueanne's family for a second Christmas celebration, the two open their mail and pay what they could in their bills.

By the time they had left Baltimore and headed on their way to Ohio, they run into some pretty heavy snow on the Pennsylvania Turnpike. At times they would have to stop and wait for the snow to slow down.

"It doesn't seem to want to slow down, do you want to continue?" asks Howard looking at Sueanne holding onto Howard Jr.

"Do you think its safe enough?"

If I don't think it's safe, I will pull over and wait it out."

They head out into the raging snow squall and carefully make their way, as once again Sueanne finds herself holding tightly to Howard Jr snug in a blanket.

The Pennsylvania Turnpike was one of the worse Turnpikes Howard or Sueanne has ever been on. Not only is it a long boring un-scenery ride, but when it snows, all traffic comes to a slow crawl.

The drive seemed endless until they approach the midway restaurant where they stopped and went in and got refreshed and Sueanne refreshes Howard Jr. then sat at the table where they enjoyed a hot meal and warmed up before Howard heads out first in the snow and cold to get gas. After getting a fill up, he reenters and carries Howard Jr. out and after Sueanne was situated in her seat, Howard hands the precious bundle where he rests gently on her chest.

After a couple more hours of boring driving and conversation, the trip seems to be coming to an end as they pull into the unplowed driveway of Korina and Brian Westford.

No sooner have they stopped the vehicle and begin to exit, when Korina dashes out of the house and through the snow pass Howard with a "Hi Howard." to embrace Sueanne.

Oh I'm so glad you made it. I figured the snow storm would prevent you from coming out?"

"It was touch and go, but Howard Jr. and I are just fine."

Howard thought to himself as he is about to grab the luggage from the car. "What does she mean her and Jr. made it? I'm the one that drove, What about me? Am I invisible to her now that she is with her family?"

"Forget the luggage, just get what you need to freshen up, I'll have Brian help when he comes home from work."

"That's alright, you three go in, there isn't that much to bring in." To himself says sarcastically, 'Thanks for helping. Hope you three get along fine. Don't worry about me. I'm just freezing out here and I have to carry all this crap by myself, damn I'm not grooving.'

The three have already entered the warm house, sitting on the sofa and coocha—cooing with Jr.

By the time Howard had entered the mudroom where he drops the luggage and brushes off the snow before removing his coat and hanging it up.

Entering the house and going into the living room where Korina has a woodstove going giving off a lot of heat. Also on the sofa admiring little Jr. are John Andrew and his brother Brian Jr. Rising from their seat, they run over to have Uncle Howard pick them up and give each other a big hug.

"Get back on the sofa and let Aunt Sueanne and Howard Jr. Breath." states Korina pointing to the sofa.

Korina escorts Sueanne into one of the bedrooms in order to care for Howard Jr. This leaves Howard sitting at the table entertaining the two boys.

When the girls exited the room, they had left Howard Jr. in the room.

"Where's Little Jr?" asks John Andrew twisting around on the sofa.

"He's asleep. You're going to have to talk with your inside voice for now."

"Want some coffee?" asks Sueanne walking into the kitchen.

"Sounds good" states Howard.

As they drink their coffee and chat, it wasn't too long when Brian tries driving up his driveway but the vehicle begins to become stuck in the deep snow. Exiting the vehicle he enters the garage where he brings out a snow blower and begins working his way down to the vehicle from the garage entrance.

Seeing what was happening, Howard dons his jacket and boots, puts on his gloves goes outside to join him in the snow removal. The noise was deafening enough that there was not much conversation going on between them.

After the snow was removed and the vehicle was driven up the driveway next to Howard's, they stomp their way into the house shaking off the snow.

"SSHH, Howard Jr. is asleep in the bedroom." remarks Korina holding a finger to her lips.

The two remove their winter gear as Sueanne refreshes Howard's coffee and pours one for Brian "I've got to go wash up first. Hello Sueanne, hello Howard." As he walks toward the bathroom Korina follows him.

After Brian had finished cleaning up and had joined everyone at the table, the foursomes talk of the trip out to Ohio.

"It was touch and go there for awhile." states Howard "it snowed the whole time we were on the Pennsylvania Turnpike."

"That pike could be very dangerous most of it is without guardrails." points out Korina.

For supper, Korina had made a nice ham with scalloped potatoes, a salad, and for desert finished it off with vanilla ice cream topped off with strawberry.

"Sure is a fine supper you make." States Howard cleaning up his plate and starting on his desert.

"I agree." Informs Sueanne as she as well is into her meal.

The evening goes on chatting about Baltimore and Sueanne's parents, as they continue sitting at the table finishing up with their coffee.

After their coffee and picking up the table, Korina states that she would do the dishes later. For now they retire to the living room where the two boys were playing with their model cars and trucks on the floor.

"Okay boys, it's time for your baths and bedtime."

"AWWWW mom, can't we stay up a little longer?"

"No! Now just march in there and get undressed, I'll be right in there to run your tub."

"I'll give you a hand." remarks Sueanne rising up from the sofa.

By nine pm, the boys had been placed into bed and Little Jr taken off the bed, still asleep is placed in a crib that Brian had reinstalled from storage. "I just knew this would come in handy someday." laughed Brian.

"Don't look at Me." replies Korina "we're not having anymore."

The three of them go back into the kitchen to do the dishes while Brian goes into the bathroom and takes a shower.

When the dishes were done, and before Korina goes and takes her shower, she checks on the boys. Korina says night to them and joins Brian in their bedroom.

Howard and Sueanne take their shower together in order to save some time, being very quiet since the bathroom was next to Korina and Brian's bedroom.

Howard and Sueanne enter the room with the crib and check on Jr. before crawling into their bed.

Lying there, Howard tries to get Sueanne to make love, but she tells him, "Not here, they will hear us."

"Just play with me and I'll play with you.' snickers Howard who hand was removed from her breast.

"No. that's my sister in there she will hear us and embarrass me."

Disgruntled Howard kisses her and rolls over so that his back towards her. At that moment, and to Howard's surprise, Sueanne reaches over him and wraps her arms around him saying softly in his ear. "Just be quiet and make no noise." states Sueanne holding him firmly in her grasp.

While in Ohio, Howard Jr. is rushed to Defiance Hospital to have an operation performed on a herniated bowel. Howard and Sueanne spend the time with him before and after the surgery.

"Will he be ok?" asks Sueanne to the doctor when he arrives in Jr's room.

"I saw no problem in the surgery. I'm sure after a couple of days rest, he will be up and running in no time."

Within two days he is discharged. The fact that being so young, he is quick to recover from the surgery and is back to being himself once again in throwing himself around the floor and being the normal little boy that he is. Unlike the hospitals in Baltimore, Howard and Sueanne notice how smoothly this hospital is run. Plus, the doctors kept you informed on everything they did.

Howard plays with Jr. and the two other boys, watching just how jr. reacts to the surgery. When he is satisfied that Jr. was going to play as usual, he has John Andrew and Brian Jr. continue playing with Jr. but keep an eye on him making sure that the two don't tire him out.

Korina and Sueanne spend the last day before heading back washing the dirty clothes and drying them before packing them away. At the same time Howard and Brian continue with his gun collection and going over his gun magazines. Howard not really interested in Brian's collection, acted interested for if it was on the other foot, Howard would have his space collection out showing Brian the entire collection he had.

An unexpected snowstorm postpones their trip back to Baltimore for another day, thus giving Little Jr. an extra day or so to heal.

The day gives the women folk spend some extra time together, while Brian takes Howard are outside in a blinding cold snowstorm for Brian to show Howard one of his hobbies: how to trap muskrats.

Not since the Blizzard of 1958 when a cold front came down from Canada and dumped snow from Maine to West Virginia and south to Connecticut closing all schools, transportation and major airports throughout, has Howard seen such snow.

At that time, he and his three brothers were living with the Caruso's in Waterford, N.H. The snow had begun falling before they had been able to complete their chores, but the boys had decided to remain outdoors to build snow forts and entertain themselves with a snowball fight becoming oblivious to the accumulation of the snow gathering about them.

After awhile, bored with throwing snowballs, Tom mentions about going down to the tree swing and jump into the snow from the rope swing.

The three were having quite a time swinging from the tree, letting go of the rope and dropping some 15-feet into the snow.

Soon the cold winds began to become more brisk blowing the snow so hard that the brothers were having trouble seeing anything below the swing. As the temperatures began to plummet, Seth, who is the first to feel the cold cries out, "I'm cold I want to go home." Looking around, Tom now notices just how bad it has gotten. "Okay, let's get going. Howard you take Seth's hand and I'll take Jr's."

As the four trudged their way through the deep snow, the cold wind blew into their faces. This caused the snow on their eyebrows and lashes to turn to ice. Seeing where they were going was next to impossible.

"I'm c-c-cold" stutters Seth trying to keep pace with Howard who was trying to keep up with Tom.

"We are all cold, but we'll be home soon." replies Tom, looking back at Howard and Seth, "try to stay close to me for I'll be picking up the pace."

"Seth can barely walk now. I'm going to try carrying him some so slow down." yells Howard getting perturbed at Tom who was carrying Jr.

"We're lost aint we?" states Seth looking into Howards ice covered face.

"We'll be alright, don't worry none." replies Howard watching Tom looking hard for any signs that they were still on trail going home.

As Howard puts Seth down, he notices that the snow was up to his waist. Howard continues picking Seth up and putting him down in order to continue himself. Tom had now begun to think that he had gone past the past and that they were entering the deep woods. He tries not to let his brothers know what he was thinking, but suddenly Seth begins crying and shaking so bad Howard couldn't hold him. This causes Jr. to cry, and the boys begin yelling at the top of their lungs in hope to be heard by someone.

"Hush" states Tom using his arm to stop them from yelling, for in the distance they hear Alberto yelling out their names.

"Here, we're over here," yells Tom waving both his arms.

Like a ghost appearing out of the blinding snowstorm, Alberto comes to the rescue. Lifting Seth, Alberto states, "Follow me boys I'll take you home." Looking at Tom Alberto says. "I've always wanted to say that."

Leading the frozen four back home, he helps to gather blankets and wrap the boys into as they are led upstairs and washed up before being placed into their pajamas

"You boys have had quite a day, now let's go downstairs to get something to eat and relax the rest of the afternoon." says Anne softly.

Before the day had closed, the snow accumulated to two-feet and ice cycles hung everywhere. The snow had covered the entire outside of all the windows. It looked like a winter wonderland. Looking out the living room window, the children shivered to think that such a pretty picture is so dangerous that neither man nor beast could be out in it.

Chapter 16

THE FOLLOWING DAY SAW A much clearer but colder day for Howards' return trip to Baltimore for his last couple days before he has to report to his next duty station at ft. Lewis, Washington and his preparation for overseas duty.

On Howards' last day, he and his family were asked to dinner by Regina and husband Alexandros Stephanotis. Arriving, Howard and family stepped up their beautiful white marble steps, the trademark of the row houses which compliment most of Baltimore. Upon looking around their home, they sit down around the table; while Regina brings over the dishes she has prepared and places them onto the table.

There were Shish-ka-bobs, French Fries, Corn and Salad. For desert Regina had made a Chocolate cake that was just too luscious.

After they had consumed their dinner, Regina and Alexandros drive Howard, Sueanne and Howard jr. to the Baltimore-Washington Airport to board his flight to Seattle, Washington. Before heading down the ramp, Howard kisses Sueanne, shakes Regina's and Alexandros hand, then plants a big kiss onto Howard Jr. saying, "You be a good boy and help your mother. I love you both."

Turning down the ramp he is out of sight. The family and friends stand by the window watching the plane leave its gate and heads over to its runway where it sits until ready for takeoff. As soon as the plane begins to head down the runway, Sueanne lets out a little cry as a tear runs down her cheek, while softly to herself, she says, 'Damn you, why did you leave me like this? What am I going to do now?'

Just as Sueanne was feeling sorry for herself, she recalls the Regina had asked her if she wanted to work with her. This allows her mother to watch Howard Jr. while she goes to work.

Before she takes the job, Sueanne heads down to the business. Getting off the bus, she enters the door where she finds Regina behind a desk doing some paperwork. "Hello Regina."

Looking up from her desk, Regina stands and holds out her hand and shakes it. "Well Sueanne, sure glad to see you. How is everything?"

"Fine, I'm fine. Waiting for word from Howard, nothing yet."

"It'll be awhile just waiting until he gets situated, you'll hear from him. Just you wait and see."

"Is the job still available?"

"It sure is when can you start?"

"I'm ready anytime. My mother can watch Howard Jr."

"Great, here let me show you what I need you to do."

"How much does the job pay?"

"At this time, business is slow and I can't pay you an hourly wage, but whenever you need money I can give you some."

"What does that mean?'

"At this moment I'm scheduling a charter to Greece We'll see about a weekly pay after the return."

Confused about when she will get paid, Sueanne agrees to go to work for her although there was to be no hourly pay, and that Regina would give her money whenever Sueanne needed it, plus she would have to wait when Regina or Stephanotis returns from a chartered flight to Greece, and then Sueanne would get two dollars an hour.

One day as Sueanne arrives at the office, she found Regina asking her to help with moving her things out of the office and move them to her house.

"But why, what is going on?"

"I need to begin another business. I believe my partner is stealing from the business."

"Can't you go to the police and tell them?"

"I can't prove it, but I know he is"

While Regina had left on a Chartered flight, her partners' mother came into the office to sit next to the partner.

Sueanne had no idea what was going on. She watched as the two go over the books, as she fig idly begin to make calls and set up a list of the next members going on the tour marking in columns of those who have paid and those who have not paid.

Sueanne calls the ones who have not yet paid to ask when they could send the money before they can get on the list to tallying up the money that should already be in, she finds that there is money missing and her eyes go directly to the partner and his mother.

She finds herself face them, she is eyeball to eyeball with the partner and his mother. Frightened, Sueanne wonders to herself, Should I run out the door or call the police. Either way she feels alone. What I should do, she wonders.

Feeling scared she begins to think of all ways in what they might do to her. Regina was right she thought. Her partner brought his mother in to cook the books and this is the reason that she has found the missing money.

At this moment, Sueanne realizes that the Chartered Flight to Greece is to be a one way trip.

Sueanne begins to sweat thinking that she has gotten between getting a job and probably getting arrested for stealing funds from the chartered members.

Approaching her were both partner and mother holding the books in her hands. In his hands were several checks, he waves them in front of her saying, "Where did you get these checks?"

Looking them over as she shook, replied, "They were given to me as payment in salary." "Did she hire you to work for her?" he asked sitting down in a chair next to her desk. "Y-Yes, she hired me to help her while she left to go on the chartered flights."

Looking at her, and shaking his head, states, "Who do you think owns this business?"

Sueanne now doesn't know what to say, but, "She told me that she owns the business with her husband Alexandros."

"It all figures now" states Apolodoris leaning back into his chair as he throws the checks onto Sueanne's desk.

"This is mine and my mother's business, and Regina is our employee my name is: Apolodoris Kotsiopoulos and this is my mother Marina, we have owned **'Grecian *Travels*'** for three years, and we just hired her this past year when we were really booming.

"b-but she told me that you were trying to take over the business, and that is why you had your mother in to cook the books." replies Sueanne with a surprising look on her face.

"I hired my mother because of her experience in bookkeeping and it was her that found that there was missing money being taken from the business."

"I thought that she was hired to keep an eye on what Regina was doing and that she was to report to you."

"Wrong again, I hired her after I discovered that you and her were stealing business equipment from the office." replies Apolodoris folding his arms behind his head.

"Stealing!" quotes Sueanne just about rising out of her seat, "Regina asked me to help move some of the office equipment to her house so she and Stephanotis could start another business and she didn't want you in on it."

Sitting back up and looking at the schedule on Sueanne's desk, Apolodoris asks, "When does the charter return from Greece/ How many on the charter?"

Looking down on the manifest Sueanne runs her fingers across a line saying, "In about three days, with one hundred twenty-two passengers, twenty-one of which are children."

"Good," implies Apolodoris, "This will give us a few days to set up a trap upon their return, put me through to the police, and I'll be over at my desk.

Sueanne sits nervously as she overhears the conversation about stealing and forgery and arrests between Apolodoris, Marina and the police, saying to herself, 'Oh Regina, what have you gotten me into. Where are you to get me out of this mess? I don't want to go to jail for something that is your fault. Some friend you turned out to be.'

After hanging up the phone, the two arrive at Sueanne's desk and asks her for her home address and phone number, then proceed to ask her to stay on until this situation is tended to. They then hand her a check and thank her for her help.

That evening as she arrives home, she tells her mother all about what had happened: the stealing, the forgery, the arrests that are about to take place in a couple of days and that she was asked to remain on the job till all is worked out, then she showed them the check for one-hundred dollars that she was given. "Let's go grocery shopping for tomorrow I'll be back to work."

On the third day, Sueanne had joined Apolodoris and his mother along with two detectives at the Baltimore-Washington Airport as the charter flight from Greece arrives. Disembarking, was no Regina, but only Alexandros and twenty-one children. When they all had entered the terminal, the two detectives approach Alexandros, asked him some questions and turned him around to hand cuff him with arms in the rear and lead him off, while the children were taken care of by the Health and Human Services.

While in custody, questions were asked of the whereabouts of Regina, and were told that Regina had no intentions of returning and that he and their son had been sent home without the adults telling them that they would catch the next charter home, but of course there was no money left to bring them back. Alexandros had come home in order to send their belongings as well as equipment stolen to be placed on a charter to Greece where they would set up a different travel agency in Piraeus.

While all this was going on at home, Howard had left the United States and had arrived at Cam Rahn Bay, South Vietnam, a protective seaward peninsula and natural inner and outer harbors form what is the best and most beautiful deep water port that he has ever seen and he has seen many a port as he traversed the world while in the navy.

Howard is aghast as such a beautiful place is turned into a major supply entrance point due to its off-loading docks for the large collection of large cargo ships as well as the warehouses to place all the supplies. Here a number of transportation units are based.

The extreme heat hits him as he realizes now that he is here in 'Kill land' Vietnam, looking around him; he mutters 'I just know I'm not leaving here.

I wished I had not joined the army a second time. Never thought I would be ordered here. God please protect me so I can go back home?'

Howard felt Billy Joy's ghost near him just knowing that Billy had gone through here on his way to Quang Tri where he met his maker. Now he was in the same predicament as he waited where they would be given him his orders for where he would be going. Some will go to the northern section while others will remain here in the Saigon area.

Howard knew that his brother Tom and his wife had served here in the Saigon area back in the early Sixties and both of them worked in the hospital where they saw a lot of death and saved a lot of soldiers and navy personnel as well as air personnel from never seeing their homes again. One such soldier was Ted Sanderson who he and Sueanne along with Ted's wife, Nancy had gone on a picnic to Sherwood Gardens. Ted had lost one eye, one arm and had shrapnel throughout his chest. Tom and Charlene almost spent ten hours mending him back so he could be returned to the states and back to his family.

While Howard was waiting for orders to his destination, back in Baltimore Regina's youngest son basil has been hospitalized after going into an epileptic seizure. As the doctors were working on Basil, Alexandros is given permission to call Regina in Greece to inform her that she was needed to be with her son. "Basil really needs you; he calls for you all day and all night. You must come home."

"Is it safe? Are you getting the stuff ready to be shipped?"

"Yes Hon and most of the packing is done."

"Has anyone contacted you about why the children were the only ones arriving?"

"I told them exactly what you told me to say."

"Good. Which hospital is he in?"

"He's in County Hospital."

"I'll try getting the next flight out. Don't tell basil I'm coming, someone may overhear you. *Kata^abaivw (Kah-tah-la-ven-oh)*?"

"*Kata^abaivw*, meaning in English, I understand."

After hanging up the phone, the detectives escort him back to Basil's room.

"Where's mama?'

"I couldn't reach her, but I will call her again. Now hush, *uttvoc (EEP-nohs)*, in English meaning, sleep."

The police hold Alexandros in custody until Regina arrives to figure out the situation, and how to return the tourists stranded in Greece back to the States to their children and homes.

For several days the Detectives, police Mr. and Mrs. Kotsiopoulos meet the arriving planes, but no Regina. Fearing a set up, she again calls Alexandros to make sure it was safe to come in."Where are you?" asks Alexandros.

"I'm in New Jersey; see any detectives or police around waiting for planes to come in."

Looking over at the Detective, Alexandros replies, "I see no cops waiting for you. You are safe, Hurry Basil calls for you."

"I'll catch next flight out of New Jersey. See you in a couple of hours."

The phone goes dead and he informs the Detectives that she is in New Jersey, wanting to know if all is safe for her arrival. "She'll be here in a couple of hours." The Detectives head to control to find out what flight and time the next plane in from New Jersey. They then wait in the terminal and keep an eye on the ramp as each flight empties its passengers.

While the lookout for Regina is going on, back in "Kill land", Vietnam, Howard is a mission through the bush, on their way to find the Vietcong who have massed for an attack on an American base that has been almost overrun on their last attack. While Howard slowly and cautiously plods along. Every now and then his mind races into the past to when he had run away from one of his foster homes and heads towards Capital City in search of his father.

Many times he had asked his foster mother or father to take him to visit his real father, only to be refused. So Howard decided one nice summer day to take it on his own to walk the 18 miles to visit with him. In doing so he would begin walking the road and occasionally finding himself on the railroad tracks which he cautiously walked.

The sun was beginning to get high in the sky when he realized that he was getting thirsty. Leaving the railroad tracks he continues through the trees until he comes to the road he had first began to walk on. Seeing a house up on a slight hill to the right of him, he approaches the house, knocks on the door where he is met by an elderly lady who asks, "Yes young man how I can help you?"

"I'm thirsty; can I have a drink of water please?"

"Come on in the house. You look as if you have been in the sun too long? Where are you coming from and where are you heading?

"I'm heading to Capital City to see my dad?"

"Are you alone?"

"Yes Maam," Taking the glass of water and taking a big gulp of it.

"Boy you have a long way to go, you want to freshen yourself up here before continuing?"

"I do have to go to the bathroom and wash up the sweat off me."

"Let me show you where the bathroom is. I'll get a face cloth and towel for you."

As Howard drops his pants and places himself on the toilet, the elderly lady approaches him and asks if he would need help.

"I think I'll be alright. But your toilet is sure high up off the floor."

"I have a disabled daughter and she needs a high toilet for she has trouble raising herself up off of it."

"If you are done, let me help you clean up."

"I'm done, thank you."

The elderly lady who says her name, "I'm Mrs. Cummings, My husband died just last year. I have three daughters and a son. One of my daughters still lives with me for she has Muscular Dystrophy and needs my help. My other children come every day when they can and help with the chores."

Wiping Howard up, and pulling his pants up, she goes to the sink where she wets a facecloth, hands it to Howard, who cleans his face of the sweat, Mrs. Cummings wipes his face and arms dry before watching him leave the house with a sandwich and some water. Thanking her as he waves to her, he turns and continues his journey to find his father.

The day's sun was just beginning to sink over the horizon when he enters Capital City. Knowing where he lived, Howard enters Carlene's Café and climbs the steps up to his fathers' room, knocking, he receives no answer.

Before Howard could finish his journey to find his father—he is suddenly brought back to his journey through the bush as it has turned into a firefight with the VC. From out of nowhere there are bullets and hand grenade blasts tearing up the bush and felling some of the troops in his group. Howard quickly readies his weapon and fires into the bush hoping to get one. The VC were invisible, "How could they hit us, and we couldn't even see them? What kind of war is this? Where are they? What do they look like? Did I hit one? I'm going to die, I just know it" thought Howard as he unloaded his carbine into the bush. Before he could reload, the firing had stopped, as the group found out, they had lost three members and four had been wounded. Looking around, they found at least ten dead VC but no trail of theirs in or out of the bush, so it must have come from underground.

Despite the intelligence gathered that Captain Skinner received prior to their journey to an American firebase where they were to aid in the defense against the VC and North Vietnamese which has been harassing them as they gathered to make a final push for the strategic area could very well decide the future of ridding the country of the Americans.

Once in the city, Howard notices how serine the soldiers looked. They were lying around in any area that would give them shelter from snipers. The city was partially devastated and had been heavily shelled. The civilian population had disappeared into the surrounding area.

Captain Skinner, who had led the group of two hundred through the bush to help save the one hundred fifty left from the twelve hundred that had been fighting back the insurgence for the past thirty six days.

Reporting to Lt. Colonel Johnson who shows the tiredness in his eyes and weary face that is hidden by his scraggly beard and could barely rise from his bed where he has been resting since the last attack some two hours ago.

"We need as many men as we can get, my men are tired they have been fighting for the past thirty-eight days straight and each attack the VC seem to get stronger and stronger. The more we kill the more they increase in size. There is no way we can defend this city on what we have."

"My men are fresher than yours, where would you like my men to defend?"

"The weakest place at this time is the eastern part of the city. The insurgence have been coming in there and just raising hell, and I have no one to free up to help hold that section."

I'll immediately take me men to reinforce them on the east side of the city sir."

Outside the headquarters, the men have found a place to sit and rest until their leader receives his orders.

Coming out of the building, Captain Skinner has his men to fall into ranks and tells them that they will be reinforcing the men on the east side and to mingle with the others that are trying to hold onto a miserable city that the enemy wants real bad.

The VC and North Vietnamese armies have amassed and swept down from the demilitarized Zone (DMZ) and have swarmed every city and hamlet all the way down to Saigon. The whole time the South Vietnamese have turned and run from the swarm that would be as an army of ants invading another's sand hill.

Upon hearing the news that there new friends were telling them, he tried phasing out what they were saying by thinking of his wife and son, hoping the army would take care of them if something would happen to him.

His fear of dying is very much on his mind as he begins remembering his youth, his half-cousins, the Orphans Home which now doesn't seem so bad. He thinks of the different foster homes, the happy ones as well as the sad ones. He recalls of his running away from the Orphans Home in search of his mother and father only to find the ones who really loved him and gave him and his brothers a home, of when he had run away from one of his foster homes in search of his father in Capital City, not finding him in his room, he had gone walking up along main street looking in all the stores in hopes of finding him. It had gotten dark by the time he had spotted his father behind a counter making frappes and serving tonic to the customers. Walking in, he finds an empty stool and waits to surprise his father.

As soon as Edward Sr. spots him, his face drops as he asks, "Howard! What are you doing here/ did your foster parents drive you here? Are you shopping here in Capital City?"

"Dad!" replies Howard as his father was asking just too many questions at one, "I ran away from them to visit and ask if I can live with you. I don't want to live there anymore. I want to be with you and mom."

Stunned, Edward finds himself short on words. Coming around to the front of the counter he excuses himself from the customers saying,"This is my son Howard; I need to talk to him." Taking hold of Howard's hand, he leads him to a quiet area of the shop where he tells him, "Howard, there is so much that I could tell you but you wouldn't understand what I'm saying."

"Dad, I'm a big boy. Where is mom?"

"Let's talk after I get out of work, here are my keys, go wash up and get into bed. I'll see you when I get off work."

Not wanting to leave him after his long exhausted eight-hour journey, Howard hesitantly takes the key. As he turns to leave, everyone was looking at a sweaty, dirty looking boy who had gotten sunburned."What are you all looking at? I'm no tar baby." Referring to when everyone was staring at him back in Penville when he had dumped the bucket of tar over his head. Continuing to the door, his father exclaims, "Howard, I love you."

The words hit Howard hard as he leaves the store and looking back to find his father talking to this older gentleman who was pointing toward the inside of the store, as he returns to the back of the counter and continues to do his job.

At the boarding house, Howard climbs the stairs to his father's room, unlocks the door and enters it.

The room consists of iron wrought double bed, a bureau containing four drawers, his father's white shirt and tan pants hanging on a hanger on the back of the door. The room looks very plain and empty with but pictures of the family on top of the bureau. With a closer look, Howard notices that the pictures have been worn down by the many times his dad had kissed them.

With the washroom down the hall and shared with other tenants, Howard proceeds down, and stops at a closet where he retrieves a wash cloth and towel. Not finding any soap, Howard is a little disgruntled as he says to himself 'guess you have to buy your own soap. That is really stupid to have to, when you pay rent.' Entering the washroom not finding anyone there, Howard approaches one of the wash basins and begins to wet his face cloth when he notices two basins down there was a small piece of soap. Going down, he takes the soap, rubs some on his face cloth and scrubs his face clean. He then proceeds to remove his shirt and washes under his arms and chest. Rubbing more soap onto the wash cloth he wets it and washes his hair. As he was drying his hair and body, a man comes in and upon seeing Howard, asks, "What are you doing in here? Don't you have a home?"Nervously and surprised Howard says, "Yes sir I have a home, but I'm here to stay with my dad."

"What's your name kid?"

"H-Howard Walker, sir."

"Are you Eddie's boy?"

"Yes sir. I'm going to live with him."

"Did you run away?"

"Yes sir."

"They won't let children live here. I know I have children too."

"But, he's my dad."

"Makes no difference, they won't let you stay.

"Well sir, excuse me I have to be in bed when my dad comes."

"Good night boy. Good luck."

"Good night sir."

Howard runs his fingers through his hair as he returns back to the room where finding no TV or radio, removes his pants and draws back the blanket and sheet and crawls into the bed to await his father.

Howard must have drifted off to sleep when he was suddenly awakened to knocking on the door. Thinking that his father was knocking to get in because he had the key, Howard jumps out of bed runs to the door saying, "Coming dad."

Opening the door, Howard is surprised to come face to face with three police officers and a woman.

One of the officers approach him as Howard backs off, "Howard Walker, you are a runaway and you are coming with us to the station to await your foster parents who are on their way to pick you up."

"No, I'm not going with you, I don't know you. My dad will be here after he finishes his work, he told me he would."

One of the officers hold Howard down as the social worker works hard trying to get him dressed. "Hold his legs; I can't get his pants on while his legs and arms are thrashing about."

Howard screams and thrashers, "Leave me alone, I'm not going anywhere with you. I want my daddy." Crying, he yells out, Daddy help me where are you? Help me please."

When the social worker finally is able to get Howard dressed, they proceed to carry him out into the hallway which is filled with spectators wondering what all the commotion was about. All the way down the stairs and out into the street Howard continues his screaming for his father and thrashing while trying to kick or hit anyone in close range.

"Where is my Daddy? I want to see him. Daddy, Daddy where are you? Help me."

Once in the vehicle, the police take him, kicking the back of the seat and screaming loudly to the station. Howard wasn't making it very easy for them to remove him from the vehicle once he was in it. Grabbing whatever he could to hold onto, he continues to kick the officers who tried getting him out. The social worker grabs Howard by the neck pulling him down onto the seat. The officers grab his legs and pull him out while the social worker holds his hands over his head. Once out of the vehicle another officer takes hold of Howard's arms and together carries him into the station and into a room where Howard is told to sit.

Once Howard knows that he could not get away, he stops his yelling and quietly sits refusing to answer any questions that are asked of him.

"Where is my daddy?" he asks.

"Your foster parents are on the way here to retrieve you and take you back home."

"That is not my home. I can't even call them my family without getting beaten up by their sons."

"Are they both mean parents to you? Do they hit you? Have they . . . touched you in any way?"

Looking at the social worker, Howard drops his eyes and again becomes silent. The questioning has stopped and they wait for the foster parents to arrive.

About an hour and a half later, the foster parents arrive, and after talking with the officers sign a paper and enter the room where Howard is turned over to them walking out to the street he looks up the main street and sees his father standing outside the Soda Shop watching from a distance of what was going on, his eyes become glassy from the tears that have swelled his eyes, just knowing that he had to call the authorities or he could go to jail for harboring a runaway even if it was his son.

Howard, not understanding what his father had done, becomes very angry with him and seeing his father not helping him to himself says, "you bastard you're no longer my daddy, I'm never coming to see you again, only when you are dead"

And as it was Howard saw very little of his father until he, his brothers and sister went to his funeral in March of nineteen-sixty-nine.

Again Howard is brought back to reality by sounds of yelling and rifle fire going on about his post. The VC is pounding the East section with heavy artillery as they get closer and closer to the city. Looking towards the tree line he spots the enemy running towards him. Raising his weapon, he takes aim and upon firing he sees his first kill fall to the ground. Looking to his left, he sees his comrades' fall as there is a sniper somewhere in the trees that have a bead on the inside of the city.

Howard raises his rifle to the tree line and scans the area until he notices movement each time his rifle fires off a round. Taking careful aim, placing his sight in the middle of the movement, he fires off a round, missing his mark, the next one he fires hits something and more movement is made until a body falls to the ground, his second kill. Howard then returns to the attackers and joins his teammates in cutting down the enemy. For half an hour the enemy attack but each time is driven off. The enemy was just testing the American's defenses as still they mass in large groups to wait the final attack.

Going over the number dead, the Americans estimate they have another twenty-three dead and ten wounded.

"We can't defend this city with what men we have. The enemy is still getting larger while we lose more men at each attack." states Lt. Colonel Johnson. "We have no communications with the outside. We need to get the gunships in here before the city falls."

"Sir, our patrol made it through, I'm sure if we send someone out they could bring back help." says Captain Skinner.

"The city is now completely encircled I can't send someone out there to be butchered."

"Sir, I could make it through." speaks up SSgt. Andrew Pineo, who happens to be part Chickasaw Indian and have made many trips behind the enemy.

"That's a big chance, we are surrounded and if they catch you there will be no one to help you." informs Lt. Colonel Johnson.

"If I slip out of the city now while it's all quiet, I could have those gunships here by tomorrow evening."

"Okay Sergeant, go prepare for whatever you need. There won't be anything left here but the enemy if you don't make it."

Saluting, the SSgt replies, "I'll make it sir. See you in two days."

As the SSgt leaves to prepare for another trip behind the enemy lines, he is told by the others that it was to be a fruitless trip and that he was going to get himself killed.

"I'm good hunter, back home I follow trail whole week. I make it back."

"Good luck Andy, We'll try to keep the light on for you."

Quietly SSGT Pineo slips out of the city and slowly is hidden in the western part of the city by the rice paddies. He is now out of sight by those watching within the city.

Chapter 17

Meanwhile back in Baltimore, the police and the detectives are watching as the passengers disembark from a flight that has arrived from New Jersey.

As one of the passengers climb down the steps from the aircraft trying to hide under a big straw hat, "There she is," responds Alexandros pointing so the detectives were able to meet her. Approaching the woman, the first detective approaches her and says, "Mrs. Regina Stephanotis, You are under arrest."

Before the woman could respond, she is held in order to be handcuffed by the police officer. Fighting the detective, Regina screams out, "I want to see my son Basil. He is in the hospital asking for me."

"First you will have to come with us."

"No, I need to see my son." thrashing her body all about that the detectives almost lose their grip on her.

With a tighter grip on Regina, she is taken to an awaiting vehicle where she is placed into and taken back to Baltimore and to the station where she is joined with Alexandros, Apolodoris and Marina Kotsiopoulos. The four are taken to a room with a lawyer and they go over what has to be misappropriations from the 'Grecian Travel' tour agency owned and operated by the Kotsiopoulos family who had hired Regina stephanotis as an assistant in getting the flights filled with tourists to be chartered to Greece and returned back later along with the same charter.

On this last flight, Regina had hired her friend Sueanne Walker to watch who she tells Sueanne were her help and that while Regina was gone on charter flights, the Kotsiopoulos family were cooking the books and stealing money from the business.

"How do you plead?" asked the detective.

"You don't have to answer that." replies the detective.

"Now I want to go see my son." replies Regina.

"Not until we get some answers."

"My client doesn't have to answer any of your questions."

"Just one more question?"

"Just how were you planning to get the rest of the tourist back home from their chartered flight?" asks Apolodoris. Looking at the lawyer, she asks, "Do I have to answer that?"

"You don't have to, but don't plagiarize yourself."

Regina looks over to Alexandros for help, but Alexandros drops his head, feeling guilty that it was he that got Regina in this mess by bringing her back.

Regina the turns to Marina and Apolodoris and states," I wasn't going to send them back, they are Greeks, and they belong in Greece. It is your business, you bring them back."

"Then why did you send back only the children?"

"Don't have to answer that." said the lawyer yanking at her arm.

Holding back, Regina says, "I had to make it look as though there were no room to send the adults back. Now take me to see my son."

"Okay, but we'll have to return you back hare after you get to see your son, implies one of the detectives, "For you are still under arrest." Climbing into two vehicles, they head up to the hospital where Regina and Alexandros were shown to the room while the detectives and police stay outside the room so as not to be seen by Basil.

Enter Basil's room, Regina and Alexandros go to opposite sides of the bed. Regina looked at Alexandros with a look that could kill she was very mad that he had trapped her into getting arrested.

Her anger turns to smile as she faces Basil and bends over his bed to give him a hug and kiss. "How is mommy's boy?"

"Where were you when I called for you?"

"Mommy was busy getting our new house ready to move into. I thought you and daddy were coming back, I would have never left you alone." Regina begins to cry on Basil's chest as he puts his arms around her.

"I'm ok mommy, I'll be fine."

When Alexandros reaches to touch Basil, Regina pushes his hand away with her elbow as she hugs Basil tighter. The two continue their talking as Regina tries to stop Alexandros from touching or talking to Basil.

The two stay for about an hour before a nurse comes into the room and informs them that Basil needs to get his rest. "Okay" replies Regina kissing Basil. Mommy will be back. I love you."

As the two prepare to leave the room, Alexandros reaches over to Basil gives his a big hug and kiss, "Love you. I'll see you later."

"Where are you going mommy, daddy?"

"I'm not going far. I have to go to work. I'll see you. I love you."

"Bye mommy, bye daddy hurry back. Love you."

Once outside the room, the detectives place the cuffs back on both of them and escort them out of the hospital and into the vehicles where they return to the police station.

Meanwhile, while Regina and Alexandros Stephanotis is being arrested for embezzlement of the funds from Grecian Travels.

Meanwhile Howard is in Vietnam fighting for his life as "Charlie", term used for the Viet Cong and North Vietnamese Army has attacked the city which he and six hundred American and South Vietnamese have been holding.

"Everyone to their stations," Commands Captain Skinner as bullets whiz past his head and explosion are seen throughout the city. Bodies are hurled through the air as direct explosions drop right on top of them. There are screams and yelling as the wounded cry out for help. Soldiers are scurrying around trying to get out of the open in order to seek some sort of protection. Howard is at his post and firing into the swarm of the enemy that has come out from their protected tree line to attack at every point of the embattled city.

Throughout the day, the fight goes on as the enemy is just mowed down before they could get too close to the city. As Twilight begins, the fighting dies down and the enemy retreats back to the tree line while the inhabitants of the besieged city go about picking up their dead and wounded.

As Howard helps carry the dead, he finds what is left of the remains of Captain Skinner had been a direct target of the enemies mortar. Howard begins feeling sick to his stomach and races away to empty sickness into a corner of the wall, With the feeling of weakness inside him and the tears flowing down his cheeks.

He turns catches his breath, wipes his eyes and returns to helping to carry the wounded inside a large room that had been used as a mess hall.

The tables and chairs have been removed in order to place them with the wounded, some crying out for help others crying for their mother's. It is a horrible scene. Looking around Howard sees his comrades, some with missing arms, missing legs, blood seeping everywhere the scene is one of hysteria.

Later that night, Howard tries writing a letter to Sueanne, knowing that he may never see her again.

Dear Sueanne;

Sorry for not writing earlier, but I have been very busy humping through the bush since arriving here in-country. I cannot tell you where we are due that the enemy may know our where about. But as it turns out they already know and they have been trying to take the city. We have fought hard all day and have driven them back. We lost a lot of brave men today. I want you to know however this ends, I am sorry for any sadness that I have caused you and Howard Jr. Forgive me for my cowardess.

I want so much to leave here and come home to you. I'm sorry I didn't listen to you when you begged me not to reenlist into this army. I thought I was doing a good deed in helping serve my country. I am sorry that it comes to this in order to show you how much I love you and Howard Jr. Forgive if I must die, for I'm in God's hands and maybe, just maybe he will protect me and bring me back home. If not than if I should die I hope someone will find this letter and get it to you. I am tired and I hate the war. Sometimes I wish-

Howard never has a chance to finish the letter, suddenly the whole blackness of the sky lights up as the enemy once again springs another attack. This time the enemy has crept even closer to city and has it surrounded. Inside the city, the soldiers scramble yet another time seeking area where they could find the most protection from the incoming mortars. This time it seems as though the city is in flames, and the cry of the enemy are now coming everywhere from within the walled city. The enemy has breached the eastern part of the city, driving Howard and his comrades into the center of the city where they hope that they could stand together until reinforcements arrive and either helps save the last stronghold of the south or be the ones that would see the south fail.

Lt. Colonel though wounded directs his men from the center of the city into the western part of the city which is the last section that the Americans hold. Yet the enemy is not satisfied with holding half the city, they want it all and they push into the middle and swiftly gather to send the Americans into the rice paddies. Huge celebrations are heard as the VC and North Vietnamese army take the city.

The Americans have nowhere to go; their backs are literally against the wall as they trudge through the watery rice paddies. Morning is beginning to arrive as the Americans look about to find how many men have left the city. Lt Colonel Johnson asks, "Who's the ranking enlisted man alive?"

"I believe I am, Sergeant Harry Facemire."

"Sgt. How many men do we have?

"I believe, looking around that we have about two hundred fifty men Sir."

'Tell the men to rest the best they can. We have to find a way out of here. The enemy is not through with us yet, they want us all dead."

As they rest in the rice paddies they could hear their wounded screaming as the enemy tortured them while the celebration continued within the city.

"Sgt. Inform the men that we are taking the offense and attack the city in order to either kill our wounded so that the enemy could not torture them or die trying. We attack in fifteen minutes."

As the Americans silently sneak up on the city, they spread out the best they could at the command, they attack the east wall of the city, catching many of the enemy off guard. With heavy losses the enemy fall back to the middle leaving what Americans still wounded where they had fallen. The majority of the VC had left the city with but a small garrison of men to clean up the mess. Hard pressed, the enemy is forced to the eastern part of the city where they strike for the tree line leaving in the retreat many of their soldiers dead behind them.

Once the enemy evacuates the city, the Americans take their wounded into the rice paddies so not to be left behind again. As for their dead, they pile the bodies the most honored way possible for they know the "Charlie" will return with a larger army than the Americans can fight off. Having accomplished what they could, they move out the eastern part of the city and join the wounded in the rice paddies and away from the lost city. Hunkering down the remaining Americans wait for either the end to come or help. Howard, sitting in the middle of the wounded has been hit in the stomach from grenade fragmentation.

The sound of yelling for the medic is barely audible as Howard lies among the wounded.

"Hey Doc am I going to make it?" asks Howard, as the doc tries to push what is left of his intestines back into place. "You are better off than a lot of the men around you."

"It hurts so b-bad."

"I know I'll do what I can for you and then I've got to help the others."

As the doc makes his rounds to attend to the wounded, the VC have attacked the city with mortars, field guns and gunboats from the eastern side that overlooked the river that was wide and deep enough to get their sampans in. The enemy was confident that they would end the American's domain over the city even if they had to annihilate the entire city and burn it down to the ground. Little did the enemy know that the Americans had deserted the city with its wounded and were hiding in the rice paddies watching the destruction of the last city and what could be the end of South Vietnam?

"This is the end. I'm never going back home. I'm going to die in this God-forsaken backward country and my wife and son will never know how. I don't want to go like this. Lord if you hear me, give me the strength to continue."

"Where is my rifle, I'm going out shooting" thought Howard to himself, until he could hear himself shouting out as loud as he was able to while holding onto his stomach, "Where is my rifle, Somebody give me my rifle, I'm not going to lie here doing nothing when they find us."

Someone bends down and lays his rifle at his side, "Here soldier, and just take it easy we will get out of this." It was Sgt. Harry Facemire. The two had arrived together and have become friends when he told the Sgt. Of knowing Sid and Barbara Anne Joy who he had watched on TV as a child. He would go to Oprey House in Randallsville, N.H. to watch their show on Saturday nights.

"Are we going to get out of this?" asks Howard looking up at the Sgt. Through tear stained eyes.

"I believe that we will be getting help as soon as Sgt. Pineo gets back."

Suddenly they stop talking. There is a rustle then sloshing of water, the enemy will soon spot them. They prepare the best they could by lying deep in the rice paddies, most of their bodies hidden under the water.

As the enemy come to within a hundred yards of them, the Americans open fire at once surprising the enemy who fall back leaving a heap of their dead behind them.

"There goes our surprise men; they will hit us with mortars and everything they have, so stay as low as you can." Yells Lt. Colonel Johnson as he prepares for the onslaught that is about to come.

Just as it looked like the VC was to make its final assault on the hunkered down Americans, American gunships suddenly arrive on the scene as though it was a Hollywood movie, spilling bullets down onto the enemy as though it were rain falling from the heavens.

Rising from their hidden positions, the survivors begin shouting and waving their weapons in the air. Soon the rescue helicopters land to help take the injured first. "Well Howard you've got yourself one million dollar wound and I'm going to miss you. You have a lot of courage doing what you did" says Sgt. Facemire sticking a cigarette into Howard's mouth so that he could take a puff.

"I'll tell the Joys about you Sgt. and how you had gone to their show to watch them. Don't be a stranger when you are ever in Capital City, I'll buy you a beer. So long Harry."

"So long Howard, take care of yourself and your family."

His litter is lifted into the helicopter just as Sgt. Pineo approaches Sgt. Facemire, "I hear that Captain Skinner got it?"

"It was sure terrible; it was as though he was the target of that mortar. We still haven't found all of him. Don't know how his family going to take this? We lost a lot of good men, damn war."

Shaking his head toward the helo, Sgt. Pineo asks, "How's Walker doing?"

"He got it good in the stomach, but I believe he'll live, At least he'll be going home, and as for us we still have some fighting to do."

Soon Howard finds himself in the air high above the ruined city and the looking below sees the enemy being pushed out of the ruins and into the tree line that has been destroyed by fire bombs from the gunships.

Though the battle of the city has been lost, and the city lay in ruins, the fighting continues, but for Howard, he is going to go through a lot of pain and anguish as he continues his grasp for life.

Howard is first taken to Saigon, to have his wounds cared for. While there he asks to make sure that his wife gets the letter that is still in his shirt pocket.

While Howard is recuperating from his wound, back in Baltimore, Sueanne who continues to work at the Grecian Travels for the Kotsiopoulos family finds herself in good standings and has been given Regina stephanotis's job, for both she and her husband Alexandros is serving their time in prison.

One evening as Sueanne arrives home, Howards' blood stained letter with an accompanying letter from now, Colonel John Johnson informing her that Howard had been wounded and to expect him to arrive at Walter Reed Hospital for more therapy. He had proven himself to be quite the soldier and had saved the lives of many men when he took out the sniper that had pinned everybody down, and that she should be very proud of him.

After reading the letter, she immediately called her mom and read the letter over to her.

"He's coming home." Sueanne tells her mom, looking at the date Sueanne notices that it was a month earlier and just maybe he was at Walter Reed Hospital now. "Do you think I should call now?"

"Probably it would be better to wait and call in the morning. Want me to go with you if he's is there?"

"Sure if he is there."

"Okay then I'll see you after I get the kids off to school. Get some sleep."

"Sleep? Who can sleep now?"

The night goes slow for Sueanne as she tosses back and forth in her bed wondering what she was going to say to Howard when she gets to see him. She tries wondering what his wounds would look like and how she was going to react when she does get to see them. As the night deepens, so does her sleep.

The following day, Sueanne and Marilyn take a bus to Walter Reed Medical Center. Upon arriving and entering the hospital they are amazed to the size of it. Approaching the information desk, Sueanne asks, "Could you please tell us where we could find Specialist Howard Walker, he's a patient here."

Thumbing through a sheet which contain the names of all the patients, the lady replies, "Walker, Howard Specialist; Third floor east wing bed eight."

Heading down the corridor that the lady pointed to the two find an elevator which takes them to the third floor. As the doors open, they see nurses, doctors and what must be aides scurrying around, going here, there and everywhere.

Stopping one of the nurses, Sueanne asks where they might find the east wing.

Pointing to the right, the nurse vanishes among the crowd.

Heading around the corner and down the hall, the two come to a four corners where they note a sign reading east wing straight ahead. Entering the swinging doors, the two are met with the sight of some twenty beds as nurses and nurse's aides scurrying back and forth to moaning and groaning patients. Heading to a main desk in the middle of the wing, they ask for Howard Walker. Looking down on a chart, she says, "Bed eleven." and points to her right.

Approaching Howard, they note he is somewhat awake but secured to his bed, as a nurse wipes his mouth with a sponge. Turning, the nurse asks, "Are you family?"

"I'm his wife and this is my mother. How is he?"

"He's holding his own, but you can visit him for a short time."

Looking down at Howard Sueanne becomes awash with fear and is unable to say anything to him.

"Mom, let's get out of here. I can't stand seeing him like this."

As the two turn their backs and leave, Howard opens his eyes and tries to call Sueanne, but his voice is just too soft to be heard. With a tear falling from his eyes, the nurse returns and wipes his face saying," It's alright. They will be back. For now, you need to get your rest.

"Once outside, Sueanne and Marilyn wait for the bus to take them back home. "Are you alright?" asks Marilyn.

"I told him from the start that this would happen, but being stubborn he had to learn the hard way."

"What has happened to you lately?"

"Mom, Its, It's because of the fact that I have been seeing someone for a while."

"Honey, why didn't you let me know? I could have helped you."

"Mom, I know what I'm doing. I'm in love with Roger Beamer."

"You don't mean the one with the motorcycle?"

"Yes, ever since he gave me that ride to Edgewood, he has been coming over for supper and he's very good with Howard Jr. I love him mom, I couldn't help myself. Howard only thought of himself and not us as a family. I'm so mad at him for leaving us to go and get him all shot up.

Howard remains at Walter Reed Medical Center for three months working his body back to health. Although Sueanne never comes again to visit, He is visited by Apolodoris Kotsiopoulos owner of the" Grecian Travels". During their conversations, word of Sueanne having a boy friend enters the discussion. "Sueanne still works for me, but I see that this man with a motorcycle is always bringing her to work and picking her up after work. I know it is none of my business, but I thought you should know."

"I had a hunch she was seeing someone, but I didn't want to believe it."

"I'm sorry to bring such sad news to you. You are coming along fine, yes?"

"The doctors say if I keep moving and exercising I'll be out of here in a couple of weeks. My stomach is getting better; I'm able to keep down small amounts of food at a time. Oh by the way are we still first in the space race?"

"I'm sorry, but I don't follow it, but I heard that NASA has had what a problem with one capsule that lost its oxygen and couldn't land on the moon so they returned."

"Have you seen or heard from my son?"

"I have seen him strapped on the back of a motorcycle when they come to visit Sueanne at the office, He looks real good. His hair is getting long like her boyfriends. Sorry I shouldn't have mentioned that?"

"It's okay, I asked you."

"Where are you going when you leave here? You go back to Sueanne?"

"I'll probably go to New Hampshire. This is the one and only chance that I can make my own mind up as to what and where I can go."

"I have to go check on the office. I will keep you informed. Take care; keep exercising so in order to get out. You're looking good man.

Three weeks later. Howard sits waiting for a bus that will take him home to New Hampshire, still upset with Sueanne, but not wanting to upset Howard Jr., he thought it best not to start an argument which would prevent him later from seeing his son.

It was a long ride to Capital City, where he calls his Uncle Fred to ask if he would pick him up and take him to Gossville to his mother.

Upon arriving to pick Howard up, He asks, "How are you? We got the word that you were injured, but we couldn't get out there to see you. Miriam is really concerned about you. Where are Sueanne and Howard Jr.?"

"Sueanne has another boyfriend; she has become a motorcycle mama, and has Howard Jr. riding on the cycle with him."

"I'm sorry that I brought it up. Your mother will be happy to see you."

As Uncle Fred drives Howard to his mother's, the conversation was mostly on his injury and that it has washed him out of the service, but with good conduct.

Howard stays with his mother until he finds his own place, a trailer in a cozy park some three miles from his mothers place. Miriam and Jeffrey help Howard move in the trailer, buys him some clothes and food for the refrigerator. Jeffrey calls the electric and Phone Company to have it put in their name until Howard could get himself together.

Howard finds work at a mill in town running cards that make yarn. Once he feels that he has a life, he writes Sueanne letting her know where he was and wishes to see Howard Jr. He asks her to come out. After several writings and calling, Howard was able to talk Sueanne in coming up where she and Jr. belong.

One day Howard receives a call that she and Jr. would be arriving in Capital City. Calling Uncle Fred, Howard explains what Sueanne has told him, and Uncle Fred agreed to meet Sueanne and Jr. at the bus station and bring them out to him.

When Sueanne arrives, Howard Jr. runs into his daddy's arms and hugs him around the neck tightly. "Where have you been daddy?"

Daddy's been on a long trip and had to finish my job before I could come home.

"Mommy has a new friend, and I ride on his cycle."

"I know, Daddy's glad mommy has a new friend. You like him?

"I do like him. He stays and helps mommy.

"Come on let's go inside and see the trailer."

As they settled down in the trailer, Howard continues working at the mill while Sueanne remained caring for the trailer and Howard Jr., who was four years old.

Howard receives notice from the New Hampshire Technical Institute that he has been accepted in the Pre-tech course under the G.I. bill, paying him two hundred ninety three dollars a month.

While Howard was going to school to try and make something out of his life, Sueanne gets a job working at an electrical shop in Penville, on an assembly line.

As the months go along, the pressure of her work and the fruitlessness of Howard's studies begin taking a toll on both of them. The evenings become long, Sueanne is bored to death there is long silence between the two. What little conversation there is turns to bickering and yelling fits.

Sueanne decides she wanted no more of New Hampshire, she decides to return to Baltimore. Howard tries to persuade her to stay and give life a chance.

But she wouldn't hear of it as she insists that he take back.

"Can we ride the cycle? Can we see Roger?" questions Howard Jr. yanking on his mothers' skirt.

"Howard Thomas Walker," yells Sueanne, "You go and play; mommy and daddy are having a talk."

Looking down at Jr. Howard watches his son walking away, sulking as he sits in the middle of the living room floor watching his mom and dad talking.

Howard just couldn't take seeing his son upset like that. "You didn't have to yell at him like that."

"Who are you to tell me how to talk to my son? You were never around to help raise him. Besides when you were left to feed him, you pushed his face into his food."

"You never forgave me for that have you, that was four years ago. I had a weakness and I got mad. Tell me, in the four years you never did anything that you had to apologize for?"

"I can't talk to you. Now are you going to help me get to the bus station or do I have to get a cab?"

Realizing that between the frustrations and the boredom of her short life in New Hampshire, that it was the missing of her family that really bothered her the most. She was so use to having her mother around that being this far from any of her friends and family, Sueanne had become scared. He knew this, for he too needs a shoulder to lean on every now and then but there was no shoulder around.

"Okay I'll call Uncle Fred one more time and see if he is free.

On Friday, October fifteenth, nineteen hundred seventy three, Sueanne and Howard Jr. board the bus one more time and the life that Howard had tried to grasp ends. As the bus rounds the corner and out of sight, Howard wanted to run after it, catch up with it, and pull his wife and son off and embrace them both while telling them how much he loved them both.

With tears flowing down his cheeks, he clenches his fist, knowing that he would only prolong the inevitable while bringing unhappiness to the three of them.

Seven years, four months and twenty-five days from the first time the two met, six years, one month and twenty-seven days from the time they had become man and wife. Howard whispers, "I'll miss you both, good-bye my love. Have a good life with your new friend. Don't let my son forget who his father is. Someday we will find each other."

Howard realizes that he still had his arm up and waving long after the bus had gone out of sight, taking with it a big hunk of Howard's life.

To be continued